A MOST
MAGICAL
GIRL

A MOST MAGICAL GIRL

KAREN FOXLEE

Piccadilly
PRESS

First published in Great Britain in 2016 by
PICCADILLY PRESS
80–81 Wimpole St, London W1G 9RE
www.piccadilly press.co.uk

First published in the USA in 2016 by Alfred A. Knopf

A CIP catalogue record for this book is available from the British Library.

ISBN: 978-1-84812-574-2
also available as an ebook

1

This book is typeset in 12pt Bell
Printed and bound by Clays Ltd, St Ives Plc

Piccadilly Press is an imprint of Bonnier Zaffre Ltd,
a Bonnier Publishing company
www.bonnierpublishing.com

FOR THE MOST MAGICAL GIRLS I KNOW:
JULIA ELIZABETH, CHLOE ROSE,
APRIL MARIA, AND ALICE MAY

It's exactly the kind of day she sees things. She knows it, but it doesn't stop her going out. Her head tells her to stay indoors, but the outside is calling: all the gray buildings and dripping eaves, all the wet stone and gleaming, rain-polished streets. The clouds are streaming, and the wind is banging at the windows. She slips out before Mercy can catch her and make her do schoolwork.

It has rained so hard that the street has filled with puddles. She mustn't look. *Don't look*, she tells herself. *Don't look*. The wind is tugging at umbrellas. It's pulling at her skirts, untying her hair. She should go inside. Her mother will be coming down the stairs. She'll make Annabel recite a passage from her Latin reader. Then they will take their places, pretty and fragile as flowers, pick up their embroidery, and wait for their callers.

Only, Annabel doesn't go inside.

Nothing in her lessons can explain this sensation, nothing in the way she is taught to walk and talk and sing and dance. There is a cord of something that joins her to a day like this. It feels like a rope that starts inside her belly and stretches up into the wild clouds. This rope tugs at her, as though at any moment she'll be dragged up into the sky. She struggles to keep her feet on the pavement. That's just what it feels like, and it frightens her, but part of her feels excited, too.

There—she's looked now.

She's looked straight into the puddle at her feet.

It's just an ordinary puddle, dull ditchwater, the wind rippling across its surface. She shouldn't bend down. What if her mother, coming down the stairs, catches a glimpse of her kneeling in the street? Oh, the shame of it! It has happened before, and her mother has been incensed. She has held Annabel's face in her hands and spoken wildly, in a way that Annabel has never heard. "It cannot be!"

But there is nothing that can stop her falling down, hands to stone. There is something moving there. She's leaning closer. Through the puddle clouds she catches a glimpse of something dark. There's a window. It's a window filled with blackness and a curtain blowing, and she wants to see inside it and she wants to look away, both at once. She moves closer, her nose almost touching the water, and sees inside.

There's a great room filled with shadows, and a man standing with his back to her. She's filled with dread upon seeing him. Cold dread, as though her heart has stopped. She cannot breathe. *Look away*, she tells herself. He's turning, that man, tall and dark and horribly thin. He's turning, and she doesn't want to see his face. She doesn't want to see the shadows in his cheekbones and the shadows in his eyes.

She hears someone crying out, doesn't know it is herself, and then there are arms around her, lifting her up and away from the ground.

The day slides back into view, the clouds twisting in the sky. Faces swim before her, fade, form again. There is the maid, Mercy, clearly, her face grimly set, holding out her arms, and, standing at the top step, her mother, darkly beautiful, trembling.

I

DARK-MAGIC GAUGE 1/3 FULL

It was dark in Mr. Angel's ballroom, but the small words etched on his invention glinted. DARK-MAGIC EXTRACTING MACHINE. *There was a cold quietness. The large machine made soft noises. It hissed in the darkness and sighed. Its inner workings rattled the floor of the room, which it filled. Its bellows opened and shut, inhaled and exhaled. The waxing moon gleamed on the moon funnel, a great brass horn that sprouted from the top of the machine and almost touched the jagged hole in the ceiling. Mr. Angel stood very still and admired his terrible invention. It had been almost thirteen years since he had fed the first tearstained handkerchief to its strange, dark heart.*

Today he offered up flowers stolen from a new grave. A black feather from a large bird kept in a very small cage. The machine sucked these things from his hand with great force, drew them across the room, and gobbled them up through a slit in its leather.

7

It was hungry and growing stronger. It wanted more. It wanted unfinished embroidery, stopped clocks, roses that a lover had refused. Mourning rings and black-bordered handkerchiefs freshly stolen from those still weeping. It wanted the bonnets of long-dead babies. The machine made Mr. Angel smile. Its bellows huffed and sighed.

Through the leather slit, sad things went in. Lost things went in. Left-behind things went in. Through the funnel near the ceiling, moonlight went in. The more he fed the machine, the faster the cogs and wheels moved, the faster its black heart spun. It was nearly ready.

He strode across the room and examined the dark-magic gauge. He wiped the condensation from its glass face and leaned his crooked body forward, his monocle pressed to his eye.

One-third full.

His breath quickened. It was working. It was filling. He could begin.

He took his Black Wand. The Black Wand. The only wand that could channel dark magic. The only wand that could raise the shadowlings. He held it to a small valve at the end of the machine. It was an ordinary brass tap, yet when he twisted it, an arc of energy connected to the Black Wand's tip and jolted him backward toward the wall. The machine thrummed loudly. The house shook. He held the wand high and marveled at the power he could feel. What would the machine be capable of at full moon? Thirteen years' worth of full moons. Thirteen years' worth of sorrowful things. Pure dark magic.

His elderly butler appeared at the door.

"I heard a commotion, Mr. Angel," he said. "I came to see . . ."

But he stopped because Mr. Angel was striding toward him, a terrible smile stretched on his bone-white face.

"Jeremiah," whispered Mr. Angel. "Perfect."

He raised the Black Wand and aimed it at the butler, whose eyes widened as a single blast of mauve light shot toward him.

Mr. Angel stepped over the pile of dust that had been Jeremiah the butler. He went down the stairs, ignoring the frantic scurrying of servants, the hurried closing of doors. The wand was still heavy with dark magic, but he did not want more piles of dust. He went down—down past the parlor, down past the kitchen, down into the cellars.

He stood in the blackness and sensed them. He knew from his books it was a place they would exist. He could smell them in amongst the turnips and apples, the bottles of cider and sherry. They smelled of emptiness. He would raise one. He would raise one from its sleep with the Black Wand and put the dark magic in it.

He pointed the wand at the corner where barrels were stacked. He uttered his raising-up words—Umbra, antumbra—quietly, coaxingly, and the wand quivered in his hand. The wood bowed and twitched as he spoke; like a fishing pole, it shivered and snagged on something invisible.

"Come now," whispered Mr. Angel, straining to hold the wand. "Come now."

In the darkness he saw the arc of deep purple light disappearing

9

behind the barrels and a grayness begin to rise. The thing emerged, its long shadowy body slipping silently from the gloom. It stretched out its thin gossamer arms toward him. Its long claws clicked. It breathed its first shuddering breath.

"Welcome, shadowling," whispered Mr. Angel.

1

*"A young lady should find, in all manner of circumstances
and predicaments, a way to be both cheerful and content."*
— *Miss Finch's Little Blue Book (1855)*

Annabel Grey arrived late in the afternoon in her best
dress and her new red town cloak. She stepped down
from the carriage and surveyed the street with her chin held
high. She smiled. She smiled the way she had been taught to
smile when things were terrible or even just a little bad. She
smiled as though she'd just seen something lovely. A beautiful painting, perhaps, or a butterfly.

It was exactly the sort of street she had imagined, although she had never once been to this side of London. It
was a mean street, the buildings leaning, holding each other
up like a mouthful of rotten teeth. It was a stinking, wet
place. There were cattle being herded across intersections,
and stone buildings and churches and factories streaming
black smoke, all crammed side by side. It was a damp and
dark street, choked with wagons and carriages and filled

with foul weather. A temperamental wind stamped up and down the road, slamming doors and stealing umbrellas and tugging at her bonnet ribbon.

She concentrated very hard on not letting her smile falter.

The costermongers were cowering under eaves, calling out, "Hot cooked eels" and "Pickled whelks," above the sound of the wind. The shop signs read USURER and MILLINER and HABERDASHER. SHIP BROKER and GRAIN BROKER and SILVER BROKER. FALCONER and FEATHER PURVEYOR and SUPPLIER OF FINE TARTAN. But before her was a shop with the words MISSES E. & H. VINE'S MAGIC SHOP neatly printed on the glass. And opening the door was a tall, straight woman with a scowl on her face.

"Annabel Grey?" said the woman.

"Yes," said Annabel Grey.

The tall, straight woman wore a dark dress buttoned up to her chin. Her hair was black and in no way matched her face, which was very old—long and thin and crosshatched with grooves.

The tall, straight woman did not smile. "I am Miss Henrietta Vine."

"My great-aunt!" cried Annabel, and she thought perhaps she should throw herself at the woman's feet, but Miss Henrietta Vine did not look as if she would tolerate such a thing.

There was nothing welcoming about Henrietta Vine.

"'Miss Henrietta' will do," she said sharply. "And you are nearly thirteen?"

"On Friday I will be thirteen," said Annabel.

"You are small for your age, then," the woman said. "And too young in my opinion to have had your skirts let down."

Miss Henrietta had grave blue eyes, and her expression was solemn, as though she were about to tell Annabel something terrible, something much more terrible than what had already happened. The terrible-news gaze was unwavering, and it made Annabel look away. She looked at her feet, at the footpath, at the shop glass behind Miss Henrietta.

"So, here you are," said Miss Henrietta. "Your mother has finally done what is proper."

Just the mention of her mother made Annabel sway.

It was her mother who had sent her here. Her mother, who had suddenly needed to go abroad. Annabel felt the smile slipping from her mouth, and she fought very hard to keep it in its place. Tears threatened to spill from her eyes.

Miss Henrietta Vine did nothing to comfort her. "You have a secret," she said, looking at Annabel carefully. "You have a secret you try to keep from the world."

"No, I don't," said Annabel. She was so shocked by these words that the tears completely dried up.

The wind blew against their skirts and it began to rain. Miss Henrietta told the driver where to take Annabel's trunk, then raised her dark eyebrows and motioned for Annabel to follow her inside.

◆ ◆ ◆

"This is not an ordinary magic shop," said Miss Henrietta
Vine when they were inside. She looked at Annabel sternly,
daring her to disagree. Annabel dared not. It was most
definitely a magic shop, and it was crowded with the most
unusual things Annabel had ever seen. There was a long
counter cluttered with greasy jars and bottles. Some contained greenish liquids; in others, things floated that she did
not wish to see. There was a long gray stick, with words
carved faintly all over it, beside a dog-eared ledger.

The shop smelled peculiar. It was pepperminty and medic-
inal and sweet and sour in equal parts. It smelled wrong, and
Annabel took a handkerchief from her sleeve and held it to her
nose, but Miss Henrietta frowned so fiercely that she quickly
put it away. She breathed through her mouth and smiled as
pleasantly as she could. Miss Henrietta glowered in return.

Behind the counter were two large specimen cabinets with
many small drawers, some of them open and some of them
shut. What looked like black feathers spilled from one and
blue ribbons from another, and gray brittle twigs spewed in
a tangle from a third. There were shelves behind the cabinets
that reached high up the walls to where a dark clock ticked
angrily, as though every second were an insult to itself. The
shelves were crammed with books and hats and boxes and
feathers and leaves and large sticks and more jars and more
wooden boxes and, on the very top shelf, several large stones.

"No, this is not an ordinary magic shop," repeated Miss

Henrietta, looking at Annabel's open mouth with disapproval. Her long black skirt made a dreadful swishing noise on the marble floor. A dark brooch glittered on her chest. Her hand reached out to the gray stick on the counter. "This is the Ondona, our wand, the Vine Witches' Wand. We do not keep any of the newer types of wands. You will meet customers inquiring after such things. They rush past to catch a late train and see the word *magic* and think they will buy tricks for their children. We trade only in high-end items that come upon the market rarely. Why, we have traveled twice to New York to purchase important wands from important witches who were about to die. These are old wands, passed down through generations. We also hold a small amount of seeing glass, most of it for the Finsbury Wizards, which must be delivered to their door, for they do not travel nowadays. They send their requests via pigeon."

Annabel closed her mouth. She tried very hard to be polite.

"In this cabinet there are some important ingredients that you will soon accustom yourself with. The drawers are alphabetically listed, as you will see—dandelion, devil's claw, dogwort—and you may in time learn to retrieve things that we ask for."

Annabel felt dizzy. Miss Henrietta Vine used the term *we*, but there was no one else present in the messy shop. Miss E. Vine's absence made her nervous. And surely she wasn't expected to work here, was she? Her mother had told her she was coming to continue her education.

She was a young lady.

"Your mother has sent you here to learn what you should have commenced learning long ago," said Miss Henrietta, as if she could hear Annabel's thoughts. "Your life has been but an illusion. Your mother has lied terribly. The sea-captain husband lost at sea? All deceit. She turned her back on us years ago, on magic—good magic, proper magic."

"But my father *was* a sea captain," said Annabel.

"Nonsense," replied Miss Henrietta. "Your mother married a magician without our consent. A magician—yes, cheap tricks in halls—and with her so divinely magical. It was a great shock, and Estella never quite got out of bed again. Then one day while your mother was very heavy with you, why, he up and died."

Annabel felt even dizzier. Her mother had always said that her father was a sea captain. That he had been lost at sea. She swayed where she stood.

"He was hit by a carriage, dear Annabel, on the Euston Road," said Miss Henrietta. "And that was not even the worst of it. But sit down if you must. There, now, don't look so shocked."

Annabel stumbled toward the counter and the stool behind it. Miss Henrietta looked most displeased.

"We will teach you the working of the shop, Annabel Grey, for we are old. We are all old in the Great & Benevolent Magical Society. The Bloomsbury Witches are ancient. They once rode their broomsticks each night, delivering love magic. The Kentish Town Wizards have such rheumatism that they can hardly stand up. I send salves each week to Miss Broughton, the Witch of St. John's Wood. Once, she could heal almost anything that was sick, much like your mother—children, especially, and birds you would think could never fly again—but she does not improve. Yes, we will teach you what we can of the shop, and then, if you show promise, of magic."

Miss Henrietta paused for a long moment. The clock on the wall ticked indignantly.

"This is what is expected of you now, although I have my doubts. I fear your mother has left all too late. You are a girl without education. A girl from a long line of witches, of good pedigree, but with no talent. It is most disappointing."

Annabel's cheeks itched and burned.

"But I've been to Miss Finch's Academy for Young Ladies," said Annabel. "I've been for two years. I speak French and Latin—well, I'm not very good at Latin, but I received honors for geography."

She had. She knew each and every European river and was very good at mapping them. The Rhine, the Seine, the Danube, the Arno. All the mountains: The Swiss Alps and the Pyrenees. The Vogelsbergs and the Carpathians. Isabelle Rutherford, Annabel's closest friend, said Annabel was the best in the whole world at knowing mountain ranges. Nevertheless, if it was possible, Miss Henrietta looked even more disappointed.

"Your mother told us that you see things, you have visions," said Miss Henrietta. Annabel's breath caught, but Miss Henrietta held up her hand to stop her from talking.

17

"Do you feel an affinity with an animal: the fox, the owl, the cat, the bird? Please close your mouth, girl."

Annabel could make no sense of it. Affinity with an owl? She quite liked Charlie, her bullfinch, who sang in their little sunny parlor. Just the thought of it and she felt homesick again.

"I am to believe your mother taught you no magic," said Miss Henrietta.

Annabel's mother and magic did not seem right in the same sentence. Her mother had belonged to the Society of Philanthropic Sea Widows. She had met with the Ladies' Lepidoptera Club each and every Saturday. She was beautiful and graceful and most unmagical.

Annabel decided she would swoon. She would swoon, and it would serve Miss Henrietta right for being so horrible. She sat very still on the stool and willed herself to faint, but couldn't. Miss Henrietta sighed. "Here is Kitty," she said. "I hope she has brought what I need."

The bell above the door tinkled, and the wildest girl Annabel had ever seen entered from the rain. Her head was held low, a furious frown upon her face, and there was not an inch of tidiness to her. Her wet black curls were tied roughly with a piece of twine, and a brown leaf dangled on a strand beside her ear. Her filthy dress was too short, and her stockings were full of holes, and her wet boots were split apart at the toes and tied around with string.

"Good evening, Kitty," said Miss Henrietta. "You are late, and I am busy."

18

The girl grunted in response. She flung her sack down on the floor. She stared at Annabel from beneath her dark brow with green eyes. The stare made Annabel blush and look away. She looked at the sack. At the counter. At the clock. The girl coughed a terrible, hacking cough. When Annabel looked again, the girl was still staring, and it made Annabel's face burn all the more.

"Annabel, this is Kitty. Kitty, this is Annabel," said Miss Henrietta, as though it were perfectly reasonable for a young lady to be introduced to a beggar.

The old woman took the sack and emptied its contents onto the counter: shells that clattered out, stinking of the Thames; a bundle of grass; several plump leaves; and the perfect body of a dead little rabbit.

Annabel gasped. "Oh," she said when Miss Henrietta and the girl glared at her. "Please pardon."

"The leaves are good," said Miss Henrietta. "From the dean's garden again? He has a fine garden, does he not?"

The girl nodded but did not speak.

"What of the world today, then, Kitty?" asked Miss Henrietta. "Bring us news."

Still the wild girl did not speak. Her cheeks colored. Her eyes grew glassy, and she scowled at the floor. Miss Henrietta waited.

"All the trees are in a fuss," said Kitty quietly at last. She seemed to struggle with each word, yet her voice surprised Annabel. It was not a proper girl's voice, but it was soft all the same. Soft and clear. "Calling, calling, calling all night through the streets. Something bad is coming, and the moon getting as big as it's ever been seen."

"So the wizards keep saying. Message after message. Calamity approaching," said Miss Henrietta. "It's a wonder their pigeons don't fall clean out of the sky with all their coming and going."

Annabel thought a little smile flickered across the wild girl's lips, but she couldn't be sure because already the girl was turning from them. She was grabbing her sack and running as though speaking had shamed her. Miss Henrietta went behind her and slipped a small parcel into her hand as she went. The girl did not say thank you. She ran from the shop, banging the door behind her.

Miss Henrietta took a deep breath when the girl was gone. She looked at Annabel with her disappointed face.

"The day is nearly done, Annabel," she said. "Hang your cloak and your gloves and bonnet. There is laundry to be done."

Laundry, thought Annabel as she stood up and walked slowly to the hat stand. It seemed the most puzzling suggestion so far. She wanted to stay thinking about the strange girl. Who was she, and where had she come from, and what did she mean about trees calling? Annabel was hungry, too; Henrietta Vine had not even offered her tea.

"A witch's dresses can be washed only at dusk on Wednesday," said Miss Henrietta. "And today is Wednesday, and it is dusk."

♦ ♦ ♦

Miss Henrietta held up both her arms. She pointed to two large dark doors on either side of the specimen cabinets.

"On no account must you ever open the door on the left," she said. "Unless it is asked of you. Do you understand?"

"Yes, Miss Henrietta," said Annabel.

Miss Henrietta opened the door on the right. Annabel followed her great-aunt down a short dim corridor and into a dismal little kitchen where a fire burned low. A blue teapot sat upon the table. She unlocked the back door and led Annabel out into a laneway.

It was a muddy, stinking laneway, and Annabel thought it was perhaps the worst place she had ever been. They stood there in the dusk, in the icy rain and the wind, which ripped straight though her pretty blue-striped town dress. Surely they shouldn't be outside in such weather. She'd catch a cold and take ill. A physician would be called for, and he'd say that nothing could be done. She would die. Her story would be serialized in the *Illustrated London News*, and her mother, who had sent her here, would read it. POOR YOUNG GIRL MALTREATED BY HORRIBLE GREAT-AUNT. There would be illustrations.

"Perfect weather for washing," declared Miss Henrietta.

She led Annabel to a washroom where there was a wooden tub and a tap for drawing water. She lit a small stove so the water could be boiled. Annabel lifted her skirts and worried for her new boots, which were made of blue leather and had blue ribbon bows. She noticed a spider high up on the wall and shuddered. A pile of dark dresses lay in a basket on the floor.

"I'm sure you have washed clothes before," said Miss Henrietta. Annabel could tell that her great-aunt knew perfectly well she hadn't. Miss Henrietta poured the water into the tub.

"I will leave you with the rest," she said. "The special soap from the Scottish Witches must be grated with a knife—just a teaspoon's worth, for it has very strong properties. When you have finished, bring the dresses to the kitchen and drape them by the fire."

Then she was gone without so much as a thank-you, and Annabel was left staring at her shocked reflection in the washtub.

"Washing clothes," she said to her reflection. She nodded, and her pretty, solemn face nodded in return. She touched a blond ringlet. "With special soap from the Scottish Witches."

Annabel picked up the purple soap and held it to her nose. It stank. She dropped it in disgust into the tub. The water turned purple and began to froth, and she yelped in fright and fished the soap out.

Would that happen with just a teaspoon of grated soap? Should she tip the whole tub out and start again? It seemed a shame. She looked at the pile of dresses and pushed them one by one into the purple foaming water. She had to kneel down on the dirty ground, which was awful. She swished the heavy dresses until her arms began to ache. When she could stir no more, she sat looking at the water.

Her mother had sent her away, and it was a dreadful thing.

Annabel supposed there had never been a more dreadful thing.

Her mother had sat her down to tell her. "I must go abroad on business. It is long overdue. I cannot explain it to you now, but you will know in time," she said. "You will live with my two aunts in Spitalfields for some time."

"Aunts?" Annabel had said. "In Spitalfields?"

She'd never been told she had great-aunts.

"If you listen well, they will teach you many things," said her mother. "Lessons you now must learn."

"What kind of lessons?" asked Annabel. "What about Miss Finch's?"

"Your education at Miss Finch's is complete," said her mother. "You will be educated by your great-aunts now."

"Complete?" said Annabel.

"I will send you a letter when I can," said her mother, beginning to cry. "Now I must go."

"I-i-is it because of the puddles?" Annabel stammered. She had rarely seen her mother cry. "I promise I won't look again. *I promise.*"

She didn't want to be sent away. She didn't want her mother to go abroad on business that could not be explained. Her mother never did anything that could not be explained.

"I can no longer protect you from your destiny," she replied. "Be brave."

23

And in the morning her mother was gone and Mercy was in a terrible state, hurrying and rushing Annabel for her trip to Spitalfields.

Be brave.

She would not think of it. She rested her chin on the tub. It was warm there, and she watched the purple water grow still. No, she would not think of it. She would not think of her mother leaving. She would not think of her father, who was not a sea captain drowned at sea, because that story was nonsense. She would not think of Miss Henrietta waiting, standing in that dark, cluttered shop, frowning.

She would think of the emerald-green ice skates she was to have for her birthday. Her mother had promised them if only she would improve her Latin. Her mother had always said Latin was very important and Annabel should never underestimate when she might need it. But the problem was Latin words made her drowsy. Mr. Ladgrove, who taught Latin grammar at Miss Finch's Academy for Young Ladies, had a voice like a sleeping potion.

She supposed she didn't need to worry about Latin now anyway. Or the green ice skates. There would be no present to open on Friday morning for her birthday. Not now that everything had changed. She began to drag the dresses, one by one, into the basket. They were the heaviest things she had ever dealt with, and none of it was fair.

She was pulling out the last dress when she saw something moving beneath the surface. It was something darker than the dresses, and it made her stop. She leaned forward.

There was her own face mirrored, rippling, in the purple water, but something moved deeper. Something coiling and unraveling. She leaned closer still. There it was, a dark wave, moving just below the surface. And just beneath the surface there was a house—the house she had seen before, the terrible dark house. Her mind screamed at her to look away.

All about the house she saw the city now, the jumble of streets and intersections and bridges and buildings. She saw it clearly, and she could not help the moan that escaped her lips as she peered closer.

The dark wave was spreading; it was rising and rising, but it did not crest. It was rushing out from the dark house, gushing from the windows, spreading out into the black streets. It was rushing out to destroy the city. It was all she knew. A great black wave of destruction ready to wipe away houses and fences and churches, schools and hospitals and poorhouses.

"Save them!" she cried.

She felt hands beneath her arms, someone dragging her backward from the tub. The wild girl's face appeared suddenly, then vanished.

"Sit up," Annabel heard her say. "Stop leaning so."

Annabel struggled to free herself, right herself. The whole washroom seemed on its side. The wild girl's face appeared again, and her green eyes were filled with curiosity.

"What's happened?" came Miss Henrietta's voice.

"Nothing," Annabel whispered.

"I was taking my victuals under the eaves and heard her

hollering," said Kitty. "'Save them!' she was shouting, looking in the water here."

"What did you see?" asked Miss Henrietta.

Annabel pulled herself up and leaned against the stone wall.

"Nothing," she whispered. She examined the mud on her
skirt, refusing to look at Miss Henrietta or the girl. "I must
have taken faint—that's all."

Here was the secret she kept from the world. She would
like to bury her face in her hands, but she stared at the tub
instead. It was just plain purple water, nothing else. The
wind whipped in through the open doorway.

"You have used too much soap," said Miss Henrietta at
last. "Our dresses are quite ruined."

It was true that in the evening light the dresses glowed
purple in the wash basket.

"Ruined!" shouted Miss Henrietta, and Annabel flinched
at the word.

"Forgive me, Aunt," whispered Annabel.

"You'll be good for nothing," said Miss Henrietta.

◆ ◆ ◆

In the kitchen Annabel helped Miss Henrietta drape the
dresses before the fire, where their purplish glow grew. Annabel's cheeks stung at the sight, but no more was said. She
shivered and watched Miss Henrietta unwrap bread and cut
the mold from it. She sliced hard cheese and handed a plate
to Annabel.

"You will be tired, no doubt," said Miss Henrietta, pouring tea.

Annabel ate, ravenous, and gulped down the tea that Miss Henrietta passed to her. She was overcome with weariness. She shivered again and wondered after the girl Kitty, who had not been asked inside. Miss Henrietta had not even bid her good night. Annabel had never been in such a place, where no one had manners.

"I hope you do not take ill," said Miss Henrietta. "Our last girl did. She faded away in a matter of hours."

There was nothing Annabel could think to say to that.

"Follow me. I will show you to your room. Take the bowl and the rest of the hot water in the pitcher."

Beside the fireplace at the end of the kitchen, there was a door, and behind the door, narrow, twisting steps. Annabel followed Miss Henrietta up three flights, past a single closed door on each turn, to the very top. The pitcher and bowl were heavy. In her old life, the maid, Mercy, would have carried them. In her old life, the maid would have said in a soothing voice, "Come along now, Miss Annabel, or you'll fall asleep on your little feet." In her old life, the maid would have untied Annabel's fair hair and brushed it out until it gleamed in the lantern light.

Here, the candlelight flickered on the walls and a cold draft rushed down the stairs. At the top landing Miss Henrietta opened a little door and crouched down to pass through. It was a mean little attic room, and the candle Miss Henrietta lit was short and Annabel knew it wouldn't last the night. The bed was plain, with one coarse blanket and not even a pillow. The tiny window showed the black sky, and the wind and rain banged against it.

"This is an old place, Annabel," said Miss Henrietta. "It speaks to itself at night. Bumps and moans. You shouldn't be alarmed. No harm will come to you here."

But Annabel felt harmed. She felt bruised by the few short hours she had been there. By everything she had been asked to do. By all of Miss Henrietta's words. She felt ruined by the day.

"The wizards have long sent messages of you," said Miss Henrietta, a little more kindly. "They think you show promise. Your mother wrote to us and told us of your visions. That is why you are here, child. They have increased, have they not?"

"I don't have visions," said Annabel.

Miss Henrietta stared at her sadly. She began to close the door.

"And who is that girl?" Annabel cried. "Where does *she* sleep?"

"Kitty?" Miss Henrietta said. "Do not worry for Kitty. She has a hundred sleeping places all through the town. She is a betwixter, Annabel. She knows all the woods that remain in London Town, the last woods, the pockets of trees where the wild things are. Much has been chopped down, Annabel. To make ships and sideboards and fancy chairs. But she knows where to find the little folk and she does our dealings with them. I have heard it said she can

28

sing up her spirit light. There are not many girls like Kitty anymore."

It made no sense to Annabel. "It's cold and rainy out," she said.

"You could not keep Kitty indoors if you tried, Annabel," said Miss Henrietta. She shut the door at that, and Annabel listened for a long time to her footsteps growing fainter down the stairs.

Annabel removed her boots and stockings and dress. She opened her traveling trunk and found her nightdress and her brush. There lay all her pretty things, all the things from her other life. Her sweet straw bonnets and her good dresses. She looked at them sadly. Outside, she could hear London: horses' hooves and carriage wheels, the lowing of cattle and the rumble of trains, ringing bells and shrieks of laughter, and, somewhere, someone wailing.

She found her little jewelry box. It was black, highly lacquered, and once, a long time ago, Annabel had had a vision in it.

You have a secret you try to keep from the world.

In the black lacquered box she had seen a funeral procession on gray streets, with a small coffin carried by old men, and she had watched it with interest for some time. She remembered it because she had told her mother, who had clutched Annabel's tiny hands.

"Annabel, close your eyes if you see such things," she had demanded. "Close your eyes—promise me—and turn away."

She opened the box now in the little attic room. Inside

winked her mother's diamond brooch. It was star-shaped and glittered on the blue velvet. It made her feel so sad that she could not breathe. Her mother had given it to her just before she left.

"But why?" Annabel had cried. "You don't need to send me away. I promise I won't look in puddles again. I promise."

But her mother had shaken her head.

"I will send word when I am to return," she replied, and took Annabel's pretty face in her hands. "Be brave."

"Mother," Annabel said now.

The candle dipped its little head.

Annabel took the star brooch from its box and blew out the flame. She lay down on the bed, and the wind and rain crashed against the little window. She thought of her long-dead father and how he had not been at all who he was meant to be. It hurt her head, so she wondered about the strange girl Kitty instead. She hoped she was somewhere safe and dry. Then she held the star brooch to her cheek and closed her eyes.

◆ ◆ ◆

The wild girl did not sleep at first. The weather lifted her spirits. The wind banged and clamored and called up and down the lanes. The world was restless and full of speaking.

Kitty walked. She walked and rested and walked again. She knew all the cobbled streets and the grand thoroughfares. She knew all the worn Thames steps and all the jagged alleyways. She listened as she went. She could hear all of London on a

30

night like this: the taverns and theaters, the organ-grinders and the balladeers, and, hidden in amongst these sounds, a wizard singing to the rain and the wild lamenting of faeries.

She wanted to listen to the trees again. The old willow in Regent's Park, thrashing its head, and the grand old lady hornbeam in Knightsbridge, whispering and shivering in her leaves. As the moon came up and peeked its head through the rain clouds, the great yew in Totteridge called far across the streets to the yew in Bromley, its old voice full of dirt and rain and greenery. She knew they were worried. Something was afoot, and she thought of what it might be as she walked. A great fire or a flood or a dragon coming. It had happened before. She knew such things.

She crept into Highgate Cemetery. The place was full of thieves, but she was swift and quiet in her worn little boots. She took refuge in a mausoleum and waited. She could smell the faeries, even in the rain. They smelled of honey, but she knew they were not sweet. They were nothing like the way people drew them or carved them into pretty statues. They spat and wailed and sang, with their sticky dresses bulging over their swollen little bellies and their nails sharp as sewing needles. Everything about them was enough to vex you. She would wait for near dawn, when they were drowsy.

She thought of Miss Henrietta's new girl, the pretty one who saw things in water. She didn't look at all magical or smell it, that one. She had a strange smell, that Annabel, blank as a page without a story on it yet or like sunlight and clean sheets. And pretending she saw nothing when she saw something, all right—something that made her turn white and nearly wet her pants! Kitty smiled in the dark at the thought of it and then began to hum a little song that she had taught herself.

It started deep down in her toes, and she hummed it up and coughed a heart light from her mouth. Kitty was full of magic that she did not understand. The light was blue, daylight blue, and it pleased her, hovering there all shimmering and spittle-covered in the dark. It was the size of her fist, and she blew it up and down with her breath, just above her nose.

She called them *heart lights* because they came from inside her, and the place they came from seemed near her heart.

She knew they were part of her. Had always known it.

Part of what was inside her—not her shell, which she knew would one day break in the cold and rain. The outside of her would break like the beetle shells she found and kept or the dried body of a blackbird chick fallen from its nest but that she knew was somewhere else, still flying. Her heart light would not die.

She swallowed her heart light, and the mausoleum grew dark. She closed her eyes to listen to the rain.

By the time the wand was empty of its power, Mr. Angel had raised three shadowlings. They swept up the stairwell after him, softly

rustling and whispering. In the machine room he commanded them to be still. They were just as his ancient books described: dreadful things, made of nothing yet brimming with wickedness, sleeping shadows brought to life with his dark magic.

They tittered and hissed when he came too close.

They changed their shapes—tall and thin one minute, stout the next. They joined together in the shape of a great tall man and towered over him so that he shivered.

"Down!" he yelled, and they were three again in an instant.

They were made of shadow, some parts ink black, others gray. In their darkness there were yawning mouths and empty eyes. On their fingers there were solid silvery claws. They showed them to Mr. Angel; they rattled and clacked them at him, rustled and hushed. When he reached out to touch one, his hand felt nothing, and they made an angry sound like the wind in long grass.

"Pass through the keyhole," he commanded of one, which sped off and slipped itself small through the tiny space, then returned again.

He took his top hat from the chair. He threw it upward and shouted, "Destroy!"

They were upon it, shredding it with their empty gray mouths and their wicked clicking claws in seconds. A fine film of hat remains drifted slowly to the floor.

The machine made a loud disgruntled noise behind him. It was hungry. It huffed a loud sigh with its bellows, and Mr. Angel smiled his strange lopsided smile.

"Follow," he said to the shadowlings, who clung together now in a black pile. They seemed fearful of the thing.

33

Mr. Angel went slowly up the staircase that wrapped about the moon funnel and ended in a small platform on the roof. Morning had come, and the shadowlings shrank themselves to hide in the folds of his cloak. He gazed out over the rooftops, at all the mean streets scratched upon the poor earth for miles and miles. All the inns and taverns and churches. All the poorhouses and asylums. The factories retched their first smoke into the sky. The great looms jiggered and clacked.

He felt the shadowlings shiver against him.

"When my wand is filled again, I will raise more of you," he said. "And in two days' time, at full moon, I will have an army. It will be the end of good magic. We will take the city."

2

*"A young lady rises early, opens her windows, and delights
in the pleasures of an industrious day."*
— *Miss Finch's Little Blue Book (1855)*

Annabel chose her rosebud-patterned town dress, which Isabelle Rutherford had said was the prettiest dress in the whole world. It had dainty short lace-edged sleeves, and it fastened with pearl buttons. Each button was a challenge. She was used to Mercy buttoning and tying and straightening and brushing. She had never once, in all her life, dressed herself.

She braided her hair, all the ringlets quite fallen out. There was no looking glass. When she opened the door, she found Miss Henrietta waiting for her on the landing. She scowled at Annabel's choice of dress. She scowled even harder when Annabel smiled as pleasantly as she could.

"We do not lie in bed once the sun is up," said Miss Henrietta Vine. "There are chores to be done, chamber pots to be emptied."

Annabel was to tiptoe into Miss Henrietta's room to empty her chamber pot in the mornings. Miss Henrietta showed her how. She was not to make a sound. No loud clanking or clinking or sloshing. It seemed Miss Henrietta Vine could not tolerate even a small amount of sloshing. Annabel wondered after Miss Estella. Where was she, and who emptied *her* chamber pot?

"Miss Estella has her maid, Tatty," said Miss Henrietta, even though Annabel had not uttered a word.

In the kitchen Miss Henrietta instructed her quietly on the starting of the fire and the making of the special yellow tea. All these tasks were to be performed silently in the first pale light of dawn.

"Now you must gather up my dresses and take them to my dresser," Miss Henrietta said. Annabel looked at them, faintly glowing where they were draped. "I will not be able to wear them for some time. At least, not until the magic diminishes."

Annabel wondered what would happen if Miss Henrietta put one on now. Perhaps she would start to float. Perhaps her feet would lift off the ground and there would be nothing she could do about it. Perhaps she would float out the back door and up into the sky. That would be Miss Henrietta gone, floating away over London, never to be seen again.

"You are loud and reckless with your thoughts!" shouted Miss Henrietta, again as though Annabel had spoken the words. She shouted so loud that Annabel jumped on the spot, her cheeks flushing, and she began to quickly gather up the dresses. They were warm from their night beside the fire, and she burrowed her hands into the pile as she carried them up the stairs.

After the dresses had been folded and put away into drawers, there was sweeping to be done in the shop.

"Goodness me, child," said Miss Henrietta when Annabel began to dab at the floor. "Have you never swept before?"

"I h-h-have," stammered Annabel.

She hadn't, except once at Miss Finch's Academy for Young Ladies, when she'd played a poor girl in a play, which she was sure didn't really count.

"Here," said Miss Henrietta, showing Annabel how to sweep.

The shop was cluttered, but the marble floor was surprisingly clean. Miss Henrietta made a great show of emptying the dustpan, which contained nothing.

"And when you are done," she continued, "you will turn the sign over and open the door to let some air and sunshine in."

Annabel did as she was told, although she was quite certain that no one would ever visit the horrid little shop. She looked at the front window and at the golden letters, which from inside spelled ꟼOHꙄ ƆIⱯAM Ꙅ'ƎИIV .H ⅋ .Ǝ ꙄƎꙄꙄIM. Annabel said the words to herself, silently, and thought they sounded quite nice backward. There was indeed sunshine, and it made her feel happy when she opened the door.

"Bearberry leaf," said Miss Henrietta when Annabel had finished.

"Bearberry leaf?" said Annabel.

Miss Henrietta opened a small drawer in one of the specimen cabinets and extracted a box containing several plum-green leaves. She motioned for Annabel to stand beside her at the counter and handed her gold forceps.

"Listen well," said Miss Henrietta. "Bearberry leaf is used for many things, for diseases of the bladder and for water-logged hearts and also for some minor skin complaints. Some say if you burn it and grind it and sprinkle it on your shoes, it will take you to your one true love. I personally don't believe such nonsense. The leaf is also used by certain therianthropes, and there is a Mr. Huxley, a member of the society, who lives in Hampstead. He requires a small amount on a regular basis so that he may change himself into a wolf. Today is the day I prepare Mr. Huxley's bearberry leaf."

Annabel, poised with the gold forceps in her hand, laughed nervously.

"It is no laughing matter," said Miss Henrietta. "Today is the third Thursday of the month, and that is the day that I must deliver him his new supply. He is old, like all of us in the Great & Benevolent Magical Society, Annabel. It will not do to keep him waiting if there is a wolf inside him to be let out.

"Take five of the plumpest leaves," she continued. "These have come by steamer from a very special tree in Manitoba, via Nova Scotia, and cost Mr. Huxley not much less than the price of gold, so it will not do for one to be dropped on the floor or squeezed too hard by the forceps."

Annabel looked at the leaves. They seemed too fresh to have come all that way. Miss Henrietta was tricking her. It was some kind of test—she was waiting to see what Annabel would do.

"When I am gone to deliver Mr. Huxley's parcel, sit behind the counter and touch nothing," said Miss Henrietta. Annabel thought Miss Henrietta's voice sounded strange. It was lower and croakier than normal. "Do you understand?"

"Yes, Miss Henrietta," said Annabel.

Miss Henrietta watched her with her brilliant blue eyes.

She did not look impressed. There was a new chill in the room. Miss Henrietta took the forceps, which hung limply in Annabel's hand, and plucked up five leaves. She folded them quickly into a parcel and tied them with string. Annabel looked away from those eyes and at Miss Henrietta's hands and then at her dress, which was dark and shiny and suddenly rustling. It was a strange noise, and it filled her ears. Annabel wanted to look away from the dress, back to her great-aunt's eyes, but found she couldn't.

She looked at the dress, and no matter how hard she tried, she could not shift her gaze. The noise of it, now a cracking and a chafing, grew. She wanted to cover her ears. *Feathers*, she thought, for that was what she saw instead of dress: midnight-black feathers. A wing stretched and then folded, and one of the black buttons of Miss Henrietta's dress was now a wild black eye watching her intently, curiously.

Annabel cried out, stumbled backward. There was a crow. Its claws clacked on the countertop, and it turned its head to

39

watch her with its dark eye. Before Annabel could scream, it picked up the parcel in its beak and flew swiftly through the open door. It sailed across the street and up into the sky.

♦ ♦ ♦

Black feathers. Annabel's only coherent thought. *Black feathers.* She wanted her old life back. She wanted to rush out of the shop. She wanted to run until her familiar pretty streets appeared. She wanted her old self back, who only had to worry about her dresses and whether she would have sugary apple cake or custard pie for pudding. She would have everything back the way it was and never look in a puddle again. Her eyes stung with tears, and no matter how hard she tried, she could not stop her bottom lip from trembling. It was wrong to cry, but she put her head in her hands and began to weep.

There were many ways a young lady might stop tears, and she had learned them all at Miss Finch's Academy for Young Ladies. She could fix her gaze on some distant object; she could press her handkerchief delicately to her nose and think of a field of flowers. She did neither of these things. She sat on the stool and cried loudly because her life was terrible. She cried because since arriving she had washed clothes and swept floors and been shouted at. She cried because her mother had sent her to this horrid little shop. She cried because her dead father hadn't been a sea captain after all, even though at night her mother had told her stories about his seafaring life. She cried because Miss Henrietta

Vine was the meanest relative a girl could ever have and she had just turned into a crow.

She let the tears drip off her nose. She was Miss Finch's worst nightmare. But she felt better for crying, and gradually the tears lessened. She wiped her cheeks with her hand because she had forgotten her handkerchief. She sat on the stool and swung her legs. It was strange that young ladies should never cry, she thought, when crying actually made them feel better. Crying was considered to be ugly, yet her limbs felt heavy now, pleasantly heavy, and she felt calmer.

She looked at the wand lying on the countertop. Miss Henrietta had called it the Ondona. She touched it rather timidly but, after what had happened with the dresses, did not pick it up. She didn't want to cause any more trouble. She sighed very loudly and opened Miss Henrietta's ledger. It smelled peculiar—vinegary—and the pages were heavy and tea-colored. They crackled beneath her fingers. The last entries were for almost three years previous, when Mr. S. Worth had paid his account in full for the purchase of two candles and Lady Pansofia Swift had ordered a new broomstick. They confirmed her theory that no one ever visited the little magic shop. She wondered if Kitty would come again. She wished she would. She was used to having other girls, Isabelle Rutherford especially, not just herself, for company.

Annabel was turning the page when she heard footsteps. She was certain someone had entered the shop, but there was nobody to be seen. She jumped down from the stool and moved from behind the counter.

She heard two more footsteps. Yes, the definite shuffle of feet upon the ground.

"Hello," she said. "Who's there?"

A low chuckle.

"Miss Vine has a new girl, I see," said a voice quite close, so that Annabel jumped back in fright.

"You should make yourself visible!" shouted Annabel. "This instant. It's rude."

There was a whoosh of purple satin and black serge, and a man appeared, his dark cloak falling around him. He held a long dark stick in his hand.

Annabel had never seen anyone like him before.

He was very tall and a little crooked at the top. He bent forward halfway up, as though he were bracing himself to walk against the wind. His luxurious black hair fell in waves around his face, and his skin was as white as a funeral orchid, as though he never, ever saw the sun.

"Oh," she said, even though she knew it was rude. It slipped out. She retreated behind the counter, away from him.

"I am Mr. Angel, wizard," he said. His voice was slow and deep. "Miss Vine might have mentioned me."

She hadn't. Or at least Annabel didn't think she had. She had mentioned wizards, though. Maybe he'd been mixed in with them all and Annabel hadn't noticed.

She didn't like to look at his crookedness, so she looked at his face, which was handsome in a way she couldn't fathom. He had very dark eyes, which were sad, probably the saddest eyes she had ever seen, with very long lashes. He had a largish nose and a mouth that was rather lopsided, one side sneering, one side melancholy. He had dark shadows in his cheekbones, as though he needed to be fed for weeks and weeks on cream buns and egg custard. Those shadows made her shiver suddenly, and a little dark memory that she couldn't quite catch flitted across her eye and was gone.

He was sad and lonely-looking.

He was wicked-looking.

As though he would pinch babies when their mothers weren't paying attention.

Or steal precious things from locked drawers very quietly.

She didn't like him. There was something about him that made her feel scared.

"I'm afraid Miss Henrietta Vine is out on business," Annabel said, and it made her think of black feathers. She closed her eyes briefly and shook her head. Black feathers and invisible men. It just wouldn't do.

"Her sister?"

Estella? Miss Estella was a mystery. She tried not to let it show.

"Unfortunately, Miss Estella Vine is indisposed," said Annabel.

"What is your name, then?" he said, and his voice was kind, but beneath the kindness there was darkness coiling.

"Annabel Grey," she replied, lifting up her chin and smiling the most polite smile she could.

"Ah," he said, surprised. "*The* Annabel Grey. Daughter of the Great Geraldo Grey?"

Annabel did not know what he meant. She did not like the way his face had split wide with a terrible tight smile. The Great Geraldo Grey? The name made her heart hurt and flutter at the same time.

"And may I ask after your mother's health?" Mr. Angel said, tilting his head, smile widening.

"My mother is traveling on the Continent," said Annabel, and she tried very hard to keep the quiver from her voice.

Mr. Angel thought for some time and then suddenly rapped his cane loudly on the counter.

"A letter for the Misses Vine, then, Annabel," he said, and took from his pocket a paper folded and embossed with a dark seal. "I have returned. I have the Black Wand and a machine already producing dark magic. When the full moon rises Friday eve, the machine will reach its potential. Thirteen years of full moons. The dark magic it will produce will be unbounded. I will raise a shadowling army and take the city. There will be no more good magic. The Great & Benevolent Magical Society, each and every member, must lay down their wands and bow down before me and pledge allegiance. If not, I will turn them all to dust."

Annabel tried very hard to keep her polite smile. It seemed to annoy Mr. Angel. He took his black stick and aimed it at the ledger on the countertop. A blast of purple light erupted from its tip, and the ledger vanished, leaving a pile of dust in its place. Annabel's smile slipped and was gone. She looked at the pile of dust and knew that Miss Henrietta would be very cross indeed. She began to cry.

But Mr. Angel was only beginning. He took his Black Wand and pointed it through the window at the sunny day. He closed his eyes and began to sing a mournful song. Annabel thought it had a very unpleasant tune. A shadow fell over the shop front as though a cloud had passed over the sun, and suddenly a torrent of soot rained from the sky. A fog rose up outside—in wispy tendrils at first, then thicker and thicker, deep brown and purplish in parts, until the street was quite clouded. The shop grew darker and cooler.

Annabel hiccuped and shivered.

Mr. Angel smiled, pleased with the result. He took a handkerchief from his pocket and handed it to her. Annabel dried her eyes, said thank you, and handed the handkerchief back to him.

"I'll tell Miss Vine that you called," she whispered.

She took the letter, and his dark-gloved hand closed over hers.

"Are you as magical as your mother?" he asked.

His gloved hand was warm and dry, and Annabel could not breathe. He spoke softly. He leaned toward her, close, with his crookedness.

"There is nothing any of you can do to stop me," he said, then turned and flicked his cloak and was gone, leaving the fog behind him.

◆ ◆ ◆

Annabel was still sitting there an hour later when Miss Henrietta returned. She did not come back as a crow but as her normal self, scowling at the weather and looking vexed.

"I've had to walk from St. Paul's," she said. "Because of all this brown fog. Where on earth has it come from? There must be a fire somewhere."

She stopped when she saw Annabel's ashen face. She glanced at the letter in Annabel's hands and the pile of dust where the ledger had been.

"I've left you alone for only two hours!" she cried. "What on earth have you managed to do?"

3

*"When calling upon a new acquaintance, a young lady will
not stare or comment upon surroundings. She will not touch
ornaments, examine paintings, or open the pianoforte."*
　　　　　　　　　—*Miss Finch's Little Blue Book (1855)*

Miss Henrietta snatched the letter from Annabel's
hands. It made Annabel feel cross and ashamed, as
though she herself had raised the fog and caused the ledger to disappear. She stood up, and Miss Henrietta took her
place on the stool, the letter undone, and her mouth open.

"All the Black Witches of Birmingham! It cannot be so!"
Miss Henrietta cried. "Mr. Angel has returned."

She turned gray, and her blue eyes filled with tears. The
letter trembled in her hands.

"Was he here?" she cried.

"Yes," said Annabel.

"And he has a terrible machine and *the* Black Wand
and . . ." She was quite overcome, and Annabel wasn't sure
what to do.

47

"Should I make you a cup of tea, Miss Henrietta?" she asked.

"No, no time for tea, Annabel. Quickly, make haste. I must take the letter to Estella. She will know what to do. We must pass through the storeroom. You are not ready for it, but there is no time. I implore you, keep your arms by your sides and your eyes on the floor. Do you understand?"

It seemed a strange request, but Annabel nodded because everything that had happened since her arrival had been strange. She felt she was becoming quite used to it. Miss Henrietta took the Ondona, the letter, and a candle and opened the door to the left of the specimen cabinets.

"Hurry, then," she whispered to Annabel. "Magical things must not be exposed to too much sunlight."

Annabel followed Miss Henrietta, who held the candle low before her. They passed through a narrow room filled from floor to ceiling with shelves. Annabel immediately forgot what she had been instructed. She looked at the shelves and the things illuminated by Miss Henrietta's candle.

There were rolled carpets and wicker baskets, boxes stacked one on top of another, large pots, peacock feathers, the staring eyes of dolls. There were glass jars and broomsticks tied up in bundles, and other things, too, although she couldn't quite make out the shapes. They were dark things, lurking things, skulking-shaped things. Things that worried her, so she quickly looked away. Finally, Miss Henrietta opened another door into the same miserable little kitchen.

It was the same little kitchen, Annabel was sure of it,

only . . . now it was different. The hearth was on the opposite side, and the door to the alleyway had changed position, and the teapot on the little table was green instead of blue.

"Quickly, quickly, or too much light will get in," repeated Miss Henrietta. "Magical objects need darkness and little air."

Annabel stood still, trying to understand what had happened, until Miss Henrietta grabbed her by the arm and dragged her forward to a large brown door that *most definitely* had not been there before.

"Now we must go down," said Miss Henrietta.

"Down?" asked Annabel.

"Down," said Miss Henrietta, and she opened the door and pointed down into the darkness.

◆ ◆ ◆

Miss Henrietta held the candle high and the light of it flared on the stone walls. Annabel gathered up her skirts with one hand and worried afresh for her new blue leather boots. The dark stairs smelled of old onions and mildew. Down they went, and with each step the smell grew. The dark stone staircase ended, and they entered a hall. Now the house smelled of rain. Annabel didn't like to admit it, but she could not deny it: it was a relief after the stench of the stone stairs. The little dim parlor they passed through, unused and lonely, the papered walls strung with cobwebs, smelled exactly like rain. Real rain, fresh rain, Annabel thought with a growing sense of alarm . . . rain falling in torrents off rooftops and filling up puddles. She stopped, her nostrils flared, her eyes widened. How could a room smell so wild and tumultuous?

A figure appeared from the gloom up ahead. She was an old lady, nearly completely bent over, holding a large crook. Annabel thought it was Miss Estella, but the woman nodded to Miss Henrietta and lowered her eyes, and Annabel realized it must be the maid, Tatty.

Tatty looked at Annabel most sternly, banged her crook down hard, and opened a door behind her. There was a noise in Annabel's ears now, a loud noise: a rippling, trickling, rushing noise. She wanted to slap her ears, shake her head, to get the sound out.

"In," said Tatty, and Annabel entered Miss Estella's bedchamber.

In Miss Estella's bedchamber there was a very large bed. It was festooned with nets and ribbons, all in tatters, all ragged and stained. Beside the bed were pink and green and brown bottles all covered in dust.

Annabel wished she had a handkerchief to cover her nose.

The room smelled of perfume gone sour. Old bathwater. Urine. And something else. . . .

Miss Henrietta pushed Annabel forward into the room with her sharp, bony finger. The something else was a river. A dark river, a black river. Annabel smelled it, and the smell of it made her gasp. It was the smell of rushing water, pungent with dead leaves and moss and the blank, airy scent of river stones. She could hear it, too, swirling and trickling and babbling, even though there was no water to be seen. The sound of the water was so loud that Annabel expected to see it cascading down the walls, but there was nothing there, just the faded pink-peony wallpaper.

"Do not be alarmed. It is only the secret river," came a withered voice from the bed. "One of the old rivers."

Miss Estella was so small that Annabel hadn't seen her. She was lost amid the cushions, her little wrinkled face half-hidden by a large lace nightcap. She peered at Annabel with mischievous dark eyes.

"It runs beneath this very place," she said, "and today it runs fast and high, and I rejoice. The sound of it gives me great comfort, for I know in my bones that I am soon to die."

Annabel thought she might faint. She would—she *would* faint—and they would have to call for a physician, and she would be taken away. It would serve them right. Her mother could never have truly meant for her to come to such a place.

"So you're the girl, then, yes?" said Miss Estella. "Vivienne's child? Vivienne has sent you back, as she should have. Finally she saw the error of her ways. Oh, the girl can feel the river, yes. See how she feels the river, Hen? It's in her blood, then. Sit her down—get the girl a chair."

Miss Henrietta sighed. She pushed Annabel toward a chair in the corner of the room.

"Great trouble is upon us," Miss Henrietta said. "A letter has come from Mr. Angel."

"Hush," said Miss Estella, ignoring her sister. "Never

mind, child; the water never comes into the room. I have a boat down there, you know, and when my time comes, I am going to sail away."

She let out a long cackle at that.

"Sail away," she said again. "What do you think of that? Speak up, then."

"I don't understand," whispered Annabel.

"Don't understand?" said Miss Estella, and she laughed even louder. "The letter, then, Henrietta. Get the child to read it. I would like to hear her voice. It will be very pleasing to my dainty little ears."

Miss Estella's ears were hidden somewhere beneath her lace nightcap. Annabel imagined they would be as purplish and withered as fallen rose petals. She needed to think of something pleasant: the green ice skates she was to have for her birthday. It was very difficult.

Miss Henrietta thrust the letter into Annabel's hands. "Read it," she demanded.

"Yes, read it, pretty," said Miss Estella, most amused. "Mr. Angel, you say? No one's heard from him for many a year.

"She is like Vivienne, is she not, Hen?" continued Miss Estella. "You know your mother was very powerful, child. Why, she could mend most anything, even what was nearly dead and gone. So magical—why, she even had her own wand, the Lydia, but she gave that away when she went and made things ruinous, all for love, and went to Mr. Angel and caused great trouble and turned her back on us."

Annabel bit her lip. Her mother was a lady, of good society. She knew her Titians from her Tiepolos. It seemed unlikely that she'd have gone anywhere near Mr. Angel.

"*The* Annabel Grey," said Miss Estella. "Remember the dreams the wizards had of her?"

"Hush, Estella," said Miss Henrietta.

"Read the letter. Go on—open the letter," said Miss Estella with a laugh.

Annabel's hands shook as she unfolded the paper. The room filled with the sound of rushing water and the smell of flood, and her head spun as though she were lost in a storm.

"To the Misses E. and H. Vine:

"It is in your capacity as secretaries of the Great & Benevolent Magical Society that I address this letter to you. I am returned to London, and the Black Wand is mine. My Dark-Magic Extracting Machine is nearly complete, and at full moon I will raise a shadowling army and take the city. Everything shall be mine. All the palaces and all the mansions. All the parks and all the estates. Each and every street. Each and every tenement. Everyone in the city will bow to me. I have raised several shadowlings already, and they are as cunning and wicked as the books describe. I implore you, send notice to all members of your society and ask them to lay down their wands and pledge allegiance to my rule before Friday midnight, when the

53

*moon will rise. I offer you all a place in my dark empire
if you obey.*

"Dated this day, 13th June 1867, Mr. A. Angel."

"You see, Estella!" cried Miss Henrietta.

"He has the Black Wand," said Miss Estella. "It cannot be so."

"And a machine!" cried Miss Henrietta.

"He will use his dark magic to raise the shadowlings," said Miss Estella. "He might turn everyone to stone."

"Dust," said Annabel. "He told me dust."

Both the great-aunts stared at her until she reddened under their gaze.

"We are the secretaries of the Great & Benevolent Magical Society," said Miss Henrietta.

"From our birth day to our day of death," said Miss Estella.

"Under no circumstances must this be allowed to happen. We must send word. We must make plans!" cried Miss Henrietta.

There was a long pause then, while the two old women thought, and the room seemed to Annabel to be filled up with their quiet cognitions. Miss Estella murmured, and Miss Henrietta wrung her hands, slowly, methodically, one inside the other. The sound of the river trickled and gushed and crooned and rushed.

"It was written somewhere, was it not, Hen?" said Miss

Estella at last. "The very rules for what the society should do if good magic was threatened. If the Black Wand was found."

"I believe you are correct, Estella," said Miss Henrietta.

"There was the book," said Miss Estella.

"The book?" said Miss Henrietta. And she wound her hands tighter, then said apologetically, "It has been long, Estella, since our mother taught us."

"The . . . big book. The very big book with the purple cover. *The Handbook of the Great & Benevolent Magical Society!*" Miss Estella spat the last words out with triumph. "Fetch it, Henrietta. And I will tell Annabel of Mr. Angel."

◆ ◆ ◆

Annabel was used to perfectly normal conversation. Who was walking out in the afternoon at Kensington and what they wore and who was to be presented in the spring. Not talk of wizards and wands and shadowlings. She had no idea what a shadowling was, but just the word made her feel worried, deep down in the pit of her stomach.

"Come closer," said Miss Estella once Miss Henrietta had gone from the room.

Annabel could think of nothing worse. She wanted to stay on her chair, where it was safe.

"Don't be afraid," said Miss Estella. "I can't hear your thoughts all the way over there."

Annabel stood and moved toward the bed. She tried a smile but abandoned it when Miss Estella grinned back at her wildly, providing a wide view of her brown teeth. Miss Estella patted the sheets beside her. Dirty, stained sheets. Annabel thought she would faint if she had to sit on those dirty sheets. But she lowered her bottom gingerly and found herself still conscious.

"Oh, but you are shaking like a little autumn leaf," said Miss Estella, as though it pleased her greatly. "Tell me, then. You see things, do you not? And your mother knew it was time for you to be educated."

"Yes," whispered Annabel.

"And what has your mother taught you of the magical world?"

"She hasn't," whispered Annabel.

Miss Estella opened her mouth and let out a long high-pitched shriek.

"Wicked thing! She should have taught you, not turned her back on us. She should never have gone to Mr. Angel. He was a Finsbury Wizard, but they sent him out of the brotherhood, for he was always making bad machines and searching for a way to make dark magic. The Black Wand is the most powerful wand in the world. It was carved of ebony by hand long ago, and it is the only wand that can channel pure dark magic. The magic of destruction. The magic of chaos. It was hidden away, but now he has it—how, I do not know. But he will do great harm with it if we do not stop him."

Annabel nodded politely to show she was interested. She wasn't. She was scared and confused.

"But there is also the good wand," Miss Estella continued. "The White Wand. Yes. It's coming back to me now. It will be in the book. The Morever Wand. There is a map for finding it where it is hidden, deep down in Under London . . . where the faeries put it. Henrietta! I remember!"

She yelled the last so loud that Annabel covered her ears.

"Oh yes," said Miss Estella. The white whiskers that grew boldly on her chin wiggled with each word. "The Morever Wand, the Faery Wand, the Witch's Wand, hidden away for years and years and the only one that can do battle with the Black Wand. Made of a Siberian rowan tree, yes! The two great wands, rulers over all the lesser wands; the Black and the White, made to do battle with each other if ever the time came."

Miss Henrietta returned. Annabel went to stand, but Miss Estella's hand closed around her wrist. Her nails were long and yellow, each one split, each one like rotting wood.

"It was small and green, after all that," said Miss Henrietta, holding the book in her hand. She glared at her sister and then at Annabel for good measure. "So it took longer to find."

"It seemed large in my head," said Miss Estella, but she didn't mention the color.

"I hope you haven't told her too much," said Miss Henrietta. "She looks pale. She's the sort who will take ill with too much knowledge. Like the last girl, who faded to nothing in a matter of days."

"She was a weakling. This girl here is strong. Don't you feel it, Henrietta?"

Miss Henrietta looked at Annabel with great distaste.

57

Annabel thought she much preferred Miss Estella, even with her wild shrieks and rotting teeth, to Miss Henrietta.

"I have recalled the White Wand and the map. Tell us what it says if the society is threatened with the Black Wand," said Miss Estella.

Miss Henrietta sat in the chair and opened the book, which was more a collection of loose and tattered pages kept within an emerald-green cover. She went through the pages one by one.

"The Great & Benevolent Magical Society," she said. "Description. Purpose. Laws. Bylaws. Membership. Members' obligations."

"Threats to the society!" cried Miss Estella. "Threats to London! Threats to the world! The Black Wand!"

"I see nothing like that written here," said Miss Henrietta, shuffling through the papers. "Here—no, wait. Sanctity of the Society: Threats, Coercions, and Forebodings. The Black Wand."

"Read it!" shrieked Miss Estella so loudly that Annabel's bottom left the bed.

"Patience!" Miss Henrietta cried back at her. "'There may come a time when those with magical and malevolent intentions gain possession of the Black Wand. The Black Wand, when filled with dark magic, can raise the shadowlings. Under no circumstances must the Great & Benevolent Magical Society allow this. At such a time, the Morever Wand must be retrieved from its hidden resting place in Under London by the youngest and most able member of the society; preferably, a most magical girl. (See appendix twenty-seven, Prophecies Related to the Morever Wand.) The youngest and most able member of the Great & Benevolent Magical Society will assume the role of Valiant Defender of Good Magic. The youngest and most able member of the society may take a companion on the journey. (See appendix twenty-seven, Prophecies Related to the Morever Wand.)'

"Oh, stuff and nonsense," Miss Henrietta interrupted herself. Then she went back to reading: "'Instructions for the singing of the map into the youngest and most able member are located in appendix three.'"

Miss Henrietta stopped there. The river gushed and hushed in Annabel's ears. Annabel tried to imagine little wizened Miss Estella being a valiant defender of anything. She wasn't sure Miss Estella could even stand. She looked at Miss Henrietta then, with her sour, creased face and her trembling hands. *Who is the younger?* she wondered.

"Appendix three," demanded Miss Estella.

Miss Henrietta recommenced shuffling through the papers. All the meanness seemed to evaporate from her face. She looked frightened. Beside Annabel, Miss Estella began to murmur again. Quite suddenly both great-aunts looked ancient and useless. A pile of papers slid from Miss Henrietta's lap to the floor.

Annabel stood up and moved toward her. "Here," she said. "An appendix should always be at the back. I'll help."

Miss Henrietta handed her some pages. She found appendix one, which was an illustration of a wand. The words

Morever Wand were printed, rather scratchily, beneath it. It looked like a stick, and not a magical one, either.

She found appendix seventeen, which was a sketch of something large and dark, a shadowy-looking thing, no more than a dark shape, really, standing in a dark space. Annabel held that page in her hand until she realized she needed to breathe, which she did. Then she put the page down. She knelt and began to go through the pages on the floor.

"Here is appendix three," she said.

Miss Henrietta studied the page and looked even more terrified.

"Time yet to read it, Hen. We must prepare the girl now!" shouted Miss Estella. "Find her a broomstick and send her to wizards so she can choose a seeing glass and they can teach her. She must be taught as much as we know!"

The girl, thought Annabel. *Who on earth is the girl?*

"The girl knows nothing!" shouted Miss Henrietta. She stood, and the remaining pages cascaded to the floor. "You cannot mean it!"

"It says it—it is written, by hands hundreds of years past. The youngest and most able member of the society, a most magical girl, must enter Under London and retrieve the Morever Wand. Here she stands, before your very eyes, Sister!"

"This child has as much magic in her as a common dormouse!" shouted Miss Henrietta. "She may be of the family Vine and she may be the youngest, but she is definitely not the most able."

The girl, thought Annabel, and then the realization dawned upon her so that it took her breath away. They were talking about her.

"She is a girl of good lineage; she is strong," said Miss Estella. "How can you not feel it, Sister? Remember the wizards' dreamings? She will go down the hole into Under London. The wand in Mr. Angel's hands will spell the end. She will save us all. She is our only hope."

"Good lineage does not make her a witch," replied Miss Henrietta.

Annabel looked down at her pretty rosebud-patterned dress, touched a stray tendril of blond hair. She let out a little laugh. A hiccup. A very small sob.

"But I don't want to be a witch," she said.

"Sometimes, dear girl, you have no say in such matters," said Miss Estella.

◆　◆　◆

They were a sad lot, those Highgate faeries, weeping over every single tree cut down. Every pond bricked over. All the fair things wiped away, copses blackened and burned, all the birds stolen from trees so that fine ladies might have a pretty thing. But they didn't move on. Others disappeared in the night, and she found their left-behind burrows filled with scraps of their lives. The Highgate faeries stayed. Their queenie was thin and vicious. Always sharpening her arrows.

Just before dawn Kitty had given them the parcel from

Miss Henrietta. They were not happy with its contents. An old plate. Lace. A tinderbox. They had all these things, the queenie screeched in her own language, but Kitty understood well enough. They were agitated. The wind and rain had died down, and they were pointing to the moon. But in the end they gave her faery twine, and she was glad to be away from them.

She had slept again in the mausoleum, and the moon had gone down. London had come to life. She felt it through her skin, pressed to the cold stone: giant looms and wood mills and carriage wheels, cooks in kitchens and poor boys sweeping streets and ladies everywhere being laced up in their stays. She smiled, coughed, slept again. The Vine Witches were always happy with faery twine.

When she woke, there was a great fog.

In the streets, shop lights blazed as though it were night and men walked before carriages holding lanterns aloft. Everywhere, people were confounded by the appearance of the pea-souper, brown in places, purple in others. And how they complained. She listened to snippets of their conversations, snatches of their concerns, as she began her long walk back. They grumbled at tavern doors and worried at windows. They covered their noses, for it stank, that fog, it stank of a thousand bad things, of peat and coal and tanning works; of sulfur, of sewers, of cigars and chimneys. Word was that a steamer had run its bow aground on the Isle of Dogs.

But Kitty did not complain. She walked. She had seen

many fogs: yellow fogs and gray fogs and black fogs. She had seen fogs this very color but knew it was not the London Particular. She touched it with her hands and knew it was something else. It was magical, this stuff, and she knew it as surely as she knew her own bones.

She did not worry. Her feet were sore and her stomach was growling, but she did not let it bother her. For faery rope, Miss Henrietta would give her new bread, fog or not, sore feet or not. She walked and walked, and there were butterflies dancing inside her, and she couldn't say why, but she felt as though the whole world were ending and beginning at once, and more than anything, she wanted to see Annabel Grey.

4

*"A young lady does not yawn or sigh but listens attentively
to any lesson or wise anecdote an elder may offer."*
—*Miss Finch's Little Blue Book* (1855)

Annabel did not like the sound of Under London. She
decided she would agree to everything her two great-
aunts suggested and, when alone, rush from the shop. She'd
take the coin in her purse and catch an omnibus to the Rutherfords' house on Park Lane and throw herself upon their
mercy until her mother returned. She could be Isabelle's sister for a while. They would wear the finest clothes and ride
in the Rutherfords' landau and ice-skate on the Serpentine in
the winter with all the other pretty young girls. She would
wear her emerald-green ice skates.

Her two great-aunts argued over her head. It was a furious argument. It crackled and sizzled and snapped in the air.
It filled that murky bedchamber. Miss Estella wore a vicious
expression on her tiny face. Miss Henrietta paced to and fro.

"We must equip her as best we can. She has the sight—we

know as much. We can give her the map. She will find the way. The Morever Wand is the only wand that will stop the Black once it is filled with dark magic," said Miss Estella. "Hours—we have little more than a day, Henrietta. Full moon is tomorrow evening!"

"But look at her mind!" Miss Henrietta cried. "Look at the clutter. She wouldn't last half a day in Under London. She has not a single wit about her."

"You are stubborn as a Tottenham Troll!" cried Miss Estella. "Henrietta . . . Sister . . . We must teach her to empty her mind. Send her to the wizards. They must be warned anyway. All the society members must be warned. They can show her how to look into the glass. That is her talent."

"Foolish Sister!" cried Miss Henrietta, moving backward and forward so that Annabel felt quite dizzy for watching it. "She has no talent."

"Mr. Angel has already raised up shadowlings," said Miss Estella. "He will raise more. He will turn London dark."

To which Miss Henrietta closed her eyes and nodded once.

"She is our only hope," continued Miss Estella. "She must go down into Under London."

"Under London," said Miss Henrietta.

"A most magical girl," said Miss Estella.

"A most magical girl," repeated Miss Henrietta, and she looked at Annabel with her most disappointed expression yet.

◆ ◆ ◆

Out of Miss Estella's riverbed chamber they went. Out past bent-over Tatty, who banged her crook very loudly. Out into the lonely hallway and the desolate parlor.

Miss Estella called to them as they left. "Teach her to empty," she cried. "Find her a broomstick. Send her to the wizards."

Annabel heard those words clearly, but then she and Miss Henrietta were on the stinking stairwell and the words grew indistinct. Miss Henrietta opened the brown door into the small, changed kitchen, with the hearth facing the wrong way and the green teapot instead of the blue. The dreadful brown fog swirled against the window and made the place very dark.

Annabel suddenly felt so weary she could fall down and sleep. At Miss Finch's Academy for Young Ladies, they would take their time warming up to the day. They would recite their French conjugations, and then they would list the capitals of the world. They would practice curtsying for a good half hour before anything difficult was expected of them.

This morning she'd already emptied chamber pots and folded laundry and swept floors, and now she'd been told she had to become a witch and go down a hole and find a wand to save London.

Miss Henrietta pulled two chairs by the fire and motioned for Annabel to sit. She raised the Ondona in her hand.

"Benignus," she said very quietly, and the flames sprang up in the fire.

She took a seat before Annabel and their knees almost touched.

"To give you the map, there must be room inside you," she said. She pointed to Annabel's head.

That doesn't really make any sense, thought Annabel.

"For you to read the map, there must be room inside you," said Miss Henrietta. She pointed to Annabel's heart.

Anyone can read a map, thought Annabel. She was quite good at it, actually. She wished Miss Henrietta wouldn't point at her. It was rude.

"For you to understand the map, there must be room inside you," said Miss Henrietta.

Fiddlesticks, thought Annabel, which was what the maid Mercy said when she burned the crumpets.

"There is no room inside you," said Henrietta. "Listen to you. You cannot control your thoughts. You are loud and careless. How will you hear the world—the real world—when all you hear are your own buzzing thoughts?"

Annabel wondered if she would get morning tea.

Miss Henrietta sighed, exasperated.

"First imagine your mind is a teacup."

"I beg your pardon, Miss Henrietta?" said Annabel.

"Impudent child," said Miss Henrietta. "To empty one's thoughts and to quiet them, one must quickly and carefully examine the cup of one's mind. What kind of cup do you have?"

Annabel stared at Miss Henrietta. It was a trick question—she knew it. No matter what she said, it would be wrong.

Miss Henrietta waited.

"If your mind were a cup," her great-aunt said slowly, each word like a stamp of the foot, "what kind of cup would it be?"

"Well," said Annabel, "it would be a little fancy. It would be a bone china teacup, white, painted all over with yellow roses, and trimmed in gold."

"Good," said Miss Henrietta. "Now that you see your cup, can you see what is inside it? What are your thoughts? Do not shout them, I beg of you. Just look into your cup and quietly list them."

So Annabel imagined her fancy teacup, and she imagined lifting it up and looking inside. *My thoughts are that you are very mean*, Annabel said to herself. That thought floated on the top like a large blob of cream.

My thoughts are that if I could go home, I'd go home this very instant. Everything would be well again. Charlie would be singing in his cage, and Mama would be dressing for a party. She wouldn't ever have been very magical. My father really would be a sea captain who'd been lost at sea.

Quite suddenly she saw a horrible thought. It was dark and oily, sitting just below the surface. The thought was: *Why did my mother lie to me? About my father, about herself. About everything.*

What did I see in the washtub? What is that part of me? The ruinous, horrid part. The part that sees things. She stopped looking in her teacup and looked at Miss Henrietta instead.

"There is more," said Miss Henrietta. It wasn't a question.

"Yes," said Annabel, but she didn't want to look again. There was much more, a thousand questions, one of them so huge she dared not look. "Are my thoughts quieter?"

"No," said Miss Henrietta.

Surely I can't be expected to go on a journey all alone? That was the next thought that rose to the surface. She'd never been anywhere alone. *What if I fail?* That was a very large thought. It was almost as big as the cup, expanding. She looked up at Miss Henrietta.

"Look again," said her great-aunt. "I know there is more."

So Annabel looked back at her fancy teacup. The thing at the bottom was worst of all. She looked at her shiny white porcelain handle instead and then at the perfect yellow roses. She looked at them carefully, even though they were completely imaginary.

"Tell me," said Miss Henrietta.

The thought at the bottom was unspeakable.

I should like to smash this teacup on the ground, thought Annabel.

She wanted to smash it because she knew that her mind was nothing like that cup. She knew this, even though she had been taught to think it was. It had been drummed into her, reinforced just as surely as she was laced up and be-ribboned, her fair hair curled with rags and arranged just so. She had been told again and again: You are pretty and frag-ile and delicate. You are nothing. This is you, Miss Annabel Grey. Pretty Mayfair girl.

She knew that cup was not her mind. She knew it, and

it made her want to howl. Her mother should have told her so. Oh, she was angry. She had never in all her life howled. She held the howl in. It hurt her insides. Her cup would be dark. Her cup would smell of unknown things. Her cup would never be empty. She would never, ever get to the bottom of it. Her cup was everything she had been taught to turn her back on. She was everything she was taught to never see.

She howled then. Her whole world was shattering around her. Everything seemed lost and found at exactly the same time. She began to cry a great wave of tears. She put her hands up to her face in horror at the force of them.

"Good girl," said Miss Henrietta. "Good girl."

Her aging great-aunt placed a large bony hand on Annabel's head. Annabel expected it to be cold and hard, but it was smooth and as light as a feather, and its touch was like the kiss of a butterfly.

Mr. Angel brought the machine a pair of shoes from a dead girl in Seven Dials, a length of black crepe stolen from a window on Gresham Street, three tear catchers, stoppers intact, stolen from a widow's bedroom. The machine huffed at the scent of them and, when he held them up, sucked them with great force across the length of the room, one by one. The shadowlings tittered and

writhed in the corner, their brand-new wings opening and shutting, waiting.

He gave the machine a small clock stopped at the death of a child. A letter of apology from one sister to another, never sent. And the machine delighted in these sorrowful objects. The things that had touched darkness. Its cogs whirred, and its bellows chuffed. The floor vibrated. Mr. Angel leaned forward, pressed his monocle to his eye, and examined the dark-magic gauge. The needle had moved—slightly but surely, it had moved. When it completed its journey around the dial, the machine would make unlimited dark magic. He would stand on his rooftop and raise his army of shadowlings.

From his pocket Mr. Angel took the handkerchief that Annabel Grey had dried her eyes with and smiled. The machine sensed it, and its gears sang in a higher note. He held the handkerchief up and felt the pull of the machine.

Annabel's mother's tears had been the first. He had fed them to his new machine all those years ago. He closed his eyes to remember how Vivienne had wept over the body of her husband. There had never been such mourning. Thirteen years of full moons, and now the daughter. . . .

"Yes!" he cried. "Of course!"

The girl was who he needed. He would feed her to the machine, not her handkerchief. She was the saddest object! As though sensing his realization, the machine's cogs whined louder and louder.

"Of course," he muttered again, and held up his hand to his

dreadful invention. "Not yet. Soon I will give you all of Annabel Grey instead."

He began to laugh then, softly first, and then louder and louder, so that the room echoed with the sound. And when he was gone with his Black Wand, the shadowlings mimicked his laughter, which was harsh and lonely and full of pain.

5

*"In education, geography is harmless, but too much history
and politics can lead to a quarrelsome nature."*

—Miss Finch's Little Blue Book (1855)

"Now you are a little emptied out," said Miss Henrietta.
"And you will remember the cup for the future, won't
you?"

It was true, Annabel felt empty and airy inside for a short
while, and she marveled at the sensation as Miss Henrietta
stood up.

"We will send you to the wizards. They will teach you
what they can. We have little time. If Mr. Angel says he will
raise an army, then an army he will raise."

Annabel wondered again what shadowlings were. She
tried to picture them in her mind, but they wouldn't form.
All she could see was Mr. Angel, with his dark, sad eyes and
his meanness. Just looking at him had made her feel terrible
and lonely.

"Pardon me, Miss Henrietta," she said. "But what are shadowlings?"

Miss Henrietta took a deep breath.

"Shadowlings are nothing creatures, Annabel. They are sleeping shadows that live in dark places and are usually no more than that. Have you ever been frightened of the shadowy space behind a door?"

Annabel nodded.

"Well, that is a sleeping shadow. A nothing creature. But if there comes someone with dark magic and that dark magic is put into that shadow, then that shadow becomes a shadowling, and it is given a life, a wicked little being, a terrible little soul. Shadows given wicked little souls, Annabel—why, they might do almost anything."

"I see," said Annabel.

"Do you?" said Miss Henrietta.

Annabel thought of Miss Finch and all her lessons. The French conjugations and the curtsying. The Latin, which Annabel could not for the life of her understand, the lacework, and the long afternoons pretending there was nothing more important than talking about what the royal princesses wore. Nothing she had learned could possibly prepare her for shadows with wicked little souls, and Miss Henrietta looked as if she knew it. How could they expect her to go on a journey into Under London? She didn't even know how to begin.

"A broomstick," said Miss Henrietta at last. "That is where we begin. We must find you a broomstick."

A broomstick, thought Annabel. She hoped she didn't have

74

to do more sweeping. She followed Miss Henrietta into the magical storeroom. This time Annabel was ready for the inside, for the odd, jumbled-up assortment of smells: peppermint and oranges and wax and old clothes. There was a place in the storeroom that smelled exactly like the sea. She did not keep her eyes to the ground—instead, she looked about herself in wonder. Near them, there was a jar filled with a silvery liquid. It made a soft bubbling sound.

"Broomsticks," said Miss Henrietta, holding up the candle to illuminate several tall hats. "Where did I put the broomsticks? Oh yes. Right beside the peat jars. Now, take the stepladder—that's right—and climb up and take one of the brooms, please."

Annabel did as she was told. She climbed the stepladder, and up close like that, with Miss Henrietta holding the candle aloft, she saw other things. She saw a pile of sticks. She saw a row of jars filled with a dark liquid. She saw a tray filled with something that looked like bones, glinting moon white.

"Are they b-b-bones?" Annabel stammered.

"Broomsticks are what we're looking for," said Miss Henrietta sternly.

Annabel reached up to where the broomsticks lay on the very top shelf. She pulled at one, but it seemed attached to the others.

"I can't," she said. "It doesn't want to come."

"Exactly right, Annabel," said Miss Henrietta. "Broomsticks are by nature stubborn and troublesome and never want to be apart from their companions. You must coax it gently and tell it that all will be well."

It seemed very silly.

"Go on," said Miss Henrietta.

"Here, then," said Annabel to the broomstick. "Don't be scared."

The broomstick wouldn't budge. The broom head, which seemed to be made of twigs, was tangled up with all the others.

She heard her great-aunt's exasperated sigh beneath her. "Say it as though you mean it, child!"

Annabel took a deep breath. She tried not to look down at the bones, rattling ever so slightly; the glass jars, chiming softly, menacingly.

"Dear broomstick, I just need you for a little while, and then I will put you back," she said, stroking it very gently. "You are very lovely. Here, now, just a little moment, that's all we ask."

She pulled gently at the handle and felt it move slightly apart from the others.

"You are made of such lovely wood, and I'm sure you can sweep the floor ever so well."

"Yes," whispered Miss Henrietta. "Try to separate it again."

Annabel tried, and this time the broomstick separated from the rest. She felt it quivering in her hands. It trembled against her heart as she began to climb back down. She suddenly felt very protective of it. So she was shocked when Miss Henrietta pounced forward at the bottom of the ladder, wrenched the broomstick from her hands, and threw a bag over the twig head.

Miss Henrietta knelt down on the ground, the thing bucking and struggling in her hands, and lashed the burlap bag with twine. "Rascal," she muttered. "Stop fighting, you rascal."

Annabel's face burned. "Why are you doing that?" she shouted.

"Keep your voice down in the cupboard," said Miss Henrietta.

"It's wrong," said Annabel, a little quieter.

Miss Henrietta stood, holding the trussed-up broomstick. "Quickly," she said.

Annabel became aware that the storeroom was starting to shake. Things were knocking. The broomsticks were banging and the bones rattling loudly in their tray. The glass jars were wobbling and the liquid was sloshing.

"Quickly," Miss Henrietta said again, and she took Annabel by the hand, flung open the storeroom door, and slammed it behind them.

Annabel looked back at the door, which was trembling. "What's happening?" she whispered.

"Ignore it," said Miss Henrietta. "Everything will calm down in a minute. For now, we must tie up this broomstick until it loses some of its feistiness."

She took the broomstick and tied it to three hooks behind the counter. The broomstick continued to struggle. It rattled and banged against the counter and caused a commotion.

"They soon calm down," Miss Henrietta continued. "You will take it to the Finsbury Wizards along with a letter I will write for them posthaste."

Annabel had no idea why the Finsbury Wizards should need a broomstick. Perhaps she was meant to sweep there as well. It was the kind of dreadful thing that *would* be expected of her. She was probably also meant to empty their stinky wizard chamber pots and polish their silverware.

Miss Henrietta sat down behind the counter and took paper from a drawer.

Annabel looked out through the window at the street, which was so dark you would think it was almost night. The fog had grown even thicker. People appeared as ghostly silhouettes passing by the clouded windows. A street crier took up his position right by the front door.

"London plunged into darkness!" he shouted. "Read all about it."

"Oh, do be quiet," muttered Miss Henrietta as she wrote.

"Fog stretching all the way to Watford!" he cried.

Annabel watched the fog swirl against the window. It was filled with soot, which came down and covered the ground. Surely she couldn't go out in it. Not alone. The broomstick trembled beside Miss Henrietta, as though with sorrow and rage, and it made Annabel feel terrible.

"I can see you are worried," said Miss Henrietta. "The broomstick will be aggrieved for only a little while. Come closer if you like. Talk to it again. You seem to have a way with it."

So Annabel knelt beside it. "I'm sorry," she said. "I'm sorry, dear thing."

"Good girl," said Miss Henrietta. She folded up her page, dripped wax on it, and affixed her seal. The last light seemed suddenly to drain from the street.

"Now it is time. Put on your cloak—you will need it against the fog. Your bonnet and gloves, too."

"But it is dark," said Annabel.

"Of course it is dark," said Miss Henrietta. "And what luck that is. It is never right to take a new broomstick out in sunshine—the thing would take fright. Here we are with a strange early night.

"I have drawn a small map on the back of the letter. The wizards no doubt will have seen you coming in their glass. Give them my letter and tell them to send out their pigeons to warn all in the Great & Benevolent Magical Society. Do not mind their quiet ways. They will tell us what is necessary for your journey into Under London."

Miss Henrietta untied the broomstick and thrust it into Annabel's hands just as the bell above the door tinkled and the sullen-faced Kitty came in from the dark. She dropped her sack to the floor. She smelled of wild sorrel from the graveyard. She coughed twice without covering her mouth.

"Perfect!" cried Miss Henrietta. "Kitty, you must walk

79

with Annabel as far as Finsbury and back. I will pay you twice your ration."

Kitty looked affronted at the idea. Annabel thought her expression very rude.

"*Three* times your ration," said Miss Henrietta.

Kitty nodded, and Miss Henrietta moved Annabel firmly toward the door.

"I shall keep a candle burning for you both," she said, and with that turned them both out into the street.

6

*"After-dark amusements should be restricted to the draw-
ing room and never the garden or the streets."*
    —*Miss Finch's Little Blue Book (1855)*

*W*hy, *I am a young lady,* thought Annabel as the door
shut behind her. *I am the daughter of a gentleman,
even if he was really a magician called the Great Geraldo Grey*
(oh, just that name, and she felt a pain beneath her breastbone), *who was hit by a carriage.*

She let out a little strangled sob. She couldn't go walking
at night!

But she straightened her back and held her head high and
refused to turn back to the door. She knew Miss Henrietta
would be watching them.

Be brave.

She stepped down onto the road . . . and, but for Kitty,
who grabbed her arm and pulled her back, would have been
run over by a carriage that clattered out of the fog with four
horses and disappeared again.

"Are you a fool?" Kitty asked, shaking her head. "Follow."

Annabel folded the letter twice and placed it in her pink waist sash. She hoped it would be safe there. The broomstick shivered against her.

"Here, here," Annabel whispered. "It will be fine."

They joined the jostling street filled with people trying to get home in the fog, men closing up their businesses and women clutching their children's hands so as not to get separated. A long-song man was taking down his song sheets and singing in a weary tone, while flower girls with hungry eyes sat in huddles with not a flower sold.

The fog was black in the places where it filled corners, purple elsewhere, with great coiling mauve clouds that drifted slowly through the streets. The soot rained down like dark snowflakes. But here and there, startling pockets of clean air appeared suddenly, holes where the golden afternoon sun shone down in little pools upon the lanes.

The fog stank. Annabel didn't think she had ever smelled anything so rotten. It caught in her throat and made her retch. It stung her eyes. It swallowed up all the street signs as soon as they were needed. Kitty walked ahead purposefully.

"Hurry up," she said to Annabel, "or I'll leave you behind."

"Miss Henrietta drew a map," said Annabel. "If you need it."

"Don't need no map," said Kitty, not even bothering to

look at Annabel. "Been to the wizards many times. Bring them their brownie tea."

"Brownie tea?" said Annabel. "I don't think brownies are real."

"Real enough if they give you a good scratching," said Kitty.

The broomstick quivered against Annabel.

She held it tight. "Hush," she whispered to it. "Don't be scared. We'll find our way to your new home."

Kitty stopped and turned to face her. Annabel in her pretty town dress, Kitty in her filthy, ragged one. There were never two more different girls.

"Can you fly that thing?" she asked.

"Don't be silly," said Annabel.

"A Vine Witch wouldn't give you a broomstick if you weren't meant to ride it," said Kitty, and she stared at Annabel for a good minute as though she were quite stupid.

The shops turned to taverns and inns with laughter and voices spilling out onto the street. People came out to marvel at the great fog and wonder where it had come from to turn the day to night. Kitty quickened her step, and Annabel had to run to keep up.

"It's very dark," said Annabel, "isn't it?"

Kitty didn't answer.

"How do you know the way?"

"All London's in my head," said Kitty, and she tapped her wild black hair.

"Where are your mother and father?" Annabel asked.

"Don't have none," said Kitty.

"What happened to them?" asked Annabel.

Kitty remembered hard, cold places. Tangled memories of rough hands and loud voices and children's faces and then the freedom of being gone from there.

"Don't know, don't care," said Kitty.

Annabel had never met anyone like Kitty in her life. "Well, I don't believe that," she said.

Kitty stopped and faced Annabel again. "Do you never shut up?" she said. "You are like a bell clanging."

It was one of the meanest things Annabel had ever had said to her. She tried very hard to think of something horrible to say back. Kitty stared at her, waiting.

"Fiddlesticks," said Annabel at last, and Kitty laughed, a wicked little cackle. She stopped just as suddenly as she'd started, and peered about her as though she sensed something.

"Quickly now," she said. There was a group of young men on a street corner, watching them. "Keep up or we'll be in trouble for sure." She pulled Annabel by the hand roughly.

Everything about Kitty was rough. Annabel wasn't sure she liked her at all.

"My mother's gone abroad," said Annabel. "And left my great-aunts to look after me."

Kitty ignored her.

"I went to Miss Finch's Academy for Young Ladies," said Annabel.

Kitty ignored her still.

"Why do they call you a betwixter?" asked Annabel.

"Just a name," said Kitty.

"But what does it mean?"

"It means I go between. This world and that world. Do dealing what others can't do."

Annabel didn't know what that meant. She stopped still to think on it.

"Good afternoon, young ladies. You've picked a fine time to take a stroll," came a voice from behind, and when Annabel turned, she saw it was one of the young men from the street corner, quite close.

"Quickly," said Kitty again.

"Don't pull me so," said Annabel.

"Well, don't stand there," hissed Kitty.

Annabel looked behind as they ran. The fog had gobbled up the young man from view. People loomed in and out of the shadows and thick smoke. Two washerwomen snarled at them to get out of the way, a butcher with a side of meat on his shoulder appeared suddenly and disappeared into the cloud just as quickly. Through the fog the shop lights shone hazy and golden, and Annabel wished, more than anything, that she could be inside.

The broomstick thrummed in her hand, gently, then strongly, in a rhythm, almost as though it had a heartbeat. She looked behind her again and saw, through the fog, the gang of young men. They were drifting slowly, hands in pockets, laughing and elbowing each other. Kitty had turned into a tiny lane so narrow the buildings almost touched. The weather played tricks with the men's voices, bringing them sometimes close, sometimes far. The fog vanished them and then reappeared them, as though by magic.

It was dark suddenly. Terribly dark. Annabel felt such fear that she stopped still.

She could not see before her or behind, but she heard the footsteps and laughter. Footsteps and laughter coming closer.

"Here," said Kitty, her hand appearing out of a dark cloud.

They ran and stumbled, turned a corner, and found themselves in a clearing of fresh air. The young men appeared through the fog behind them. The broomstick shook violently in Annabel's hands.

"There's no good running," one of them said. "You've got your pretty selves into a dead end here."

It was true. They stood at the end of a tiny bricked lane.

"We only want to stop and say hello," said another.

"We is only being polite," said a third.

◆ ◆ ◆

Now! the broomstick said, not in words but in the way it bucked in Annabel's hands and yanked her half off her feet. Annabel knew that *now* was what it meant.

"Quick," said Kitty, ripping the burlap bag from its head as the young men gathered in a circle around them.

When the bag was off, the broomstick jolted in Annabel's hands, lifting her feet clear off the ground.

"Get on!" shouted Kitty. "You must."

The broomstick was already going up. It dragged Annabel and Kitty, and they clawed themselves onto its back as they plowed through the circle of young men. Annabel kicked out at one who was trying to grab her foot, but the men's sneering faces soon turned to astonished. Annabel screamed as the broomstick shot straight up.

The broomstick rose so fast Annabel was sure they were heading to the moon. It flew through the sky at such tremendous speed that her bonnet blew off. She felt Kitty's arms around her waist, and they both looked down to catch one last glimpse of the men before the fog covered them over.

◆ ◆ ◆

The broomstick flew them up until they were over the rooftops, above the clouds, into clean air. They flew above London into a strange purplish afternoon light. Annabel thought she heard Kitty scream, not a terrified scream but a wild whoop of delight, but the wind took all noise and threw it far behind.

Annabel clutched the broomstick hard, hoping she wouldn't fall. They could see glimpses of London through the fog: tiny snatches of the great parks and giant trees, a sliver of the glassy Thames, the glimmer of lights on grand roads.

"I need to deliver you to Finsbury!" shouted Annabel over the wind.

She had no idea how to stop the broomstick. No idea how to make it go up or down. She tried to lean backward to see if that would help, but it almost performed a somersault. She pulled the letter from her sash and nearly lost it to the wind. She turned to the map that Miss Henrietta had drawn and read out the address neatly printed there, as though it might help.

"Number Three Sun Street!" she cried to the broomstick, although she wasn't sure it understood such things.

She felt the broomstick slow. "I really have to take you there," she said as gently as she could.

The thing stopped in midair and began to plummet.

"Help!" screamed Annabel.

"Do something!" cried Kitty.

They went straight down.

They fell through the clouds.

They fell through the fog.

They fell past the chimney tops.

Then the broomstick stopped. It stopped with a lurch so sudden that their bottoms lifted clean into the air. Then it shot forward at great speed. It sped down roads and streets and laneways until they disappeared in a blur. It hurtled through a church nave door and careered back out again. It skidded beneath a bridge. It fishtailed between factory smokestacks. It flew through parks and along avenues until it set its heart on a street and a lighted window at the very end.

The broomstick raced toward the lighted window. There was no time to think. It raced toward the glass, not stopping or slowing. It hit the window, and the glass fell apart in great shards around them, and they scooted across the floor, rolling up rugs as they went, crying out in fright, right into the middle of a group of ancient men—all of them stooped and bowed—who were at that very moment taking biscuits and tea.

◆ ◆ ◆

It wasn't how Annabel thought a wizard's house might be, dark and gloomy and filled with cobwebs and cauldrons. She and Kitty lay in a tangle in an ordinary sitting room. All around, on chesterfields, were very old men with astonished expressions on their faces.

The Finsbury Wizards didn't wear cloaks or hats but, instead, dark morning coats. The coats were dusty on the shoulders, as though the wizards had sat in the same place for a very long time. Most of them held a biscuit halfway to their mouths, so that Annabel wasn't sure at all about Miss Henrietta's idea that they would know of her coming. They looked very surprised indeed.

"Ouch," said Annabel, and she began to cry.

She couldn't help it. It was the third time in one day. She couldn't stop the tears. She couldn't think about a flower or a pretty painting. She wept loudly and her nose ran. It was her mother gone, and her father not a sea captain after all, and flying on a broomstick with a wild girl. It was finding herself lying on the floor in a strange house with dusty-shouldered gentlemen gazing upon her with open mouths. It was how she was no longer Annabel Grey. Not the Annabel Grey she had been. She would never be that girl again.

Be brave.

Kitty sat up. She had a little gash on her head. Annabel looked at her own hand, which was throbbing, and saw that she, too, was bleeding. The sight of blood made her let out a long wail. The wail seemed to make the Finsbury Wizards spring into action.

"Goodness gracious me," said the tallest and the oldest, and he jumped up in a befuddled fashion. "Quickly, Mr. Crumb. Fetch the magic bag."

Mr. Crumb looked as if he had never done anything quickly in his life, but he shuffled as fast as he could out of the room and returned with a small black bag. The other two wizards put their biscuits down and stood up and sat down again and did not seem sure what to do.

"Well, now," said one of them, who had only a few tufts of hair on his head. He handed Annabel a very stiff handkerchief from his pocket, and she dried her eyes. "You mustn't cry."

"Stay very still," said the other, who had a decaying carnation pinned to his lapel. "It appears you're both bleeding."

Confirmation of this fact made Annabel cry even more until the tallest and oldest offered her a withered hand and pulled her to her feet. Mr. Crumb extracted a small bottle from the magic bag and waved it under her nose. It had a horrible smell, but the room was suddenly clearer. There were the wizards smiling at her kindly. Their faces glowed in the firelight and through her tears. There was Kitty standing staring at the shattered window. She looked terribly uncomfortable in a sitting room, her hair all tangled by the wind and a little trail of blood disappearing down into her ear.

"But you're bleeding, too, Kitty," said Annabel.

"It's just a little cut," said Kitty, and she refused any help from the wizards. She crossed her arms, retreated closer to the window, and looked out at the fog, which at that very instant was winding dirty tendrils into the room.

"Good evening, Kitty," said the tallest wizard, who had cornflower-blue eyes.

Kitty wouldn't look at him.

He took a plate of biscuits and placed them on a small table near her, the way one might give a cat some milk. "Thank you for delivering Annabel Grey to us safely," he said very softly. "And thank you, Mr. Crumb, for kindly administering the smelling salts. Annabel, I am Mr. Bell."

"Mr. Crumb," said the wizard with the magic bag.

"Mr. Bourne," said the wizard with the wilting carnation.

"Mr. Keating," said the wizard with very little hair.

"And you are Annabel," continued Mr. Bell very solemnly. "The magical world is very noisy tonight. There is much chatter and calling and confusion, but your name and young Kitty's name above all ring clear."

Kitty had sat on her haunches to eat a biscuit, even though

there was a chair right near her. She ignored Mr. Bell, who made no mention of the shattered window or of the cold draft that blew through it now and lifted up strands of Kitty's hair and ruffled the fuzz on top of Mr. Keating's head.

It made Annabel weep afresh into the old handkerchief she'd been given. "I'm so sorry," she said. "We didn't mean to come in through the window. It's just that I've never ridden on a broomstick before."

"Never mind that," said Mr. Bell. "All that matters is that you have arrived, and with not a moment to spare."

"I have a letter," said Annabel. "From the Miss Vines."

She gave the letter to Mr. Bell, who sat down and read in an ancient, quavering voice.

" 'For the Finsbury Wizards. Regards, etc. We write as a matter of great urgency to inform you that Mr. Angel has returned. He has the Black Wand and a machine that can produce dark magic. He has raised shadowlings already, and at full moon Friday he will raise an army and take the city. He requests that all members of the Great & Benevolent Magical Society lay down their wands and pledge allegiance to him. We have sent you Annabel, the daughter of Vivienne. She is the youngest and most able member of the society. According to the handbook, she must retrieve the Morever Wand for the society. She has sight but no discipline. We implore you to teach her what you can and then send forth your pigeons to spread the word. Yours, etc., E. & H. Vine.' "

92

"So it is true. The whispers are true," said Mr. Crumb. "He wishes to raise an army and take the city!"

"Our glass told us as much," said Mr. Keating.

"But before us is the girl," said Mr. Bourne. "Do not forget it."

And then they all paused and gazed upon Annabel very solemnly.

◆ ◆ ◆

They gazed upon her for so long that Annabel felt embarrassed and her cheeks burned and she looked instead about the room, which was small and comfortable and cluttered. She noticed that some of the wallpaper had begun to peel and the pressed ceiling had flaked and dropped its paint like snowflakes on the floor. She noticed Kitty, but Kitty refused to notice her. Kitty ate her biscuits and stared out the window as if she would much rather still be flying on the broomstick through the sky.

Everywhere, there was a thick layer of dust. Dust on the sideboards and on the mahogany table and chairs and even, she noticed with horror, a thin layer over the biscuits. Just looking at those biscuits made her stomach grumble.

"Please," said Mr. Bell, pointing to the biscuits, "while we think."

So Annabel chose a biscuit and shook the dust from it. She chewed thoughtfully. Mr. Bell and Mr. Bourne and Mr. Keating and Mr. Crumb . . . they really were very unwizardly names. And four was a very unwizardly number. *There should be three or seven*, she thought, and she took another bite and waited for them to finish their gazing.

"You must choose a glass for us first," said Mr. Bell finally, and he creaked up and to the bookshelf and retrieved an old wooden box. "Sit here, somewhat closer to the fire."

He took a large brown stick from where it was propped beside his chair. It was smooth and covered half over with strange symbols. He pointed it at the fire and closed his eyes and said the word *Benignus*.

"Benignus," he said again, and the flames grew up tall and the room grew warmer. There was that word again, thought Annabel. It sounded Latin.

"This is the Adela," he said. "The Finsbury Wizards' wand."

"And my great-aunts have the Ondona," she said.

"And the Bloomsbury Witches have the Delilah, and the Kentish Town Wizards have the Kyle, although they are very old now indeed. Mr. Huxley—you may have heard of him—has the Little Bear, a very strange wand, made of driftwood, but very good for making fine weather. The Old Silver belongs to Mr. Hamble in Stepney, and it is a tree-healing wand. He can bring new buds to dying trees . . . but he can barely lift it anymore. All members of the Great & Benevolent Magical Society are very old, Annabel, and now Mr. Angel has returned, not aged at all and wanting us to lay down our wands and do bad with him. To practice terrible dark magic on the good people of London."

It did seem very wrong to Annabel, and she remembered Mr. Angel's pale skin and the way he had looked at her when she told him her name. It made her shiver.

"We have the lesser wands, Annabel, and above the lesser wands there are the two powerful wands, the Black and the White, although the White is sometimes known as the Morever. The Black Wand has long been prized by those wishing to do wrong. He has searched the earth for it, no doubt, and now it is his and he has a machine that can produce dark magic. Not just a small amount, Annabel, the way a wizard might make a drop, but the quantity produced by a machine like the great steam engines and the great looms. Why, he might do almost anything now."

"He has already succeeded in raising shadowlings," whispered Mr. Keating.

Annabel thought of them then, tried to picture them in her mind. *Shadows given wicked little souls, Annabel—why, they might do almost anything.*

It made Annabel feel scared. She looked to Kitty, but Kitty looked to the window and refused to be involved.

"You, dear child, must go into Under London to retrieve the Morever Wand," said Mr. Bell. He said it calmly and quietly, as though he were saying she must go to the High Street and choose a new dress.

"The White Wand, the good wand," said Mr. Bourne. "A most magical girl is required. The Valiant Defender of Good Magic. Everything is threatened, Annabel. Everything. From the smallest babies to the most ancient witches. Only the Morever will defeat the Black Wand with dark magic in it."

That did not help her fear. Not one little bit.

"Now for your glass," he said. "Please open the box."

Annabel knelt beside the fire and opened the lid.

"Anyone who has the talent of sight can usually find a seeing glass that will suit them," said Mr. Bell, as though Annabel were trying on hats at Harrods.

Annabel thought of the dark house and the dark wave, ready to wash over the city, and it was so violent in her mind that she flinched. Were they the shadowlings? It was such a terrible thought!

"You do see things," said Mr. Bell, "don't you? In puddles?"

The wizards looked at her so kindly and the fire was so warm and the taste of the biscuit still so sweet in her mouth that she nodded.

"Yes," she admitted. "Yes, I do."

"Well, then, you must find a glass and learn to see in it. Puddles are not always at hand," said Mr. Bell. "Your sight will help you on your way. . . . Both of you on your way."

He looked at Kitty then, and Kitty looked back from the window. "I've only got to take her back to the witches' shop," she said. "That's all I said I'd do. For three times my ration."

Mr. Bell nodded kindly.

Inside the box were many small parcels of fabric. Annabel unwrapped the first and found a palm-sized piece of green glass, quite jagged. She held it on her hand and then to her eye. The wizards nodded approvingly. It changed the room to a turquoise color and the fire to a dirty yellow. But did it suit her?

She wrapped the green glass back in its cloth. *Go on a journey to find a wand and defeat Mr. Angel with it,* she thought. She didn't know anything about wands. It was not the same as being asked to balance a book on her head and walk to the door and back. It was not the same as mapping the Danube. It was not at all the same as decorating a bonnet with yellow ribbon. But there was a faint tremor of excitement, deep down, within her. She looked up and saw Kitty watching her, and looked quickly down at the box again.

There was brown glass and clear glass and yellow glass. There were pieces of pottery with glaze, which were only a little shiny. There was the brown bottom of a jug, which she held up with disdain. It wasn't at all how she expected magical seeing glass to look. Finally she unwrapped an old rag and found a piece of ruby-red glass.

It was thick, and it fitted snugly inside her palm. She turned it and watched its light play on the ceiling. It caught the reflection of the flame in the fireplace. Annabel felt something inside her, a faint shimmer of recognition.

"You sense something with this one?" asked Mr. Bell.

"I feel it is mine," whispered Annabel. "Although I don't understand how."

"Is it the one you choose?" asked Mr. Bell.

"Why, yes," said Annabel, not admitting that it really felt much more as if the ruby-red glass had chosen her.

◆ ◆ ◆

"Now, some rules for looking in it," said Mr. Bell. "Mr. Crumb, if you will?"

Mr. Crumb took the seat closest to Annabel. It took some time on account of his not being able to stand at first and Mr. Bourne and Mr. Keating having to heave him up. Then Mr. Bourne and Mr. Keating had to sit down, which took some doing. A pair of glasses was lost and found again. Annabel wondered if anything much ever happened in the magical world, between the Vines and the Finsbury Wizards.

"Well, now, the rules are simple, my dear," said Mr. Crumb. "One, visions require a quiet mind. Two, in visions the future is never colored and there is often not any sound. Yes?"

Annabel nodded.

"Three, the past is often colored and often very loud," he continued. "Do you agree?"

"Well . . . ," began Annabel.

"Four, something seen in the present in another place—why, that is often very murky."

"I see," said Annabel.

"And finally, if someone speaks to you directly from a vision, then that person is dead or very close to death, hovering between the two worlds. Yes?"

"Oh," said Annabel, and she felt glad that no one had ever spoken to her in one of her visions. Indeed everything was always dark or colorless and without any sound, which meant she saw into the future, she thought, and she felt quite pleased that she had remembered the rule. She smiled at Mr. Crumb. He blushed fiercely.

"Perhaps Annabel should try to see in her glass," suggested Mr. Bell.

The wizards nodded encouragement and murmured softly.

Annabel looked at the glass that she held in the palm of her hand. She felt very self-conscious.

"Empty out your mind," whispered Mr. Crumb. "The way Miss Vine taught you."

Annabel wondered how they knew such a thing. She imagined her cup, which wasn't fancy this time—more of a dark earthenware mug, which surprised her and made her shudder. She looked at her thoughts that were in it. Number one, it felt good to say truthfully that she did see things in puddles, but, too, it made her feel very afraid. Afraid like being in a blustery wind that was going to tear her feet off the ground and blow her away. Number two, there was Kitty. She was never out of mind. How she was standing there, waiting to take her back to the magic shop, even though Annabel could tell she wanted to run away. Number three, could she really be expected to go on a journey all alone to retrieve a wand? She'd never done anything like that before. She'd only been on organized expeditions and trips to the country with her mother. She felt the wizards shifting on their chairs. Her cup seemed to always be very full.

But finally she felt her mind grow quiet.

She looked into the glass.

Part of her told herself to look away, so she knew she was right. She knew she would see something. She felt the cord that joined her to the sky, even though she was indoors, inside, warm beside the fire.

She saw shadows moving in the glass. Annabel leaned closer, and a small moan escaped her lips.

It was murky in the glass, like looking through a smudgy window. There were things flying. Shadowy winged things. A swarm of them against a pale gray sky. She watched them, and she wanted to look away. She watched them and wanted to see closer. They were birds. They were men. They were shadows. Her vision took her down suddenly, as though she were flying above. In the dim murkiness she saw the dark Thames first, a jumble of streets, then the magic shop and Miss Henrietta, her blurred face looking up at the sky, her mouth opening in terror.

Annabel dragged her eyes from the glass, covered her face with her hands, and breathed one great breath.

"What did you see?" the Finsbury Wizards asked in unison.

Annabel told them.

"Her talent is strong," said Mr. Bourne.

"She sees the immediate future well," said Mr. Keating.

"The seeing glass and her vision may help her somewhat on her journey," said Mr. Bell. "But time is of the essence. Mr. Angel has raised more shadowlings. His magical machine must be growing in power."

Annabel did not like the sound of *somewhat*. *Somewhat* meant not entirely. Not exactly. If she was lucky. The Finsbury Wizards were full of *somewhat*s and *perhaps*es. She thought wizards should be more exacting in their magic. She had finally seen a shadowling, and she did not like the look of it at all.

"You do not seem aware, young Annabel, of the wondrous magic that is inside of you," said Mr. Bell. "It is not your fault, of course. You have been taught to believe otherwise. But you have your seeing glass."

Kitty sighed softly near the window.

"Your mother was once the youngest and most able— why, she had her very own wand, the Lydia," said Mr. Bell.

"But she gave it away to the Witches of Montrouge," said Mr. Crumb, and all the wizards shook their heads slowly.

"She turned her back on magic," said Mr. Bell. "But she has made the proper decision and sent you to us, and in time perhaps she will come, too."

"But . . . ," said Annabel. She pictured her mother far away, and her heart ached again. A real ache. She hadn't known hearts could hurt so much. The wizards looked at her thoughtfully.

"But why did she turn her back on magic?" asked Annabel. "And why did she tell me . . . lies?"

Their faces looked infinitely sad.

"Please," said Annabel. "What happened after my father was hit by the carriage?"

Daughter of the Great Geraldo Grey.

Mr. Bell cleared his throat. "Now, then," he said. "Hen and Ettie never got over Vivienne going against their will, but your mother loved your father. There was no doubt of it. When he died so suddenly, she was wretched and wild with grief and she wanted him brought back."

"But how?" said Annabel.

"There is no good way, Annabel," said Mr. Keating very quietly.

"What is gone is gone, and that is the way of life," said Mr. Crumb.

"But there was Mr. Angel, once of our brotherhood, the very youngest, expelled for the wickedness that grew in him slowly but surely over the years," whispered Mr. Bourne. "He, dear Annabel, had made . . . a resurrection machine."

"Your mother, Vivienne, took the body of her husband to Mr. Angel's dark mansion," said Mr. Bell. "And we do not know what happened there, but afterward, when she emerged from the house alone, she turned her back on all magic forever."

There was silence in the little warm sitting room.

"And now you must both return to the shop quickly," said Mr. Bell. "If what you see is true, then the shadowlings are afoot and Mr. Angel is beginning to raise his army. He is a dangerous and damaged man, Annabel. He wants to rule everyone. Hen and Ettie will put the map in you."

In me, thought Annabel, like a spoonful of tonic that Mercy sometimes gave her. And to hear their names as such, as though they were girls. Then she realized that the wizards wanted her to stand, and Mr. Bourne very timidly held out the broomstick for her, which was disappointing because she had thought perhaps they'd go home in a carriage.

"But I thought I was to deliver it to you," said Annabel.

"The broomstick is yours," said Mr. Bell most kindly.

She looked at it and worried. What if she couldn't stop it again and she went in through the glass of the magic shop? That wasn't the kind of thing that Miss Henrietta would tolerate. Yet she also felt relieved when the broomstick was in her hand, and it shivered in response to her relief, an old friend.

Mr. Bell nodded to Kitty, and Kitty glared at him from under her dark eyebrows.

"When all is done, young Kitty," he said, "you must fetch us some more of the magnificent brownie tea. There are not many girls like Kitty anymore, young Annabel."

And he looked at Kitty with such sadness and tenderness that Annabel had to look away.

They were guided down a long hallway, where, in the gloom, a grandfather clock showed it to be early evening. Annabel tucked the ruby-red seeing glass into her bodice. She felt the broomstick, which she was becoming increasingly fond of, tremble against her.

"Above all, be good, Annabel Grey, for all of good magic depends upon you tonight," said Mr. Bell, and then the door

103

was open and she and Kitty were deposited once again into the dark.

The moon rose and shone like a dirty coin through the fog. Mr. Angel listened to the Dark-Magic Extracting Machine. He listened to its inner workings, churning and grinding, winding and unwinding. Sometimes it stopped. Sighed. He remembered what was at its black heart, the first sorrowful thing, and that made him smile.

He stood and fed the machine black-bordered paper taken from a widower's desk, a flogging strap stolen from a home for waifs. Six feathers stolen from the museum, from a bird long extinct. The machine took deep breaths, sucked these objects, one by one, down the length of the room. A chief mourner's sash. Blackwork embroidery. A long-gone baby's booties, kept for years in a bottom drawer.

Mr. Angel raised his monocle and peered at the dark-magic gauge. The needle pointed to two-thirds full. He took the Black Wand and filled it, bracing himself for its force.

He strode down the stairs.

He turned his two footmen to dust because they stood in his way.

He went into empty bedrooms and raised shadowlings from long-unopened wardrobes. One, two, three of them. He strode down the stairs and into the library and raised them from behind the black velvet curtains. He swept them up the stairwell and or-

dered them beside the others that swayed like dark candle flames. They rose and fell at the sound of his voice.

He held up the handkerchief Annabel had cried upon. The shadowlings rustled and whispered to each other in their strange airy voices. He let them sniff at it, and their long claws came out, wanting.

"The machine was made first with the tears of the mother." He spoke softly. "And now it shall be complete with the sad little daughter. One more day, and the full moon rises."

They grew tall then, the shadowlings, stretched themselves upward, and made an angry noise like buzzing hornets.

"Fly now, shadowlings," he said. "Bring me Annabel Grey."

And they were off; they were flying, all of them, in a stream toward the ceiling, sliding themselves up the steps past the moon funnel, slipping into the rusty moonlight and away.

7

*"A lady should walk demurely in the streets. She should
pay little attention to that which does not involve her."*
—*Miss Finch's Little Blue Book (1855)*

In the street the fog was brown as mud, thick and choking.
Annabel looked at the broomstick and then at Kitty.

"Don't deny you enjoyed it," said Kitty.

"I didn't," said Annabel.

"You lie a lot for a young lady," said Kitty, and she laughed
her wild little laugh that made Annabel's skin prickle. "It
were like being a bird."

But the trouble with broomsticks, thought Annabel, *is that
they're undisciplined and stubborn.*

They straddled it, but nothing happened.

"Go," said Annabel, but it stayed where it was.

"Up," said Annabel, but it refused to take off.

"I insist," she demanded, but it would not move an inch.

Yet when Annabel thought of Miss Henrietta in the ruby-
red seeing glass, the broomstick shot into the air without

warning. They had to grapple as they wobbled, and hold on for dear life. They soared up through the stinking fog; they rocketed past roofs and chimney tops; they broke through a cloud and into the night sky. This time Annabel *did* hear Kitty let out one long screech of delight that was most unladylike.

Through the fog they glimpsed Parliament and palaces, parks and avenues, and St. Paul's, deep below, like a toy discarded at the bottom of the sea.

"We must go down soon, good broomstick," said Annabel, but it only lurched wildly in response and curved playfully around a steeple.

"Now, then," she soothed, "we mustn't smash anything at Miss Henrietta's shop."

The thing bucked so wickedly that they nearly fell off in midair.

Annabel decided the best thing to do was to tell it she didn't want to land at all.

"Let's fly all night!" she shouted to it. "All the way to the sea and definitely *not* to the magic shop."

The broomstick hesitated, waggled its twig tail disconcertingly, and then zoomed forward.

"What's that?" shouted Kitty. "Look!"

She pointed toward the horizon, where, through the clouds, the near-full moon was rising. A clump of dark shadows moved there. Annabel wanted to speak, but fear seemed to have stolen her words.

She knew what they were.

They grew clearer in the sky, those dark winged things. They came closer. The wind picked up the sound of their voices and threw it across a distance. They sighed one single word. *Annabel.*

"Quickly, we must away!" shouted Annabel finally. "Quickly, dear broomstick!"

Now was not the time for stubbornness. She thought of Miss Henrietta's upturned face again in her vision, and the broomstick plunged suddenly. Their skirts flew up into their faces, and they plummeted at such speed that Annabel was sure they were about to die. They screamed in unison. Screamed and screamed and screamed and screamed until the broomstick stopped and, with utmost politeness, lowered itself gently through the fog until a street appeared, with Miss Henrietta standing outside the shop looking anxiously at the sky.

◆ ◆ ◆

"Hurry! Mr. Angel has sent shadowlings," said Miss Henrietta, and she rushed them into the shop, locking the door. She grabbed the Ondona from the countertop and pointed it toward the window. Out on the street the shadowlings descended slowly, like black angels.

Annabel stared at them and could not move. She heard Kitty's breath quicken beside her. They were shadows, it was true, but they constantly changed their shapes. First they were tall, thin men in top hats, peering through the window, and then they shrank themselves down to eerie gray copies of Miss Henrietta holding up her wand. Finally they formed themselves into a black mass pressed against the window, black wings beating like a swarm of moths'. Their claws, their only solid parts, drummed and scratched on the window glass.

Miss Henrietta raised the Ondona and closed her eyes. She closed her eyes for so long that Annabel wondered if she knew what she was doing, but then her great-aunt shouted.

"Benignus!" she cried.

She fired the word and the wand at the window. A great golden light grew there, and the shadowlings drew back, swept upward, disappeared.

"They do not like the light," she said, "but it will stop them only for a little while. Quickly, follow me."

They took the left-hand door through the magical storeroom, which seemed to be humming softly to itself, as though worrying about a complicated problem. Annabel looked at Kitty and saw that her eyes were also wide with wonder. They rushed down the stairs behind the large brown door, Miss Henrietta in the lead, the candlelight rushing down the wall beside her.

Miss Estella was propped up in her bed with a look of wild excitement on her face. "Look at her, look at her," she cried. "The most magical girl, as magical as can be. And the betwixter girl as the one who will help her on her way."

"I'm not going anywhere," said Kitty. "I took her to the wizards and back. That's all you asked for."

"But you saw the shadowlings, Kitty!" cried Miss Henrietta. "You know enough of such things, and the handbook itself says the youngest and most able of the Great & Benevolent Magical Society should have a companion on the journey to retrieve the Morever Wand."

"Don't care what no stupid book says," said Kitty, and she stayed near the door, as if she might run away.

"Sit on the bed," Miss Henrietta demanded of Annabel. "We must sing the map into you now."

"Has she got room in her?" asked Miss Estella.

"Enough—hopefully enough," said Miss Henrietta, and she took one of Annabel's hands in her own and placed the other on Annabel's forehead. Miss Estella did the same, and as she did so, she let out one of her wild shrieks, which Annabel would have responded to with a startled jump if she could have.

But she couldn't.

She couldn't move at all.

She was completely paralyzed by her great-aunts' hands.

A light began to fill her, a terribly bright light, and then a sudden rushing, piling, screaming, pushing source of energy. It was as though her head were a little bottle and it was being filled with a raging river. She wanted to cry, *Stop!* but she could do nothing.

Into her went the streets of London, the well-tended, paved, pruned, manicured streets of her childhood and also the wilder ones, the jagged, rotting tenements and staggering lines of slums. Into her went the streets that petered out into the fields and the cemeteries and the woods that she had never known, pushed and shoved and squeezed into her mind. Old churches and new churches and railway stations and factories and cathedrals and charnel houses and mansion houses and hospitals, until she thought she would explode. Then sewers, suddenly, and tunnels and rivers rushing loudly in her ears, and stone stairwells turning and corkscrewing down into darkness.

And into her went several catacombs, pressed down deep inside her until she could bear no more, and into her went dimmer places, the roots of the great trees of London—she saw them—and deep, dark places with holes at the bottom leading to blacker places still. She looked down, and she saw, where the hands of her great-aunts lay upon her skin, lines appearing.

She looked at them in horror, but there was nothing she could do. The lines appeared upon her left palm first and then spread out—the lines of passages and tunnels and stairwells. Strange words appeared, and arrows and dotted lines and chutes and chambers and, here and there, wild, lopsided writing.

She felt the lines growing over her skin, traversing her arm—caverns and cliff tops and sudden abysses—and they snaked and crept slowly up her neck and onto her left cheek, unstoppable.

"There, now," said Miss Henrietta, and they released

their hands from Annabel. They looked at her and couldn't hide their dismay.

"I do not remember it being told as such," said Miss Henrietta.

Annabel turned her left arm, heavily mapped, this way and that.

"It is what it is, what it must be," said Miss Estella, although she seemed terribly shocked.

Annabel stood then and moved toward the dressing table beside Miss Estella's bed. She stared at herself in the mirror, at the lines and passageways and chambers drawn all over her arm and face.

"What have you done to me?" she wanted to shriek.

She would have, if not for the crashing sound above and the sound of a rushing wind outside.

"Quick—latch the door, Kitty!" cried Miss Henrietta.

Kitty had the latch down just as a great pressure thumped against it.

Annabel . . . , sighed the shadowlings outside.

Their voices slipped under the door, and Kitty backed away, her eyes on the floor. There was a thin darkness spreading through the crack.

Annabel turned back to the mirror. She felt as though she moved within a dream. She stared at her ruined face. Surely her mother had not wanted *this*. Surely her mother had only wanted her to learn how to look in the specimen cabinet or perhaps how to see in her glass.

But there was no choice.

Be brave.

There was no choice, and everything was changed, and everything was different.

Be good.

I am Annabel Grey, she thought. The seeing glass was tucked safe in her bodice. The map was on her and in her. The broomstick was in her hand.

I am Annabel Grey, she thought. *Valiant Defender of Good Magic.*

She willed herself to believe the words. She wished herself to believe the words. Oh, how she did *not* believe those words!

But she did not want those terrible things and Mr. Angel to take London.

"Make haste!" cried Miss Henrietta, flinging open a trapdoor beside Miss Estella's bed.

Miss Estella had her hands outstretched to Annabel. She clutched at Annabel's shoulders, kissed her cheek with her papery, dry lips.

"In here are the answers," she said, touching Annabel's head and then her heart. "This is where you will find your magic."

Miss Estella turned to her sister. "Give her the Ondona, Hen. They will need it. I feel it."

"She will not know how to use it," said Miss Henrietta.

"She *will* know," said Miss Estella. "I am sure of it."

Miss Henrietta pointed the Ondona at the trapdoor. "Benignus," she shouted, the way she had in the shop. "Benignus!"

Her face was fierce, and light erupted from the end of the wand and coated the perimeter of the trapdoor so it snapped and sparkled and sizzled white.

She thrust the wand into Annabel's hand and herded her toward the space. Annabel peered down through the glow at a ladder that disappeared into darkness. Would the magic light burn her?

"Go!" screamed Miss Henrietta, and Annabel knelt down quickly. She tucked the broomstick under her arm and turned to feel for the ladder. She clambered onto it and watched Miss Henrietta's solemn face.

"But you will need the wand," said Annabel. She'd just realized it. "Against those things!"

"Go quickly," cried Miss Henrietta. She grabbed Kitty, who was frozen, staring at the black shadow seeping under the door. She thrust her toward the ladder.

Kitty started down after Annabel, her eyes still on the spreading shadow stain upon the floor. She did not want to go, but there was no other way out of the room, away from those things.

Annabel . . . , whispered the shadowlings, and the sound filled the room in the draft sliding its way slowly though the crack. Miss Henrietta snapped the trapdoor shut after the girls.

It was dark.

Terribly dark.

Just a thin square of spell light up above.

Be brave. Be good.

Annabel heard Miss Henrietta cry out in a high-pitched voice. Loud words. Wild words. Magic words. She heard Miss Estella shrieking with her. Spell words. Heart words. Saving words. Annabel clambered down the ladder with Kitty. They climbed down, down, down into the darkness.

II

DARK-MAGIC GAUGE 2/3 FULL

8

"When traveling, a young lady should always take care to wear dark clothing and to ensure a quiet and courteous demeanor."

—*Miss Finch's Little Blue Book (1855)*

Down they went into Under London. The broomstick trembled beneath Annabel's arm as though afraid of the darkness, and Annabel trembled against the ladder because she was just as frightened. And holding a broomstick and a wand and descending a ladder and shaking all over at the same time made things very difficult. It reconfirmed in Annabel's mind her theory that the Great & Benevolent Magical Society was very wrong indeed to have chosen her as the most magical girl.

It was a very long ladder, and Annabel's and Kitty's eyes adjusted to the darkness as they went. At first the bricked-in space was narrow, but halfway down, it opened out into a much larger tunnel. There, they could see the ladder plunged toward water. Far below, Annabel could see a tiny rowboat:

Miss Estella's rowboat. Oh, just the thought of her great-aunts made her want to cry.

I am the Valiant Defender of Good Magic, she told herself sternly, but her bottom lip quivered. Far above, they could hear the trapdoor begin to wobble and bang.

"Can those things get through?" Annabel asked, and the brickwork took her voice and magnified it.

Oh, she did not want those terrible things to hear.

Those dark things. Those things she did not understand.

Those things that whispered her name.

"If you keep stopping, they will," said Kitty, climbing down fast and stepping on Annabel's fingers occasionally, adding to her vexation. "We need the river."

The fast river would take them away. Kitty could hear it beneath them. Its urgent rushing voice said, *Quickly, quickly, quickly.* She was a girl who knew water: the sound of the tide turning and the streams covered over and chattering all night through culverts and ditches. She knew the voices of forgotten wells and fountains. Ponds that held the sky on the marshes. This river said, *Hurry, hurry, hurry.*

When they stood together on the bottom rung of the ladder, the river touched their boots. It was loud, this river. It slurped and slapped and shouted, *Quickly, quickly, quickly.* It stank. *If this is Under London,* thought Annabel, *it smells rotten.* It made her eyes water. It smelled of human waste and dead things. Even worse, the boat was not close to the ladder at all but two body lengths away, its rope tether pulled taut by the racing river.

"What now?" whispered Annabel, and high above them the trapdoor rattled.

"Try pulling," said Kitty, and they grabbed at the rope together, but the force of the river was too strong. Up above, the trapdoor jolted several more times.

Annabel felt scared, terribly scared, and her legs felt wobbly.

"We'll have to jump," said Kitty. "It's not too far."

Annabel looked at the boat and the dark wash of water that rushed between them and it. The river that smelled like a thousand chamber pots. She nodded her head, even though she had never once even jumped across rocks in a pleasant stream. She took a deep breath and tried very hard not to let out a sob.

"It's the only way, Annabel Grey," said Kitty, and in the dim light Annabel saw her green eyes gleaming. Kitty looked like a girl who could jump across wide spaces and climb very tall trees. "Here—give me the broomstick and the wand."

Kitty took them from under Annabel's arm before she had time to protest. Up above, the trapdoor banged loudly.

"You know you can," said Kitty. She could hear the river in a way that Annabel couldn't. It said, *Away, away, away,* with its restless voice. "Watch me."

Kitty sprang out from the ladder like a cat from a wall. She yelled a little yell as she went. It was a rough sound, and it seemed to propel her across the space. Annabel saw her land in the boat, *smack!* and the thing pitch wildly side to side.

"Jump," called Kitty.

"Yes," said Annabel, but she didn't move.

"Now!" shouted Kitty.

High above, there was a pounding against the trapdoor.

"Yes," said Annabel again.

Be brave. Be good.

She closed her eyes. She tried to yell the way Kitty had yelled. She yelled a smallish yell and leapt. She leapt out into the space between the ladder and the boat. She leapt out and felt herself falling. She yelled and waited for the feeling of a wooden boat.

She longed for the feeling of a wooden boat.

She thought in those tiny seconds that stretched out like minutes that perhaps she had never longed for anything more.

She waited for the comfortable slap of herself hitting the wooden boat, but instead she felt water, the sudden shock of cold, stinking water.

◆ ◆ ◆

The river took Annabel under. It took her head and held it down. It filled up her mouth. It roared in her ears. It snatched her and snagged her and somersaulted her. It wanted her for its own. Annabel had never swum. She flailed against the force of it. She tried to raise her arms, but the river grabbed her from below. It pulled at her skirts and the cloak, yanked her and tugged at her and twisted her down.

"Help!" she cried once, and Kitty heard her before she went under again.

Kitty was tearing at the rope tether, cursing the pretty girl all mapped over, the magical girl, who would drown before she even got a chance to look in her stupid red glass. She had the rope undone then and the boat was rushing away on the back of the river.

"Annabel!" she called as she went, and she peered into the blackness.

The river released Annabel momentarily, and she gulped mouthfuls of air. It slammed her into the brick wall and raised her quite suddenly onto a brick ledge, where she grasped a metal grate and remained.

"Help," she said, coughing, and she saw Kitty go sailing past in the boat.

"Stay there!" shouted Kitty, and she cursed the girl again. "I'll try and stop."

The river gushed through the brick tunnel; it sped Kitty away in the little boat. It banged her against the walls and spun the boat like a leaf on a stream. Kitty grabbed an oar and tried to row against the current, but the boat would not be slowed. She heard Annabel's calls, farther and farther away in the darkness.

"Stay there," shouted Kitty once more, and she paddled as hard as she could. She paddled and paddled, until she managed to turn the boat lengthwise. The tunnel obliged by growing narrower at that very point, and the bow and stern wedged against the walls so violently that she nearly fell out.

"Annabel," she called when she had recovered herself. "Let go of the wall and let the river bring you down. I'm stopped here—you'll find the boat."

"Don't be ridiculous!" cried Annabel. She was out of the water, shivering against the grate. There was no way she was going back in.

"You must!" she heard Kitty shout from somewhere far away. "You can't just stay there."

Annabel looked at the dark water surging beneath her toes.

She didn't like the river, the secret river, hidden away so long ago beneath the city. Rivers were meant to be clean and pretty, with grassy green banks, like the ones she had gone boating on with Isabelle Rutherford. Rivers were places where you giggled behind a parasol and admired the view.

She had never had anything so terrible happen to her.

She closed her eyes and wished it all away.

"Hurry up!" came Kitty's voice. "The boat's nearly gone, and that'll be the end of you."

"Fiddlesticks!" shouted Annabel, and she jumped into the stinking black water again. She didn't think she'd ever been crosser.

Kitty heard the splash. "You'll hit the boat!" she shouted to encourage Annabel but heard nothing, just the river's loud voice against the brick walls. "Annabel?"

Nothing but the river racing by.

"Annabel?"

Then a thump. A definite thump, with the little boat tilting to one side and Annabel's face appearing in the darkness.

"Here," said Kitty, and she dragged Annabel forward until she had her beneath the arms. She hauled Annabel's stinking, sodden mess into the boat and laughed.

"Stop it!" shouted Annabel, and then she coughed so violently that she spewed over the side.

Kitty had never seen a young lady so thoroughly ruined. She looked at Annabel's fair hair, all undone and tangled; her rosebud dress, all muddied.

Annabel stared back at her with disbelief. She'd never met anyone so rude. She'd nearly drowned, and the terrible girl had laughed.

"Beg your pardon," said Kitty, and she replaced her laughter with her solemn green-eyed stare. "You just look a mess, is all."

"Well, I nearly drowned," said Annabel. All she could smell was the terrible river. It was stuck up her nose and down her throat. She could taste it, and just the thought made her begin to wretch again.

"Nearly, but you didn't," said Kitty. "I saved you."

◆ ◆ ◆

Annabel should say thank you, she knew it, but she didn't want to. Not to someone who had saved her and then laughed at her. The green-eyed girl never stopped looking at her.

"I'd be very pleased if you stopped staring at me," Annabel said instead, very politely.

Kitty laughed her little laugh again. She took an oar and pressed it hard into the brick wall until the bow of the boat loosened and spun and the boat was moving again.

"We have to find a way up out of here," said Kitty. "We'll need your map."

Annabel held her hand to her face. She remembered her reflection in Miss Estella's mirror. They were in the boat for a purpose, to find the Morever Wand, and deliver it to the Great & Benevolent Magical Society and save all of London, including her home. The remembering quite took her breath away. *Home!* She wanted her house and her mother and Mercy calling her for supper. The boat raced along on the dark river. It was taking her farther and farther away from all those things. She had never seemed so far away from everything that she knew.

"B-b-but we've got to go to Under London," stammered Annabel. "To find the wand and stop Mr. Angel."

"You can do all the looking and saving you want," replied Kitty. "I want up above. I only said I'd take you to the wizards and back, and now I'm down here where I don't want to be."

She was a girl who needed air and sky.

"But remember?" said Annabel. "Remember what the wizards said? The whole of good magic depends upon us."

"Upon *you*," said Kitty.

"But you saw those things!" cried Annabel, and the boat

banged them against a wall for good measure, spun them in a circle, and flushed them out suddenly into a wider open place. "Mr. Angel wishes to raise an army of them and march on the city. You must help."

"Do you never stop talking?" said Kitty, as though Annabel had said nothing of importance.

Annabel shivered with the cold. She had never felt so bad. She was on a stinking underground river, with the worst girl ever—who said she would not help her—and she had to find a wand and save everything by herself.

She peered into the darkness at the place where the water had slowed. She would have to find a way. She knew she would have to. She just had to think. She tried to empty out the cup of her mind, the way Miss Henrietta had taught her, but there was one huge thought in the way of everything: she really didn't like Kitty.

Kitty began to hum softly, and that made Annabel dislike her even more. She blinked back tears in the dark. Yes, she disliked the girl very much. Miss Henrietta and Miss Estella were positively endearing compared with this girl. She disliked having to dislike someone. She wasn't used to it. She was accustomed only to pleasant things. It seemed such a violent emotion and poked at her insides.

Kitty hummed.

"Stop that," said Annabel.

But Kitty didn't.

Kitty hummed for another minute, gradually getting louder, until she opened her mouth and out popped a blue

127

orb of light, shimmering and starry, the size of her fist. Annabel fell back, astonished. By the orb's light she saw Kitty's solemn little face, the Ondona, the broomstick lying at the bottom of the boat, and her hand and arm all mapped over.

"How did you do that?" whispered Annabel. Now she could see the dark water and the arched brick ceiling above. They were in a large underground chamber. The water dripped and trickled loudly.

"I just raised it up with a magic song of my own making."

"Where does it come from?"

Kitty shrugged. "My heart, I believe."

Annabel remembered Miss Henrietta. *I have heard it said she can sing up her spirit light. There are not many girls like Kitty anymore.*

"You can do magic?" whispered Annabel.

Kitty didn't answer. Instead, she made a loud hawking noise and spat over the side of the boat. Annabel shuddered. Kitty bobbed the light up and down. Her face disappeared in and out of the dark.

"Well, I'm going to find the wand," said Annabel. "I have to. I have the map. I'll find my own way."

But her voice sounded weak and small.

They rocked on the river, and Kitty laughed again, but softly this time. She took a deep breath and expanded her heart light so that they could see better the place they had come to. The river had widened and slowed. The chamber was circular, the ceiling vaulted. Opposite them three arches stood like dark mouths.

Kitty thought. She thought of how the night would be up above. How the moon would be climbing the sky and the dirty fog might have lifted and, everywhere, the secret places of London would have woken. The great trees would be sending their shivering messages. A badness was coming, it was clear now. That was what they had been saying. The wild grasses at Hackney Marshes would be singing a warning song. The meadows hidden and tucked behind gasworks and factories, the places where the farms pressed their edges against town would be calling, shrill with summer bluebells and dog rose.

A darkness is coming. A blackness is coming.

The shadowlings scared her. The thought of them gliding over her places, wiping them away. She had seen dark things and known treacherous places, places brimming with bad feeling, but nothing had scared her as much as those shadowlings.

Annabel would not get far at all without her help. Kitty knew it just as well as she knew the river was singing to them of danger. It annoyed her, for she was hungry and tired and had not counted on her day turning wrong in such a way. But it made sense now, the strange feelings of endings and beginnings. She sighed.

"They've gone and ruined your pretty face with all that writing," she said at last.

"You shouldn't say such things," said Annabel.

"They have," Kitty said. "I never saw a girl all written over with words and lines."

"Stop it!" cried Annabel.

"Let's see what the map shows," said Kitty, and she made her heart light small and hovered it just over Annabel's hand.

"Will you help me, then?" asked Annabel.

"I will help you find your way," said Kitty, and her stomach growled, and she thought of her lost evening. "You would never find it on your own."

In Islington there was a tavern where the music had stopped. On the chairs there were piles of dust, and on the floor there were more. Mr. Angel kicked at them with his shoe. He raised the Black Wand and admired it. He was more powerful than any man had ever been. He was sure of it. He was full of darkness and ruin, and he laughed and wiped terrible tears from his eyes.

He walked the streets submerged in his strange magical fog. London was filled with disgruntled sounds. Out on the Thames, foghorns lamented and anchored boats rang their bells. Men cried frantically to one another at the great intersections, guiding carriages with lanterns that barely pierced the cloud. It was a sooty, stained, drowning London.

He raised seven shadowlings in dark lanes. Seven more that had been sleeping for centuries in the cloisters of a great church. He sang them up, Umbra, antumbra, from sewer grates. He raised them up, and they gasped their first breaths. He commanded they carry him to the magic shop, and they seethed and writhed and grew themselves into the shape of a chariot. With their claws, they made a seat for him to sit upon. They carried him off the dirty road and up into the sky.

"Annabel Grey?" he said to Miss Estella and Miss Henrietta where they lay. "I need her. When I feed her to the machine tomorrow night at full moon, its power shall be complete. I will raise my dark army."

Of course they would not tell him where she was.

The shadowlings crowded around the trapdoor to the secret river, though. The light from the Ondona still burned there.

Mr. Angel looked on the two old women sadly. He tut-tutted softly under his breath.

"You think she can save you?" he said quietly.

He aimed the Black Wand at the light and extinguished it.

"Good magic is finished," he said. Then he bent down and unlatched the door and let the shadowlings beneath.

9

"If a young lady finds herself vexed by passengers of ill-breeding, she should turn toward the window to admire the view."

—Miss Finch's Little Blue Book (1855)

There was constantly changing weather on her face. It seemed to Annabel that most often Kitty frowned or looked ashamed, but sometimes brief outbreaks of sunshine appeared, tiny half-smiles accompanied by the little wild cackle, so filled with pleasure. There was a tiny smile now as Annabel watched the orb that hung between them.

"I don't understand what it is," said Annabel. "I mean to say . . . where does it come from?"

"Here," said Kitty, frowning, and she pointed to her chest. "Inside me."

"But who taught you how to do it?" she asked.

"None did."

"But what kind of magic is it?"

"How should I know? *My* magic," said Kitty.

There was the little smile again, quickly replaced by a frown as she leaned forward and took Annabel's hand. She dug her dirty fingernail into the skin, marking the path. The line began on Annabel's left palm, and both of them knew it was the magic shop, the dark stairwell, the ladder to the secret river.

There was a maze of lines that spread away from the entrance, tiny tight lines showing the underground river coiled and corkscrewed deep beneath London. And then on the fleshy part of Annabel's hand there was a wider space and three arches drawn in a fine, magical hand.

"This is where we are," said Kitty, touching the place where the three arches were. "And there is only one way we must choose."

They had been in the little boat for some time, and yet the line had only twisted across Annabel's palm. She knew about map scale from geography. The map stretched over her forearm, along her upper arm, and onto her neck and face. Under London was not only stinky but very big. Kitty ran her finger from the first arch along a path that stopped at Annabel's wrist. A dead end. She traced the path from the second arch. It snaked to the opposite side of Annabel's wrist. There were waves drawn there.

"The sea," said Kitty, and she thought of the marshes and birds circling and the way the wind spoke of faraway places there.

"But we don't want the sea," said Annabel.

Kitty ran her finger over Annabel's lower arm.

The third line wound its way through myriad other lines that led to other places. It coiled off Annabel's wrist onto her forearm.

"What does that say?" asked Kitty.

There was a thick black line and words that Annabel needed to read upside down.

"The . . . Singing . . . Gate," she said. "That's a strange name."

"The Singing Gate," repeated Kitty, running her finger over the words. "I've heard of it."

"How?"

"They talk of it," said Kitty. "The little folk—always singing and crying about it in the way they do. The wizards speak of it, too. It protects Under London. Stops anyone from entering that's not meant to go there."

Annabel had never heard of it. She wished the Miss Vines had mentioned it if it was such a difficult thing. Kitty knew much more than she did—Kitty, who fetched tea from the brownies and dealt with faeries. She wanted to speak to Kitty of such things, but, as if sensing it, Kitty let go of Annabel's hand. She stood up, and the boat rocked to one side until she sat down beside Annabel. She took the oars and handed one to Annabel.

"Row," she said.

No *please.*

They rowed across the still water until they were at the dark, dripping mouth of the third arch. The opening was so tight that the little boat bumped against the walls. They pushed at the brickwork with their hands.

"What if it isn't the right one?" whispered Annabel as they entered.

She felt she should know. She felt that if she were truly magical she should know. The knowledge should be very solid and bright. She shouldn't be filled with such uncertainties.

"You're the map," said Kitty. "You're the most magical girl, Annabel Grey. There's no turning back now."

◆ ◆ ◆

Annabel was frightened. There was no way around it. The boat groaned and complained as it scraped against the narrow walls. Hidden objects bumped against the little hull. Each sound made her jump. Each sound made her shiver.

There was a current again, and Kitty put away her oar and moved to the bow. The blue heart light glowed between them. Annabel picked up the broomstick and held it to her chest. She didn't understand, but it made her feel safer just to know it was there. She could never explain such a thing to Isabelle Rutherford. To anyone from her old life. She wished Miss Henrietta were there to tell her what to do. Her strange great-aunt, who all her life Annabel had not known existed. Who was not at all the way a great-aunt should be, kindly and doting and full of sweet wisdom.

She thought of her mother then. Her mother, who had pressed flowers and embroidered handkerchiefs but had really been very magical and had never told her. Her mother, who had lied to her. She pictured her on a railway platform in Paris in her dark traveling clothes, so beautiful and graceful that everyone stopped just to see her go. Annabel stifled a sob. She desperately hoped the betwixter girl wouldn't hear. She trembled with cold.

"Here," said Kitty. "I can only do it for a while."

She closed her eyes and turned her heart light a deep red. She blew it toward Annabel, and the heat of it was real and warm. It burned Annabel's cheeks in a comfortable, prickly way, and in minutes her dress and the cloak were stiffening dry.

But then Kitty let out a gush of breath, as if the exertion was too much, and the light turned blue again, much paler, and Kitty brought it back close to herself.

"Thank you, Kitty," whispered Annabel. *Thank you for the warmth. For saving me. For staying with me.* She wanted to ask again where the light came from, who had taught her such magic, how she stayed calm when they were in darkness deep beneath London.

She said nothing.

Kitty yawned and curled herself a little at the bow of the boat.

What if those things have come down into the darkness? Annabel wanted to ask. *The shadowlings.* She peered behind, into the blackness beyond Kitty's light. The broomstick, sensing her fear, quivered against her. She held out her arm and looked at the strange writing on her mapped arm. The Singing Gate first and then other small words higher.

"What does it say?" asked Kitty, and her voice sounded sleepy.

"I'm not sure," said Annabel. It was difficult to read upside down.

The light was too dim, and Kitty did not move her heart light closer.

She heard Kitty laugh softly, and it made her feel cross again.

"Can you read it?" Annabel asked and knew in asking that she wanted to shame the wild girl.

Kitty shook her head. "Can't read," she said. "But I know the way the sun shines a little different every day and how it hits the grand old lady hornbeam straight on in summer but on her left cheek only by the winter, and how it changes her mood. And I know which birds sing first at Kensal Green and what their song says. Not everyone has a need for fancy letters, Annabel Grey."

Annabel sat very quietly, ashamed.

Kitty stared at her sullenly. The boat slid through the dark tunnel, pulled by the strange current. The river made a new sound, but only Kitty heard it. It said, *Come, come, come.*

Annabel thought perhaps she should look into the glass. Maybe it would tell her what to do. She took it from where it was tucked into her bodice, glad it had survived her time in the rushing river. She peered into it and tried to empty the cup of her mind, but there was nothing. Nothing at all. It was just empty ruby-red glass.

Kitty frowned and looked away.

"What if those shadowlings are coming?" whispered Annabel. There, she'd said it at last. She was scared, panicked. Why had they sent her on such a journey? They obviously needed a much more magical girl.

"Hush," said Kitty. "You saw what the Vine Witch did with her wand. That is all we need do if they come. You will point the wand at them and make fire come out of it, and that will keep them away."

Annabel looked at the wand. She had no idea how to make anything come out the end of it and knew Kitty knew that. The tunnel widened and the current quickened further. The boat felt lifted, carried by the river. The stench had disappeared. The place smelled of rain.

Annabel looked at her arm to be sure they were in the right tunnel. The line of the passage they were in twisted and turned. It led to the Singing Gate, sure enough, and she reached out her finger to touch the line but stopped. The place felt strange. Even just looking at the line drawn upon her skin, she felt a trembling and lightness. She shook her head. After the Singing Gate the line threaded off to the side of her arm. She turned her arm in the dimness to see what was above her elbow.

It was impossible. They should have given her the map on a piece of paper. She would have been able to read a proper map. She was very good at reading ordinary, unmagical maps.

"The river will take us now," said Kitty, curling up further in the bow. She coughed her harsh cough. "I must swallow my light because I cannot have it out of me so long."

"Please," said Annabel.

"I must," said Kitty. "The river will take us."

"But how do you know?"

"Can you not feel it?" said Kitty. "Can you feel nothing?"

That made Annabel's cheeks burn. "I can feel it," she lied.

Kitty swallowed her heart light.

"The river is singing to us," said Kitty in the darkness. "Listen, and up above, London is still dreaming."

"I know," lied Annabel.

"You don't know nothing, Annabel Grey," she said.

Annabel closed her eyes and tried to think of the emerald-green ice skates she'd had her heart set on. She tried to conjure them up, but it was no good. However much she tried, they dissolved and she saw Kitty instead, and shadowy things in Miss Estella's bedchamber, her mother standing on a faraway railway platform. She felt the map stinging upon her skin.

She began to cry.

"Stop crying," said Kitty before she fell asleep. Or she thought she said it. She was already dreaming.

"But we're both crying," she dreamt Annabel Grey replied.

The shadowlings slipped down the ladder, their claws click-clacking on the rungs. They scampered up the brick ceiling and formed themselves into the shape of something huge, something

unspeakable. The thing stretched out its shadowy tentacles through the tunnel.

They came to the place where the three arches stood.

At each entrance they opened their mouths and breathed in to catch the taste of her.

At the third they moaned and hushed and laughed against each other's dark cheeks.

They whispered the word, one word, the only word.

Annabel . . .

And they slipped into the tunnel like black water into a drain.

◆ ◆ ◆

In London Above, the Finsbury Wizards made preparations as quickly as they could. As quickly as they could was not very fast. Mr. Crumb needed to rest halfway up the very long staircase to the pigeon room, but they could not leave him, for he was the pigeon master.

"Not far now," said Mr. Bourne encouragingly, and they all nodded and agreed that it wasn't far, only three more flights.

But they were used to sitting for long hours.

They were used to days passing with nothing to occupy them but their thoughts.

They were used to creaking slowly up the steps to their beds and arising twelve hours later to think again.

Now that the magical brown fog had swallowed the city, there was a more dreadful worry in the house. The feeling of endings was very strong. Word must be sent to all in the society. It exhausted such elderly wizards. At that very moment they would normally be taking their evening tea and biscuits.

"I always knew he would do something like this," muttered Mr. Keating when they started moving again.

"We all knew it," said Mr. Bell. "But there was nothing that could be done until now."

"Why, though?" said Mr. Crumb, who was quite breathless. "Why must he always do wrong? His resurrection apparatus, and now this machine that can make dark magic. Why this badness—where did it come from?"

They themselves had seen it appear and grow in Mr. Angel, this desire for power, for others to bow down to him. They had seen it grow and had been confused by him. By his blackness. By his coldness. Until they could do no more but turn him away.

Could they have done more to stop him, to help him, to save him? These were the questions that filled their heads on the very top stair. They shook their heads, deep in thought.

"But there shall come a most magical girl," said Mr. Bell at last. "Or so the prophecy says. . . ."

And they all nodded and smiled quite sadly.

Mr. Crumb prepared his birds as swiftly as he could, which was not swiftly at all. He talked to them softly, attached the tiny scrolls to their necks. There were messages for the Kentish Town Wizards, with their terrible rheumatism; the Bloomsbury Witches, faded and ancient in their yellowing lace dresses; Miss Broughton in St. John's Wood; Mr. Hamble in Stepney; Mr. Huxley in Hampstead.

Beware, Mr. Angel in possession of the Black Wand and dark magic.

Raising an army of shadowlings.

Demanding all lay down their wands to him.

Youngest and most able member of society sent into Under London to return with Morever Wand. A most magical girl.

Our only hope.

He sent forth five pigeons into the London night, where the near-full moon had risen and was shining feebly through the fog. One pigeon remained on the sill. Mr. Crumb's arthritic hands hesitated over it.

"Shall we send a message to the Miss Vines?" he asked. "To see whether the girls made it back to them safely?"

His voice was old, so very old.

Mr. Bell lowered his head and shook it slowly.

"There will be none there to receive it," he said.

10

— line divider —

*"When traveling, a young lady should answer questions
politely but spend little time talking to strangers."*
— *Miss Finch's Little Blue Book (1855)*

Annabel woke suddenly and sat upright. Someone had
called her name. She had slept in the tiny boat, woken,
and slept again. How much time had passed? In the beginning it had been a brick ceiling curving over them, passing
minute after endless minute. But then the brickwork was
gone and the tunnel was roughly cut, and they passed beneath jagged rock dripping with water.

"You hear it now?" Kitty had asked sleepily from where
she lay, a little messy mound in the bow.

Annabel had heard it. The river sang. It sang a song of
water drops and the hushing of the river touching rocks. It
sang a sighing song of falling water and secret places. The
bow of the boat dipped, and the river sang them down.

"Yes," Annabel had whispered. "I hear it now."

When she slept, she dreamt of Miss Henrietta, and in the

143

dreams her great-aunt's face was very bright, like Kitty's light, hovering above her, and it made her feel safe. But when she woke, there was darkness.

"Kitty," she said.

The dark-haired girl did not rouse.

"Kitty," whispered Annabel. "I thought I heard something."

She picked up the broomstick and prodded Kitty with it.

"Leave off," snarled Kitty, and she sat up scowling.

There it was again, a murmuring, a low sighing. A rushing noise, like a wind coming from far away.

"Please, a light, Kitty," whispered Annabel.

Kitty began to hum her heart-light song, but she was frightened and her humming seemed uncertain. The whistling, rushing noise grew louder. Annabel took the Ondona in her hand and turned toward the sound behind her. She saw nothing but blackness, but she was certain something was coming through the tunnel after them.

What if it was the shadowlings?

The Ondona felt like a stick—that was all, a thin, brittle stick—and Annabel wasn't sure how to get light from it. Not in any of the ways Miss Henrietta had in the shop, nor the way Mr. Bell had in raising the fire. Both of them had said something, she was sure of it. They had uttered a word. If only she could remember the word!

The sound was growing louder now. It was an angry droning, a violent hissing coming after them through the tunnel. Kitty hummed louder. Still no heart light.

The word was . . .

Annabel tried to picture Miss Henrietta raising the Ondona to the shop window. She was uttering the word. Annabel saw her in the kitchen, raising the wand before the hearth, and the word was . . .

The noise was deafening now, one long sigh that brushed against their ears.

Then silence.

Nothing but the sound of their own breathing.

Then a word. One whispered word.

Annabel . . .

Kitty made a small noise, and from her mouth came her heart light, pale pink and weak. She grew it in the air before her and illuminated the tunnel, where several huge black shadows skittered backward along the rock ceiling, their claws scraping.

"Benignus!" shouted Annabel, pointing the wand, for she had remembered the word.

"Benignus." Her voice was a squeak, the wand a stick—nothing more.

The shadowlings crept forward, slowly, tentatively, out of the blackness, over the walls toward them.

"Benignus!" cried Annabel again, holding the wand up. It was Latin, she was certain of it. If only she could remember what it meant.

"Benignus!"

Nothing. The shadowlings reached their long gossamer arms down from the ceiling and whispered her name.

Kitty's heart light flickered, faltered . . . then grew suddenly huge.

It grew so huge that Annabel turned her eyes from the terrible creatures to see what had happened. It grew so great that she had to shield her eyes. But it was not Kitty's heart light at all. The little boat had entered a great cavern. It had slipped suddenly out of the tunnel and into a cavern filled with the brilliance of a million chandeliers.

◆ ◆ ◆

The shadowlings did not follow. Not at first. They hung back inside the tunnel, hissing and writhing in horror at the light. Annabel and Kitty stared at the place they had entered. A vast wall shimmered before them. It sang a strange song, a throng of tremulous, chiming, whispering, weeping sounds. The song made the boat shake; they felt it in their feet and hands, and their lips shivered. It was bright, so bright that they had to cover their eyes. Kitty scrambled backward in the boat, pushing the dark tangle of hair from her eyes. She swallowed her heart light.

"It's the Singing Gate," she whispered. She had never imagined how it might shine.

The shadowlings called out from the tunnel but did not brave the dazzling light. They moaned and writhed and called Annabel's name. The little boat floated across the space, its bottom scraping against the shallows until the two girls stood and stepped out into the clear water.

"What is it made of?" asked Annabel, still shielding her eyes from the light. It was not a wall made of brick or stone or earth but of some other, shining substance. It sang louder as they went toward it.

Annabel looked behind her toward the shadowlings. One stretched out a giant arm toward the cavern but pulled it back just as quickly, as though it had been burned.

"They won't come now," said Kitty.

"I don't trust them," said Annabel. "They'll think of something."

They called her name across the cavern and the gleaming wall sang louder, as though it did not like their voices. Annabel held the broomstick and the Ondona and looked up at the wall, high as the cavern's ceiling. It was tall as a church spire, and it glittered with light, singing to them as they approached.

Their feet crunched over the white stone of the shore. Annabel picked up some from the ground. It was bone, and she felt faint with the realization. She was standing on finger bones and toe bones and femurs, rib bones and skull bones and arm bones, all pulverized. She went to say so to Kitty, but Kitty put a finger up to her lips to silence her.

When they were close enough to the wall, they saw it was made of the same material. Millions upon millions, trillions upon trillions of tiny bones. The bones were laced together, twisted and twined and fallen and crushed like overgrown vine, so dense that Annabel and Kitty could not see through it. But at the same time, the wall moved. It seemed to Annabel

147

that it bulged toward them rhythmically. It trembled and fluttered.

The shadowlings called out; they blew a desolate wind across the cavern. They stretched out their arms, and their shadow wings opened and shut toward the cavern. They grew bolder. Annabel did not like to keep her back turned to them.

Kitty looked at the wall. In amongst the bones there were scraps of other matter, iridescent tatters and ribbons. She knew the stuff, had seen it and touched it with her own hands up in London Above. She reached her hand out now, and the wall sang a loud song and swallowed the strange material up. The bones clicked and cracked and closed over the shining stuff.

"Whom do the bones belong to?" whispered Annabel. "Children?"

"The faeries," whispered Kitty. "This must be where they are buried, then, down through a hole who knows where, and their bones do the job of guarding Under London and the wand."

The wall sang a low, lilting melody of bone scratchings and shiverings.

"But how do we pass?" said Annabel, looking nervously behind.

The wall was complete. There were no gaps, no doors. It stretched from their feet to the cavern roof. There was no way under or over. Mixed in with the tiny bones, Annabel now saw, were larger bones, human bones, caught in places in the wall. A leg bone held tight by the small bones. A skeleton hand hanging just before her.

"Oh," she said, and looked away. She closed her eyes.

Green ice skates, she said to herself. *Green ice skates.*

Behind them the shadowlings were huddled together, whispering and arguing just inside the tunnel opening.

"Can you use your magic, Kitty?" Annabel whispered. She didn't know what other magic was inside Kitty, but she was sure there'd be more.

Kitty didn't turn to her. She stared up at the wall. She reached out again to touch some of the shimmering material, and the wall snapped loudly at her hand.

"We don't need magic," said Kitty, nodding at the finger bones dangling from the wall. "Those that came before us thought they needed spells and such, but I've seen enough of the faeries to know them. They are tricky and cunning, but their weakness is loyalty. They cannot bear to be apart. They sleep together, sing together, bathe together. They are always combing each other's hair with their fingers. And if one is troubled, why, the others, they cannot bear it, and they move together to put it right. I think perhaps they are the same when they are no more than bones."

The Singing Gate did not like Kitty's words, it seemed, for it shook and sang up several octaves to a crescendo of chimes and sighs. Annabel watched Kitty. She seemed sure of herself. She had never spoken so much.

Kitty turned and frowned at Annabel.

"I am right—don't you think, Annabel Grey?" she asked. "If I take a piece of bone here, the whole lot will come at me and the rest will be weakened for us to pass through.

149

It will take some jumping, and you must be ready when I say to go."

Annabel didn't know. She wished the Finsbury Wizards or the Miss Vines had mentioned what to do in such a case. She looked behind and saw the shadowlings sliding out of the tunnel into the cavern. They spilled into the shape of a dark net, a huge net, forming across the cavern roof. Annabel watched as the shadow net slowly began to lower.

"Kitty!" she cried.

But Kitty wasn't listening.

"I know faeries," said Kitty. "And sure enough, I know their bones."

She reached toward the wall, and the whole thing snapped in unison toward her. She did not flinch, only gave a little laugh.

"Kitty!" shouted Annabel. The shadow net was lowering, casting a pattern across the water. The wall sang a frantic song.

"Yes, I know faeries," Kitty said, and she reached forward again, without warning, and snatched a bone from the wall.

◆ ◆ ◆

The wall screamed. It sang one long note of panic. It relaced and renetted at terrifying speed toward Kitty's hand. Annabel saw a large hole open up before her and then more, everywhere—great tears appearing in the bone lace as it closed toward Kitty's hand.

"Go on, then!" shouted Kitty, pointing to the largest gap.

She was racing toward Annabel, the little white bone in her hand, the wall snapping and clicking after her in a shimmering white wave. Annabel threw herself through the hole, and Kitty came after her just as the wall closed behind them with a monumental *crack*.

The wall sang an enraged song. It screamed and pulsated white-hot. Annabel sat up, scurried backward on her bottom away from it. Kitty didn't follow. Kitty lay very still with her eyes closed.

"Are you hurt?" Annabel asked.

There was something terrible in Kitty's pale face.

"It's gone and got my foot," she said.

"It's *what!*" cried Annabel.

She lifted Kitty's skirts to find that the bone wall was knitted tight around the wild girl's ankle. There was blood dripping onto the cavern floor.

"Let go of the bone," said Annabel, but it made no difference. Kitty dropped the bone, and the wall held her tight. It would not let go of her ankle.

Annabel took the bone and threw it back at the wall, and it clicked into place, but still the wall did not release Kitty. It sang in earsplitting waves of sound. The look of agony on Kitty's face grew. She covered her face with her hands and sobbed.

"It will be fine—I'll get you free," Annabel said, but she didn't know how.

What could she possibly use against the force of that wall?

"Release her, please!" she cried at it, but it held Kitty's ankle tight.

Annabel snatched a bone from the wall, thinking it might open up another hole or weaken its grip on Kitty. But the wall held even tighter, as though it had learned its lesson. They had escaped the shadowlings only to be captured by the wall. She felt tears again but instead made fists with her hands and stamped her foot.

"Fiddlesticks!" she cried.

She thought of the ruby-red seeing glass. No good. The broomstick? No use whatsoever. She looked at the Ondona in her hand. When she had held it up in the boat at the shadowlings, nothing had happened. When she had said the word *Benignus*, nothing had happened. Yet she knew this was the Ondona. It had to be the Ondona. Miss Estella had known they would need it. Miss Henrietta had pushed it into her hand for a reason. Annabel had seen Miss Henrietta raise the fire and make light with the wand. She had seen Mr. Bell do the same with the Adela. They had used the word *Benignus*. She was sure of it. Benignus. It was Latin, she was positive. Benignus. Benigno. Benigni. Benignum. Benignae. It meant . . .

She needed to know the meaning of that word.

Annabel stood up, but, oh, she felt awfully shaky.

She pointed the wand at the wall where Kitty lay sobbing.

"Benignus," she said, but she sounded very unsure of herself.

Nothing.

Her voice was like a tiny insect's drone against the wall's concerted effort to keep hold of Kitty. Annabel closed her eyes, concentrating on the word, the shape of it. Oh, it was a strange word, like a mouthful of stones. She did not like the feel of it. She doubted herself, and the word meant nothing. Perhaps there was a certain way to say it?

"Benignus," she said very sternly.

"Benignus," pleadingly.

Kitty whimpered on the ground.

Maybe there was something else she had to do? Miss Estella had pointed her split-wood fingernails at Annabel's head and heart. It wasn't very helpful. Magic should have instructions. Wands should come with rules, like the ones for embroidering the edge of a handkerchief.

Annabel took a deep breath. What she needed were the bones to loosen around Kitty's ankle. That thought was clear in her mind, and clearness, she decided, was what she needed. Instead of trying to simply get magic out of the wand with a word, perhaps she had to give the wand instructions.

Yes. That felt right. She straightened her shoulders the way she had been taught at Miss Finch's Academy for Young Ladies. The wand did not know what to do if she did not tell it, she decided. The word alone meant nothing. You had to be particular with wands. You couldn't just point them at things and say a word and hope for the best.

She wanted the Singing Gate to release Kitty's foot. Kitty with her hands over her face, crying but trying not to. Kitty, the wildest, fiercest slip of a girl that Annabel had ever met.

Kitty, who made Annabel's skin prickle and sting with her ways. Kitty, who had chosen to help her. Annabel did not want the wall to keep Kitty. Kitty would not become one of those human bones resting in the wall. Just the thought of it enraged Annabel. She wanted the wall to release Kitty.

The strange sensation she felt before one of her visions flooded through her body. The excited, terrified feeling. The joined-to-the-sky feeling. *I want the wall to loosen around Kitty's ankle*, she thought, louder. *I want to raise the bone wall around her ankle. Let go of her, wall.*

"Benignus!" she cried, with that thought very clear in her mind.

Nothing.

But she didn't give up. *Benignus* meant . . .

Benignus was . . .

She tried to picture Mr. Ladgrove, her Latin teacher at Miss Finch's Academy, saying the word. Oh, that was horrible, for he did indeed have a voice like a sleeping potion, but it jolted something in her memory. *Benignus* meant "kind"!

She straightened her spine even more and raised the wand. *Singing Gate, you will release Kitty's ankle. Kitty is my friend.* She wanted this with all her heart. She wanted it ten thousand times more than emerald-green ice skates.

"Benignus!" Annabel cried, and the voice was nothing like her own. It was strong and clear. *Benignus* meant many things, Annabel knew, but in that moment, it meant, *By good, kind magic, by the magic of my kind heart, release my friend.*

She felt a jolt in her hand.

A gushing sensation.

It seemed her hand melted into the wand, and suddenly from its tip there surged an arc of white light that hit the wall around Kitty's ankle.

The wall made a stunned sound.

It gasped a deep breath, then paused.

The bones rattled around Kitty's ankle, and she was released.

It was over. The wall relaced, and its great voice subsided. Kitty turned on her side, stifling her tears with her fists. And Annabel fell to her knees, staring at both her hand and the Ondona with wonderment.

◆ ◆ ◆

"Let me see your leg," said Annabel when she had recovered.

The large cavern on this side of the Singing Gate took her question and repeated it several times. The cavern was round and empty, and the floor swept clean. The shimmering light of the Singing Gate danced on the ceiling, but there were also torches burning in brackets on the walls. Someone tended to the place.

"Get away from me," snarled Kitty.

She had sat up and was holding her ankle and was glaring at the Singing Gate. *It's just like them, those stupid faeries*, she thought. *Always doing things painful, always argumentative and spiteful and saying everything is theirs: every stinking tree and river.* She needed her leg to walk. She needed her leg to visit all her places, to touch all *her* trees and stones.

"Did you see what I did?" asked Annabel, and she couldn't help the smile. "I got the light to come out of the wand, just like Miss Henrietta. I felt it in my hand. It came from—"

"I don't care," interrupted Kitty. She moaned and held her ankle and hated the wall.

Annabel's smile disappeared. "But we did it. We're through, and the shadowlings are on the other side," she said, softer now. "I must look at your foot."

"Leave off," said Kitty, staring at her stocking, which was soaked with blood. "Unless you know the spell for stopping blood, too."

Annabel's hand still felt heavy with magic. Comfortably heavy. She wondered what her great-aunts would think of her . . . or what her mother would think. Perhaps she *could* learn a spell for stopping blood, but for now what she needed was a bandage. The red cloak would do. It was her brand-new town cloak and she hated to ruin it, but with some trouble she tore a largish strip from the hem. She asked Kitty to remove her boot, and Kitty cursed her, of course, but pulled off her very old shoe. It was full of dirt and leaves.

"Your stocking, too," said Annabel, which made Kitty swear even more.

There was a line of deep puncture wounds around Kitty's ankle, and Annabel wound the red bandage there. Kitty's ankle was thin and pale. Kitty had never known a bed or sweet puddings, and there, in the cavern behind the Singing Gate, that made Annabel feel very sad. She wished there were healing magic in the cloak, and she thought of the wand again and the word she had used.

"Should I try?" she asked. "With the wand?"

"Don't point that thing at me! You'll do it wrong and give me a chicken's leg to walk on."

That made Annabel laugh, but Kitty did not smile. She snatched the boot from Annabel when she tried to tip the leaves out.

"They keep my feet warm," she said, and Annabel felt ashamed for not knowing such a thing. Sitting there in that strange cavern behind the Singing Gate, bathed in its softer, less angry light now, Annabel thought there was so much about the world that she had never known.

"Well, if you won't let me try some magic on it, we must see if you can walk," said Annabel.

"Of course I can walk," said Kitty, refusing Annabel's hand. She stood alone, limped a few steps, and stopped.

"Lean against me," said Annabel.

"Why would I do that?" snapped Kitty, but she leaned heavily on Annabel's arm all the same.

"You saved me from the river," said Annabel as they began to walk slowly across the cavern. She couldn't help herself. "And now I have saved you in return."

"Oh, shut your gob," said Kitty.

That made Annabel smile, truly smile, for the first time since her mother had left her behind.

157

On the other side of the Singing Gate, the shadowlings turned back into the darkened tunnel. They could not pass through its light and had to return to their master. They wept as they flew, moaned, screeched in frustration at their failure. They came back to Mr. Angel, who stood in the London fog with his growing shadowling army.

They whispered the words they had heard. They whispered the words into his ears, folding and unfolding their claws. Well, if you won't let me try some magic on it they keep my feet warm I know faeries and sure enough I know their bones can you use your magic kitty, please a light, Benignus, Benignus, Benignus, Benignus.

Mr. Angel put his hand up to hush them and motioned them back among the others.

"Follow," he said to his army, and they rose up after him now, a dark flock, a black fluttering cloud.

"Down!" he cried, and they slipped behind him, one hundred of them small into the folds of his cloak.

"Up!" he cried, and they erupted from the fabric, grew large, grew monstrous.

"Destroy!" he shouted, and pointed to a carriage that had turned onto the road.

Afterward, he stood among the remains, the tiny fabric scraps still raining. He tasted wood splinters and dust and horsehair, and he smiled his terrible smile. The girl had gone down into Under

London, but she would come up again. He would have her then to feed to his machine.

His wand was nearly empty.

The moon was high.

He would need to feed his machine again. It needed a lonely china doll that a girl no longer loved or a little pauper's coat that never gave warmth. It needed black hatpins from a widow's veil. It needed flowers from a new grave.

But first he would visit the Finsbury Wizards. He would have the Adela. The old men would bow down before him or he would turn them to dust. He would have all the lesser wands: the Delilah, the Kyle, the Old Silver, and the Little Bear. He would have all the good wands, and he would destroy them one by one. He would destroy them so that good magic was gone for good.

11

"When visiting town, a young lady should walk with her carriage erect and her bonnet straight."

—*Miss Finch's Little Blue Book (1855)*

In the cavern behind the Singing Gate, there was an opening. It was an arched entrance, quite tall and grand. It looked like a tunnel that led somewhere important.

"The map," said Kitty, and the room filled with her demand.

"Say please," said Annabel, even though Kitty was leaning against her and had a very sore ankle. The girl had no manners.

"Please, Miss Grey," Kitty snarled.

Annabel smiled.

"Get your gigglemug off me," said Kitty. She supposed that smiling must be something that all rich young girls were taught. Smiling as though they owned everything, even the weather.

The stone walls took their argument and repeated it several times.

Annabel held out her left arm. Straightaway she saw that the lines from her left palm to the Singing Gate had vanished. They had been erased from her hand.

"Perhaps what we pass disappears," Kitty said, taking Annabel's hand.

"I would be very glad for that," said Annabel. Oh, to be herself again, with pure white unmapped skin.

"But no good if we have to find our way back," said Kitty.

Beyond the black line of the Singing Gate, there was the large circle of the cavern, and beyond that only one line that marched neatly across her arm.

"Well, that makes it simple," said Annabel cheerfully. "We just go down this tunnel."

But Kitty didn't release her. She placed her finger on the line that threaded away to the edge of Annabel's arm. When she reached the edge, she turned Annabel's arm over. The line continued, but it was lost in a vast web of tunnels and chambers and hollows and spaces that covered Annabel's entire forearm. In the center of the complicated maze were four neat words.

"The Kingdom of Trolls," whispered Annabel, and she felt quite winded. "Oh, I see."

She tried not to sound too scared.

"We must find our way through Trollingdom," said Kitty.

On Annabel's upper arm there was a body of water. Annabel could see tiny waves drawn there and, up high, the words

The Lake of Tears. She went to touch that part of her skin but stopped. The feeling was terrible there, so lonely and empty.

"The Lake of Tears," she whispered.

"Through the Kingdom of Trolls—if we can find our way through—and across the Lake of Tears somehow," said Kitty. "And then . . ."

She peered at Annabel's shoulder, trailed her eyes up onto Annabel's cheek, and looked away.

"What?" asked Annabel. It was awful to be mapped in places she could not read.

"Through the Kingdom of Trolls first," said Kitty, avoiding her gaze. She winced when she went to take a step.

Annabel looked at the grand opening opposite them. It was most definitely the way into the Kingdom of Trolls, and into the Kingdom of Trolls she must go. *I am the Valiant Defender of Good Magic. I am a most magical girl.* She tried to think those thoughts with certainty, but they were still shaky in her mind. She looked at the Ondona in her hand and remembered how she had made the good magic come out of its end. That made her stand a little taller.

Be brave. Be good.

They must go forward. The shadowlings must be stopped. All she need do was think of what she had seen in the washtub, the darkness about to sweep over London. They had to keep moving until she reached the Morever Wand.

"We will fly," said Annabel.

Her broomstick was there beneath her arm. It thrummed softly against her. She had not called it hers yet, but it felt right to, although just having such a thought made her bite her bottom lip. What would Isabelle Rutherford think of such a thing?

Kitty shook her head. She took a torch from the stone wall. "The passages will not stay high for long. Not if it is a place for trolls. Trolls are short and fat and like to crawl."

"Well, then," said Annabel, and she could not disguise the little shiver she gave. "We will fly for as long as we can."

◆ ◆ ◆

The broomstick did not like the passages. The broomstick, they learned, liked air and open places. At first, it would not budge. It was like a stubborn donkey that no amount of carrots or cajoling could move. Kitty sighed and made it worse.

"We need to find the White Wand," Annabel said to the broomstick, tucking the Ondona into her sash. "The Morever Wand. It's very important.

"We need to save London," she added.

"You are on a very special journey, dear thing," she said. "Please fly."

She tried other encouragements. "Imagine when we are home—why, we will fly together into the sky."

Threats. "If you don't fly this instant, I shall be very cross indeed."

What worked in the end was not words. She imagined having the wand in her hand and climbing back up the river ladder and seeing the Miss Vines. Just the thought of them filled her with longing: Miss Estella's wild smile and Miss Henrietta's frosty blue eyes. She didn't know how she could miss two people so much whom she had only just met.

The broomstick shot off through the entrance to the passage so fast that Kitty nearly fell off.

But it did not like to be hemmed in. It flew close to the stone ceiling, and they needed to crouch low to avoid banging their heads. It was skittish. It did not like twists or turns, and the passage abounded with them. The tunnel bent back on itself, the ceiling lowered, the walls narrowed. For some time the Singing Gate's glow stayed with them, but then the light leached from the passage. Occasionally in the distance a torch flickered, and they passed where it cast its pool of orange light upon the ground.

Kitty held up her own torch to darkened places.

In the dimness they saw that finally the tunnel was branching ahead. The broomstick hesitated, faltered, stopped.

Kitty flinched when she stood.

"Map," she said. Then, remembering, "Please, Your Royal Highness."

They sat on the ground, their backs against the narrow tunnel wall, and looked at Annabel's arm. By the torch flame Kitty's eyes were very green. She took Annabel's arm and peered at it. Her hair was a wild tangle, and she had her knees drawn up to herself. She smelled of blood and green grass.

"I wonder if I could learn to sing up a heart light," said Annabel.

Kitty did not answer her but looked at the map.

Annabel thought of what light she might have inside herself and what song she might have to sing to get it out. Perhaps something strange would happen. Perhaps it would be like the cup of her mind, which was not fancy china after all but dark pottery and bottomless. Maybe fire would come out of her nostrils instead. She smiled in the dark.

"I wish I understood it, though," said Annabel. "How you do it."

"Perhaps some things are not meant to be understood," said Kitty.

"But have you met someone else who can do it?" asked Annabel.

"No," replied Kitty. "But I've met all magical types that can do the strangest tricks. Mr. Huxley turning into a wolf right before my eyes, and Miss Henrietta, too, half out of her crow clothes. The Bloomsburys looking into their magic mirrors and mending broken hearts."

"Oh, tell me more," said Annabel.

"Hush," said Kitty, and again she frowned her fierce frown and pulled Annabel's arm closer.

She touched the line, followed it until it came to the place where they sat. Here, the path divided into two. They saw that each of the two passages branched. The map became a nest of lines, crisscrossed and crosshatched. An impossible maze. An unsolvable tangle of lines and caverns.

"Now what?" Annabel whispered.

"*You're* the most magical girl," said Kitty.

Annabel knew there must be something she was meant to

do. Something magical. This was what was expected of her as the Valiant Defender of Good Magic. Yet all she felt was stupid. Kitty watched her.

Annabel put her own finger against her skin at the place the tunnel divided.

She didn't want to.

She didn't like the way the map burned upon her skin. Her head said, *Look away*, but her heart said, *Touch*.

Annabel traced the lines with her fingertip, and a terrible thing happened.

The tunnels and chambers and caverns and chasms filled her head as her finger moved.

"Oh," she said.

The places filled her head with rock and moss and water dripping on walls. Her mind raced through these places. Past stone and straw and dark lichen. Dirty troll washing on sagging lines. The sudden close face of a troll: lumpen, gray, its rotten mouth smiling. Annabel wrenched her finger from her own skin and looked to Kitty, breathing hard.

"You see it as you touch?" said Kitty. "It makes sense if you have the sight and the map is magical."

"But up close. I see the walls," said Annabel, and there was a restless panic inside her, as though the whole map wanted to burst off her skin or burrow deep—she wasn't sure which. "It makes no sense."

"Your problem is you're always looking for sense," said Kitty. "If you see it close, you must be able to see it far. Try again. Move from the walls; move your mind."

"I don't want to look again," said Annabel.

"Oh, save us," said Kitty. "Look again or I'll bang you on the head. You aren't much of a valiant defender of anything if you don't."

It was true, Annabel knew it, so she touched her finger to her arm again, and immediately the rock wall rushed up to her face. If it could, that rock wall would climb inside and fill her up. She was the map and everything in the map, and it was a dreadful thing her great-aunts had done to her. The rock wall all lined with mud and straw and the saliva of trolls rushed past her. Her mind careened and crashed through the tunnels until she heard Kitty's voice.

"Slower, Annabel Grey," Kitty said. "Slower."

Her voice came from a long way off, but Annabel listened and slowed her breathing. Her vision slowed. She breathed deeply and fought against the urge to lift her finger. She didn't want to see a troll. Not its gray teeth or skin. She breathed deeper still, shifted her mind a little. She was away from the wall now but still cramped and close to it.

"Above," she said quietly to herself.

Then she was looking down on the tunnels, looking down on the passageways corkscrewing and doubling back on themselves—empty places, places filled with echoes. She caught a glimpse of a troll rushing along a path beneath her and then of troll houses—rough pockets cut into the earth, roundish, lumpy, devoid of any comfort—and, inside, trolls eating and sleeping and dancing and weeping.

And quite unexpectedly she saw herself in one such house, and Kitty as well.

They were there, huddled on the floor, looking frightened. But she had rushed past that place before she could stop. She tried to backtrack, reverse her finger on the map, but she could not find the room again. She decided it must have been her mind playing tricks. That's all it could be, and anyway, she felt she was on the right path now. The tunnels were untangling. There was an airiness to them. They were wider. A huge open cavern appeared and a vast dark lake within it. Another little boat was waiting on its shore. She knew that was the right place to be. The Lake of Tears. She removed her finger from her arm.

"The first path," she said.

"You're certain?" asked Kitty.

Annabel thought of them huddled in the troll house but shook the image away. The boat at the end felt right. It was the correct path. She knew it in her fingertip and in her heart. It felt good to trust herself. She had asked of her vision and been rewarded. She took a deep breath.

"I am certain," she said.

◆ ◆ ◆

In the chosen passage Annabel and Kitty could not stand upright. They had to walk bent over with their hands stretched out before them. Soon they needed to crawl.

Annabel had never crawled on her hands and knees

through a troll tunnel while carrying a broomstick and a wand before, and she never wanted to again. Even worse, Kitty made her go first and kept treading on Annabel's cloak and skirts. Annabel was almost certain it was on purpose.

"We must be careful," whispered Kitty, carrying the flame. "Trolls are vicious."

"Have you met one?" whispered Annabel.

"I have. In Tottenham. Well, the back of one, going down its hole. That was enough. The smell of it went up my nose and didn't come out again for weeks. They have tiny sharp teeth that can rip you to shreds."

"Raise the flame so I can see what is ahead," whispered Annabel.

"No, I must keep it low in case we come upon one," said Kitty.

Which made Annabel feel even more frightened. She didn't want to meet a troll.

"I heard they eat pretty rich girls for tea," said Kitty quietly from behind.

"Stop it," said Annabel.

Kitty was mean and ungrateful for a girl who had been saved from the Singing Gate. Annabel felt the pull on her cloak again and was about to become very cross indeed when she heard Kitty whisper, "Stop."

Up ahead, there was the sudden glow of a light and the sound of gruff voices. Kitty tugged Annabel back against the wall and extinguished their torch into the earth.

"What Gruen should like very much for supper is rotten apples," came one very clear voice.

Annabel saw the light ahead stop. A short silhouette appeared, standing at what seemed to be a passage crossroad. Another shape materialized in the light.

"Filled up with juicy worms," said a second voice.

"Yes, full of worms," said the first. "Does Mab smell something?"

"What?"

"Gruen caught a whiff of something strange!"

The flame went higher, and light rushed down the tunnel toward Kitty and Annabel. It stopped just short of where they huddled.

"Probably naught," said the first. "But Gruen could have sworn there was a sweet smell."

The light went up again, held higher, so that it came within inches of their knees.

"Gruen has rotten apples on his brain," said the second with a laugh, and then they were moving again, taking another fork in the passage, turning away from Kitty and Annabel, who held each other in the darkness.

◆ ◆ ◆

They crept forward again, and Annabel's knees felt terribly wobbly. She fumbled in the dark until she found a way to tie her broomstick to her back using her sash. She tore a hole in her dress high up near her collar and pushed the handle through so it stayed close to her skin. It felt wrong to rip her dress, but she also felt clever. The broomstick shivered there quietly, and she was glad for it. She was a girl with a broomstick tied to her back and a wand tucked in her sash. A most magical girl. She whispered those words and remembered the sudden gush of magic that had moved the Singing Gate.

At the places where the passages branched, there was always a torch burning on the wall. The trolls must have a network of them, Annabel supposed, like the gaslights in London Above. At each intersection they consulted Annabel's arm by the flame's light. Annabel traced her finger over the map but never again saw themselves huddled on the floor in a troll house, which made her feel better. She would hate to make the wrong decision.

Sometimes the tunnels went down almost imperceptibly. Other times they plunged, and Annabel and Kitty scrambled on their bottoms to stop from falling. Sometimes they heard voices, troll voices, far away, coming closer. Laughter sometimes. Once, the thundering of footsteps up ahead, with the shouts and cries of a celebration. But the map took them away from these places. Deeper and deeper. It grew quieter and quieter.

"I don't like it," Kitty whispered.

She was used to the roar of London. The churning and thundering and rattling of factories. The tenements, the turning wheels, the street criers, and the drunkards singing and the bells ringing. The voices of the trees and grass. The sudden upward rushes of birds on the marshes. Down here the quiet hurt her ears. It was a deep-beneath-the-earth quiet.

Finally they reached an open space where they could un-crouch themselves. There was no torch, so Kitty hummed in the dark until she had a heart light, and she threw it into the air and grew it so their shadows leapt out before them.

The cavern was filled with pebbles, and a shallow stream ran through its center. They moved as quietly as they could across it, there being nowhere to seek cover, but the noise of their feet was loud. The little stream chattered, and Kitty was glad for the sound. She limped, and Annabel watched her lift her skirts and examine the bandage.

"I could try magic again," said Annabel. "It might work."

"They say your mother was a healer," said Kitty, sitting down and touching the bandage.

"Have you heard them speak of my mother?" whispered Annabel. Just the sound of the word *mother* and she felt tears.

I can no longer protect you from your destiny.

"Don't start your bawling again," said Kitty.

"I wasn't," said Annabel. "It's just . . . What do they say?"

"That she was the mender of bird's wings and other such wild things, and small children about to die—she could tend to them and mend them in time."

"Let me try," said Annabel

Even though they whispered, their voices echoed in that place.

Kitty stretched out her leg for Annabel.

Annabel closed her eyes and thought of what she wanted.

172

She wanted the pain to lessen in Kitty's ankle and for it to heal. It was very clear.

"Benignus," she said, very slowly, and she thought she sounded very magical.

"Benignus," she said again, but nothing happened. No light blazed from the Ondona. Her hand felt very empty. Magic was a puzzling thing.

"I'm thirsty anyway," said Kitty, moving her leg away. She knelt down beside the stream and scooped water with her hand to taste.

"Go on," she said to Annabel. In London Above many streams were poisoned, but this tasted clean. It was sweet and clear. "It's good. I wouldn't drink it if it weren't."

But Annabel's expression had changed. She was looking into the water.

There was something dark flickering and twitching just beneath the surface, and Annabel thought it was a fish. She leaned closer. The stream was not deep, but she felt she was looking into the ocean. The depth confounded her. She worried over it, and her mind said, *Look away*, but her heart said, *Look closer*. The black thing twitched again. She watched its tail, and she saw that it was not a tail at all but part of a wing and that the wing was part of a horse flying through the night sky. The dark horse was drawing a dark carriage.

Deep in the shallow stream it was murky.

It was the shadowlings and Mr. Angel.

The shadowlings had formed themselves into a black chariot, and he rode upon their seat of claws. He rode through the London dawn shining feebly in magic fog, the chariot skating down streets, rising and falling, faster and faster. It undulated over rooftops and slid along lanes; it flattened the grass in gardens. The great fog opened up before it and closed behind it.

Annabel wanted to look away, to shout into the water, *Stop!*

But it was no good. There was nothing she could do but look.

The shadowling chariot slowed. It glided to a stop in a street she knew.

Mr. Angel stepped down and walked through the swirling fog to a doorway. He looked at the window above. A window that had been shattered and mended, the cracks still clear. He smiled.

Annabel felt Kitty's arms beneath her shoulders. She took a gulp of air, realized that her face was wet.

"Are you trying to drown yourself, fool?" asked Kitty, pulling her back from the water. "You fell right in."

Annabel tried to focus on the betwixter girl. She shook her head.

"I saw something terrible," she said when the cavern stopped turning. "I saw Mr. Angel and the shadowlings at the house of the Finsbury Wizards."

"Is it now or is it to come?"

Annabel tried to remember what Mr. Crumb had said. The past was colorful and noisy. The future dark and soundless. "To come," she said.

Kitty turned and made her heart light small so Annabel could not see her face. "Well, we have time, then," she said.

Annabel looked at the map on her arm. They had made their way through only a tiny part of the maze of lines. They were only halfway toward her elbow. She could not even see what was written on her face. *Did* they have time? How long had they been in Under London? All the darkness and endless tunnels conspired so that she could no longer tell. She was tired and she was hungry.

I am the Valiant Defender of Good Magic, she said to herself sternly. She smoothed down her muddy rosebud dress and straightened her newly torn red town cloak. She checked to make sure the broomstick and Ondona were safe.

"Thank you," she said to Kitty. "For saving me. I might have drowned."

"You'd never get anywhere without me," said Kitty, but there was no anger in her voice. Instead, Annabel thought she saw a flicker of a smile, the quick passage of sunlight across her face, but Kitty was turning already, moving across the cavern, and the only sound was their feet crunching over the pebbles deep beneath Under London.

◆ ◆ ◆

In London Above the pigeons flew through the night. They flew through the great brown fog, to Bloomsbury, to Hampstead, to Stepney. To St. John's Wood and Kentish Town. The wizards sat down on their chesterfields to wait.

Mr. Bell took the Adela, which lay on the tea table between them.

"Benignus," he said gently, lowering the fire.

He took the wand and turned to the window and made it whole again except for one sliver of glass. He took that sliver, still cool from the night air, and held it in his palm. He gazed upon it and wished for a sign that Annabel and Kitty had entered Under London and were safe. But the vision did not come.

He saw Mr. Angel and the shadowlings. He saw them rushing through the streets. The army was growing— there were hundreds of the nightmare creatures now. They swarmed behind Mr. Angel, whispering to each other strange empty secrets, stories without endings, snatches of conversation they had heard in the world. They moaned and cried and giggled to each other. Their claws scratched against the sides of churches and tapped on children's windows.

Mr. Bell looked up from the glass and shook his head.

They waited then. They sat very still on their chesterfields and waited. They were accustomed to waiting. Wizards wait for signs and omens. They wait for the sun or the moon to be at just the perfect place in the sky. They wait for the sugar to slide to the bottom of their brownie tea and dissolve. They wait for a prickly feeling in their ears and, when it comes, know it is the right time to look into their seeing glass.

But this was a terrible waiting. They waited during the first hours of that strange dark day. Londoners choked upon the fog. They closed up their windows, greasy with soot, and lit their fires and huddled round. Warning bells sang up and down the river, and birds flew into windows, and men walked off bridges by accident and carriages collided on street corners.

They waited solemnly.

They waited sadly.

Finally it came. The knock at the door.

Mr. Bell stood and made the journey down the stairs. Down past the ancient books and boxes. Down past the peeling wallpaper, his knees creaking and groaning. The shadow in the glass at the door was huge, but he did not cower. He opened the door to his visitor.

"Mr. Angel," he said.

"Mr. Bell," said Mr. Angel, and then he began to laugh. Mr. Angel laughed at the old wizard's politeness and his fear. He laughed at the dark day he had created. He laughed at the ride he had taken through the sky. He laughed because night would come and the full moon would rise. He raised his wand and pointed it at Mr. Bell, and the shadowlings crowded in behind him to watch.

12

*"When out calling, a young lady never touches the cups
and saucers until tea is served."*

—*Miss Finch's Little Blue Book (1855)*

Annabel and Kitty found a lone torch burning in a passageway that seemed to stretch for miles. Kitty took it and swallowed her heart light. They were glad for the new warm glow. There were hundreds of passages, all stinking and sticky, all empty. At each turn they consulted the map.

"Yes, this is the right one," said Annabel when she knew, when her finger and her heart and the map told her. She tried to sound cheerful, as though choosing one slimy hole over another were a normal occurrence. *Keep going*, she told herself silently each time she thought of the shadowling chariot sliding to a stop before the house of the Finsbury Wizards.

The passage narrowed. Annabel and Kitty crouched and crawled in the silence.

"Where could they all be?" whispered Annabel.

"Perhaps they have gone to a troll wedding. Trolls are always getting married," whispered Kitty.

"How do you know?"

"Miss Henrietta always says it," said Kitty. "'It's as muddled as a troll wedding.'"

Annabel pictured Kitty and Miss Henrietta talking this way. Miss Henrietta could not look at Annabel without seeming disappointed, yet she looked at Kitty with a strange reverence. The wizards, too—a reverence and a sadness.

I have heard it said she can sing up her spirit light. There are not many girls like Kitty anymore.

They crawled and crawled and crawled until their knees hurt. They wriggled on their bottoms through tight spaces. They looked at the map on Annabel's arm until their vision blurred. Hours passed. Kitty raised the torch and shone it into the many rooms that opened off the tunnels. Each time, they scarcely breathed until they saw the room was empty. They were rough little earth rooms, with no furniture at all. Annabel thought if these were troll homes, the trolls must be very uncomfortable indeed.

But in one of the small rooms the light caught on something in the middle of the floor. The girls held their breath, thinking it was a troll, but the thing did not move, and they crept toward it. It was a rough sack, filled to the top with apples. They were old apples, some of them very soft, and the smell of them was strong and ripe. Annabel's stomach lurched, and her mouth filled with saliva.

There were more sacks. One contained a grayish vegetable that smelled blank, like potatoes; another contained
stones. There was a sack in the far corner that contained
things that looked like pale carrots.

"I'll eat an apple," said Kitty, going back to the first sack.
"I'll eat the whole lot."

"Should we?" whispered Annabel. "I mean, they aren't
ours."

In the dimness she saw Kitty's incredulous face.

Kitty was a girl who ate where she could: in the orchards
and vegetable gardens of grand houses, at the baker's bins
where children with empty eyes fought over scraps of dry
bread.

"I'd be eating new bread if it weren't for you. We haven't
eaten for hours and hours," she said. "Who cares who they
belong to? Have you seen any apple trees on our journey,
Annabel? These are troll apples, stolen from cellars up above.
We're only stealing what has already been stolen. Here."

She thrust an apple into Annabel's hand and retreated to
the far corner of the room. She chose a place between two
large sacks.

"In case anyone comes," she said.

Annabel took the broomstick from her back and the wand
from her sash. She couldn't properly see which parts of her
apple were brown and which were good. She was reluctant to
start eating, but her stomach growled. The torch flame was
low; it cast a small orange glow.

"I wonder what color my heart light would be," said Annabel, sitting cross-legged in the darkness.

"How would I know?" said Kitty. She ate noisily. Her first apple was already gone. She spat out a bad bit, and it made Annabel feel queasy. Then she was up and returning with several more in her skirt. She passed two more to Annabel, who hadn't started on the first.

"How do you learn to do it?" said Annabel. "I mean, how did you know to even try?"

"Well, how did you know you could see in puddles?" replied Kitty. "You just looked in one, didn't you?"

Annabel took a small polite bite. For a rotten apple it tasted wonderful.

"I didn't really understand what was happening," said Annabel.

"Nor I," said Kitty. "I only knew that inside me is a part separate to this outer skin, and one day when I was a wee thing, I sang to that part and the light came up. And I worked at it, see, just the way you are getting better at seeing things. I can sing the light up, is all. And when the shell of me is gone, then the light will stay out wandering."

"Oh, don't talk of such things. It makes me sad," said Annabel.

Kitty laughed and spoke with her mouth full. "Can you feel what is inside you, Annabel Grey?"

"What do you mean?"

"I mean, what's in here," said Kitty, reaching to touch

Annabel's heart. "Not the dress and the fancy knickers and the manners, but in here."

"Yes," said Annabel, and then to sound certain she said, "Yes, I can."

"Liar," said Kitty, and she laughed her sudden joyous, wicked laugh. "You don't know nothing, Annabel Grey."

Her mood was improved by food.

"We should rest," she said. "Close our eyes for just a little while for strength."

She drove the torch into the ground.

Annabel thought of her vision in the cavern stream. The terrible black chariot and Mr. Angel looking up at the poor Finsbury Wizards' window. She shook her head. They shouldn't stop. But even as she shook her head, she began to feel drowsy. The apple was heavy in her belly, half-fermented, sticky on her lips. She rubbed her eyes.

"Just a little while," said Kitty.

"Yes," said Annabel. "Yes, I suppose you're right."

"We must," said Kitty. "You know we must."

Annabel took off her cloak and lay it on the ground between the two sacks.

"Share the cloak with me," Annabel said in the darkness. It was softer than the ground.

She didn't think Kitty would, but she felt her shifting closer. She had a wild smell, this girl. She smelled of the streets and the leaves and the sky.

"I wonder who your mother was, how you came to be alone," whispered Annabel.

Kitty remembered red hurting hands and children in a line, the closeness of bodies, the cold.

"I don't recall. Perhaps I was stolen" was all she said.

Annabel imagined that. No mother. Not even a tiny memory of a mother.

"My mother had to go away," she said. "On . . . business abroad."

"She had to go away so you could learn your talents," said Kitty. "She is magical, and you are, too. Perhaps she's gone to fetch her wand back."

Annabel pictured her mother fetching her wand, the Lydia. She imagined her taking it back from the Witches of Montrouge.

She is magical, and you are, too.

Annabel smiled in the dark. "I miss her," she said.

She said it to Kitty but just as much to the darkness. She wanted to see her mother, to meet her, her real mother, the one who had been hidden away Annabel's whole life. There were a thousand questions she wanted to ask her. Questions she *must* have answered.

"You'll see her again," said Kitty, and then she was overcome with coughing, and Annabel felt the feverish warmth beside her.

"What other magic is in you?" asked Annabel when Kitty had settled.

"Hush," said Kitty. "You never stop talking." She yawned a giant apple-scented yawn.

"Why don't you live with the Miss Vines?" asked

183

Annabel. "They could teach you and help you with your talents."

Kitty didn't answer for so long that Annabel thought perhaps she had fallen asleep.

"That's not my place," Kitty said at last.

Why? Annabel wanted to ask. It was there on her tongue, which had grown heavy and thick. Why? Where was her place? But sleep was taking hold of her already. It was taking hold of them both. It was taking them and plunging them further down, deep down into darkness.

◆ ◆ ◆

"There is no need for that, Mr. Angel," said Mr. Bell, and he bowed sadly. "We have the Adela and lay it down before you. We have sent messages to the other members of the Great & Benevolent Magical Society, and I know that they will do the same."

"You are sensible, old wizard," said Mr. Angel, nodding. He held a hand up, and the shadowlings shrank behind him into the folds of his cloak. He followed Mr. Bell up the stairs.

The wizards waited in the parlor, the Adela on the tea table before them.

Mr. Crumb took it and slowly stood. He handed it solemnly to Mr. Angel and looked very frightened.

"Very wise, gentlemen," said Mr. Angel. "When the clocks are all stopped and the darkness comes, I will have all the palaces and mansions, all the churches, all the Parliament rooms. I will keep whom I choose, destroy whom I choose, and if you serve me well, you shall have your own spoils. But first . . . the girl. The Vine Witches have sent her into Under London to find the Morever Wand?"

Mr. Bell nodded.

Mr. Angel gave a small laugh. He raised his hand again to the shadowlings, as they slipped from the folds of his cloak and spun and eddied about the room. They whispered and wept so that the old wizards held their hands to their ears. When they were done, one of the terrible dark things held Mr. Keating's handkerchief on its glinting claw.

The handkerchief that Annabel had dried her tears on.

"I sent the shadowlings to bring her back. They have not returned. She is alone? Do not lie to me."

"She travels with another girl. A betwixter by the name of Kitty. You will have heard of her."

Mr. Angel gave it thought.

"And you think she can save you all?" said Mr. Angel. He looked at the Adela in his hand. "You think that she can save good magic? You think she will return by moonrise and defeat me? Do not lie."

There was nothing to be said but the truth.

The wizards bowed their heads.

"We believe she will," they said.

13

"At the dinner table, a young lady should never contradict her host. In all circumstances she must put forward an agreeable and graceful countenance."

—Miss Finch's Little Blue Book (1855)

In Annabel's dream there were maps: paper maps unfurled and fluttering down from the sky; the maps from Miss Finch's Academy, drawn with her own hand; and the map written in magic upon her body. The world could be mapped—she knew it in her dream—yet there were always places uncharted. In her dream she knew she would travel to such places.

"All of good magic depends upon you," the wizards said, just as Mr. Bell had in real life, and they peered over her with their kindly blue eyes in their wrinkled, worn faces.

"Yes, I am the Valiant Defender of Good Magic," she said to them, and her voice sounded very sure. But then she felt herself drifting the way one sometimes does in dreams,

186

drifting upward, slowly, as though coming to the surface of all things. Then she was there, and she opened her eyes and was surprised to find the wizards' faces still above her.

She was even more surprised to see they had grown little beards, and she wondered at that for a moment. Then she pondered the rags tied in their long straggly hair and thought that was quite strange. Finally she considered the rotten teeth in their mouths and realized she was not looking at the Finsbury Wizards at all but that, above her, were three trolls looking down.

"Ooh. She be ugly," said the middle troll, in a yellow dress. She had a flat gray face and a squished nose. She fingered the little beard on her chin and grinned.

"Very ugly be she," said the trolls on either side.

Each held a torch with a flickering flame. They were equally gray-faced and squishy-nosed. One had tufts of hair protruding a good inch from her nostrils.

Annabel opened her mouth and tried to scream but found she could not. All the air had been knocked out by fear. But Kitty rose up, kicking and screaming. It gave the trolls a surprise, although not for long. Two of them leapt on her.

The trolls were short and fat, but their shortness and fatness were no impediment to them. They were tremendously strong and swift. Annabel was spun by the hair before she even knew she'd been touched, and a coarse rope was lashed around her arms and waist. Kitty went to release a heart light, perhaps to scare them, but the hum was punched out of her by a troll. The light orb fizzled and evaporated as the rope was strung round her.

"This one does magic!" cried one of the trolls holding Kitty. The broomstick and the wand were picked up from the ground and examined.

Kitty called them "greasy mutton heads" and "fat galoots" and several other bad names, which they listened to with interested expressions.

"We'll take them both to Aunty," said one when Kitty had finished.

"What about the king?" said the middle one, who had trussed Annabel up. She was the smallest of the three, and she wore a thoughtful expression as she stroked her little dark beard.

"The king be busy getting married again," said one of the others. "We'll take them to Aunty first."

Annabel and Kitty were bundled together, and with the little troll in the lead, lighting the way, and the other two behind, they set off to be shown to Aunty.

"Now what are we going to do?" whispered Annabel.

It was all wrong. Mr. Angel was going to the Finsbury Wizards and she was meant to be finding the Morever Wand, and now she was all tied up with rope.

"Did you see this in your map?" hissed Kitty.

"No," said Annabel, although perhaps she hesitated too long, for Kitty stopped and stared at her until she was prodded from behind by the two trolls.

They were Erta and Marta. Annabel knew this because, it seemed, trolls spoke of themselves incessantly.

Erta said, "I cannot believe Erta found some humanling children. Aunty will be pleased, she will."

Marta said, "Marta found the humanling children. Marta sniffed them out."

The troll at the front, guiding the way, said, "I found them. You both know I did."

Annabel thought it strange that the little thoughtful-looking troll did not refer to herself by her own name.

"Hafwen found naught!" shouted Erta.

"Naught Hafwen found!" shouted Marta.

Then they giggled very loudly, so that it echoed up and down the tunnels, and before them Annabel saw Hafwen's shoulders slump a little.

Annabel had been raised very well and Kitty's wild-ness hurt her senses, but nothing had prepared her for the misbehavior of trolls. Trolls do not say *Please* or *Thank you*. They do not say *How do you do?* or ask after your rela-tives. They do not say *Excuse me* when they burp or break wind. They both burp and break wind with alarming fre-quency. Hafwen broke wind in front of them. A loud break-ing of wind. It stank, and Kitty called her some more names that Annabel had never heard. She thought she would faint. Erta and Marta prodded her from behind.

"Keep walking, ugly girl," they said.

Never in her life had she been called ugly.

They went up and down troll tunnels. They went in and out of troll caverns. They walked and crawled. Trolls were very good crawlers.

"Hurry, before the king's wedding feast is finished," said Erta.

"Hurry, hurry, hurry, or they'll see our treasure," said Marta.

Finally in the far distance they saw a tiny glow. Erta and Marta began to call. "Aunty, Aunty," they cried, getting up to their feet. "Erta and Marta have a surprise."

A voice came from afar. "A surprise! You haven't killed Hafwen, have you?"

"No!" they shouted with glee. "Wait till Aunty sees it!"

They pushed Annabel and Kitty through the troll hole and placed their torches in brackets on the walls. The space was tiny, the floor littered with remnants of food. There was another hole leading from the first room, and from there the voice called again. It was a loud, gravelly voice.

"Show Aunty, then. Is it the biggest worm you ever saw in all of Trollingdom?"

Annabel and Kitty were pushed through the second hole, and there on the floor, on a pallet of straw and hair and the tops of root vegetables, lay a very large troll. She was roughly the same height as the other trolls, Annabel guessed, but twice as wide. Her tummy bulged inside her heavily stained nightdress. Her eyes grew huge when she saw what her nieces had brought her. Erta and Marta took an arm each and pulled her to a sitting position.

"By all the trolls in Trollingdom," she gasped. "You have found humanling children."

"Erta found them," said Erta.

"Marta found them!" screeched Marta, and she struck her sister troll a blow to the cheek.

"I found them," said Hafwen, and she scowled at her captives.

Annabel saw intelligence in this troll's eyes, which were a murky green. Something else, too: a tiny pearl of sadness. Yet when she went to look closer, the little troll had turned her face away and was staring at the wall.

"Bring them to me," said Aunty. "The dark-haired one is very bony and will be good for naught, but look at the fair one. Bring it so I can see. Aunty will feel its arm and tell you exactly how to cook it, what kind of sauce to use, and what kind of night vegetables to serve it with."

"What of the king?" asked Hafwen.

"Pah! The king—what of him? He has just had a wedding feast. Aunty will send him the skinny one and keep the fat one!" shouted Aunty.

Annabel had never been called fat! No one had ever told her how she was to be cooked! She wanted to speak, and she was beginning to speak when Erta interrupted.

"This one does magic," said Erta, and she prodded Kitty with her fat, dirty finger.

"Oh, does she?" said Aunty. "Even better! The king will give us a reward for her. Do some now, humanling child."

"I can't when I am tied up," said Kitty.

Aunty laughed and her belly heaved.

"Aunty is not stupid," said Aunty. "Untie you and you will magic us to death."

"And this one lay with these two pieces of wood," said Marta.

"They're my broomstick and my magic wand," said Annabel. Then, hopefully, "I can do magic, too." She didn't want to be cooked in a pot with night vegetables.

Marta clipped Annabel on the head for speaking.

"Ouch!" shouted Annabel. "I beg you, please stop."

Erta and Marta raised their eyebrows.

"Please," repeated Annabel. She felt very cross. "We must pass through the Kingdom of Trolls and we must continue on our journey. We must find the Morever Wand. I am the Valiant Defender of Good Magic and the youngest and most able of the Great & Benevolent Magical Society, and the whole of London depends upon me."

Erta and Marta laughed so hard that they both broke wind.

They pushed Annabel close to Aunty, who pinched her arm.

"Delicious," said Aunty. "But look—she has lines all over her. Will that ruin the taste? Tell Aunty again where you have come from with a broomstick and a magic wand and what is the purpose of your journey."

"I come from London," said Annabel, and she would have pointed above her head if she had had a free arm. "Have you heard of it? And the world is in danger, you see, because there is a gentleman by the name of Mr. Angel and he has built a machine that will produce dark magic, and already he is raising shadowlings. They are terrible things. I don't think you'd like to see one. And when the moon rises tonight, he will raise an entire army of them and everything will be in darkness and he will turn everything to dust. At least I think it is tonight in London Above."

Oh, it all sounded wrong. Kitty did nothing to help her. Kitty would be glad she was not for the pot but to be taken to the king. Just the thought of that made Annabel feel even angrier. She made a small angry noise.

"So, yes, the world, all the world, will be in darkness. And I am the Valiant Defender of Good Magic, and I must find the White Wand and take it back to the Great & Benevolent Magical Society so they can defeat Mr. Angel. I beg you to let us pass!" she cried, exasperated.

"Yes," said Aunty, scratching her large belly and then her large hairy chin. "Of course."

Annabel breathed out a sigh.

"Only, we are quite fond of darkness, us troll-kind," Aunty continued. "And this gently-man wants more of it, you say. And you on your way to save the world, and this scrawny one here, being magical."

"I am a little magical, too," said Annabel eagerly.

It sounded as if she were making it up.

"Yes, both magical now," said Aunty. "Let Aunty think. . . . The skinny one was seen to do magic. The golden-haired one with the two sticks says she has magic and she is the valiant defender of the magic, here to save the wide world, upstairs and downstairs. . . . Let Aunty think."

Erta and Marta leaned toward her, waiting for the decision. Aunty chewed on her bottom lip like an enormous cow. Hafwen stared at the wall, unmoving.

"No," said Aunty at last. "We will eat them both. With a black sauce. The skinny one will add flavor with her magical bones."

She began to laugh then, and she laughed so hard that bits of clod fell from the walls of the little round room.

"Keep them tied while Erta and Marta go to the night garden. Hafwen can watch over them," directed Aunty. "Humanling children are cunning. They are very good at getting away."

"They won't get past me," said Hafwen.

◆ ◆ ◆

Hafwen pushed Annabel and Kitty back into the first room, with the broomstick and wand placed beside the door. She prodded them into a far corner and then sat before them, her flat, warty knees an inch from Annabel's. Annabel thought of her vision. She had seen this, and it made her shiver and close her eyes. Hafwen did not look at them. She stared at the wall. Annabel looked at Kitty, and Kitty nodded in agreement.

"Why can't you do magic with your arms tied?" said Hafwen to the wall.

"Arms are needed for magic, it seems," said Kitty. "I have never been tied up to notice it before."

"Well, now you are," said Hafwen to the wall, quite pleased.

Hafwen stared at the wall, and Annabel stared at Hafwen's eyes. They were no darker or lighter than her troll sisters' eyes, but they were different. They contained a twinkle. It was a tiny twinkle, hardly there at all, but a twinkle all the same. Trolls are not known for the twinkle in their eyes.

"And what can you do with that wand?" asked Hafwen, staring at the wall.

"Much magic. I got the Singing Gate to release Kitty's foot," said Annabel. She nodded at the bandage on Kitty's ankle. Hafwen looked briefly at Kitty's leg.

"Not many get past the Singing Gate," said Hafwen. "Does it hurt?"

"Of course it hurts," said Kitty.

"Good," said Hafwen.

"Do you like it here, Hafwen?" asked Kitty.

Hafwen ignored her.

"Have you always lived here?" asked Annabel. Very gently. Very politely.

"I don't know why you are speaking to me," said Hafwen. "I will speak to you only when you are in a stew."

"That doesn't make sense," said Kitty.

"Shut your little humanling trap," said Hafwen.

Annabel took a deep breath and closed her eyes. She knew Hafwen was their only hope. How she knew it, she wasn't sure, never having dealt with trolls before, but she knew it all the same.

"Is she still fat, Hafwen?" called Aunty from her room. "Perhaps we should feed her something."

"She is still fat, but I'll feed her some night turnips," replied Hafwen.

"Good!" shouted Aunty. "Aunty can smell her from here. She will be like eating wedding cake."

Hafwen did not stand. She did not fetch night turnips.

"Perhaps I can do some magic for you, Hafwen," said Annabel.

"What kind of magic?"

"Perhaps I can look into my special looking glass and tell your fortune."

"I already know my fortune," said Hafwen, and there was something very sad in the way she said it. Her troll face was quite crumpled and angry.

Something melted in Annabel's heart. "You can never be sure of that," she said. "I never could have guessed I was going on such an adventure. My glass is in my bodice, tucked in just here. You could get it out and place it on my knee."

Hafwen looked uncertain. She wanted to, Annabel could tell. A little pulse jumped in her hairy troll throat. Finally Hafwen stood and pulled the ruby-red seeing glass from where it was tucked. She placed it on Annabel's knee.

Annabel looked into it.

"What can you see?" asked Hafwen.

"You must be patient," whispered Annabel.

She felt scared. What if it didn't work? She remembered the teacup of her mind, and she began to empty it out. What had happened to her great-aunts? What would Mr. Angel do to the Finsbury Wizards? Would she find the wand? Was she strong enough? Kitty, always Kitty—who had come to help her when she needn't have. The time. The moon. Her mother. Finally her mind grew still.

Annabel looked into the glass and felt a strange sensation in her belly, as though she were joined to the sky—a sensation she detested and loved in equal parts. She felt the peculiar falling feeling, the lifting feeling. *I should like to see the future of Hafwen the troll,* she said to herself very carefully. She had never asked before; she had only ever accepted what came. *Please,* she added, so as not to forget her manners.

She saw something in the glass. Something strange. She saw grass. Long grass, wet with night dew.

Well, that's not very helpful, thought Annabel, but then she realized that the grass was very green, and she could smell the grass, all green-grass-smelling, and suddenly, a head appeared quite close. It was Hafwen the troll, with her crumpled, angry face, coming out of a hole, crawling on her hands and knees. Hafwen sat down, *plonk,* flattening the grass, and looked up at the sky.

Annabel heard the night then. She heard the night all around Hafwen, the chanting of insects and the sighing of the grasses. She saw the big, clean, sparkling starry sky. That was where Hafwen was looking. She was looking upward, sitting now, her head resting on her knees, looking up with a most un-troll-like expression of wonder. She was watching the stars, gazing at them, reaching her hand up as though she could pluck one, and then looking guilty and frustrated that she had done such a thing.

"Why so long?" said Hafwen, and Annabel was suddenly rushing upward and out of her vision, seeing the crown of Hafwen's head receding, and then nothing but plain red glass.

"You shouldn't interrupt, you big oaf," said Kitty. "She was in the middle of seeing."

"What's going on out there?" cried Aunty.

"Nothing," said Hafwen. "She just doesn't like the taste of turnips."

She was clever, this little troll.

"What did you see?" Hafwen whispered, leaning forward.

"Well . . . ," said Annabel, and despite everything she smiled. "I saw beautiful stars."

She heard the breath catch in Hafwen's throat. "I saw one of them belonging to you," said Annabel.

"To me," whispered Hafwen, but then her face hardened. "You're lying."

"Wouldn't you like to have an adventure?" asked Annabel. "If you helped us, you would have a star of your own. I know it. I have seen it."

It wasn't entirely the truth, but she knew it was their only chance.

No reply. But there was a faint twitch in Hafwen's cheek. "How could I have a star?" she asked.

"I know where some are kept ready-plucked," said Annabel.

Kitty watched them both, a rare smile breaking out on her face.

"If Annabel has seen it, then it is so," she said. "Do you think they'd send someone with no talent on a perilous journey such as this?"

"I saw you up above," said Annabel.

"Of course I go up above," said Hafwen. "The troll tunnels go everywhere, right into your cellars. Why do you think I wear a humanling dress?"

It was true. Hafwen's yellow dress was definitely the wrong shape and size for the troll. Annabel imagined trolls in her cellar, maybe creeping up her stairs, rifling through her drawers. Oh, the things she had not known!

"But I saw you outside, looking up at the sky," said Annabel.

Hafwen narrowed her eyes. "With the stars?" she asked.

The way Hafwen said *stars* made the gooseflesh rise on Annabel's arms.

"But how did I take one from the sky?"

"I didn't see you take one, but I told you that I know where they are kept for just such a troll as you."

Hafwen looked terribly sad and guilty. She shook her head. "We should not look upon the sky," she whispered. "Stay inside. Stay deep, they say. Eat the worms and marry; do not tarry. Tend your garden. Have a baby. But I go up to a place where there is grass, a field of it, and naught but the sky filled up with jewels shining."

"Yes, I saw it," said Annabel. "And you shall have one if you come on an adventure with us."

"Don't be stupid," hissed Hafwen, and she closed up her face and the twinkle in her eye, turned toward the wall, and would talk to them no more.

In another life, the life of two days ago, Annabel would have given up. She would have cried. She would have shouted, "I want to go home!" But there in that troll hole, the little torch flame flickering on the wall, she knew Hafwen was the answer to their predicament. It was a good thought and it made her feel buoyant, like a kite being tugged on a breeze. Kitty looked at her, not with a frown but encouragingly. The kite tugged even harder.

Aunty called out as Erta and Marta stumbled back in through the doorway.

"I hope you haven't forgotten stones and worms."

Erta and Marta carried a large black pot filled with river water and night vegetables.

"And I hope you have enough water!" shouted Aunty again from her room. "There are two for the pot. Is Halfwen still watching them?"

"She is sulking in the corner with them," said Erta, and she pinched Annabel on the arm. "Poor miserable Hafwen," said Marta, and then off they went to collect worms and river stones.

Annabel knew that Hafwen was the least miserable of

them all. Of Erta and Marta and Aunty and all the trolls in Trollingdom. They had had the good fortune of finding a troll with a twinkle in her eye.

"Say you'll help us. Come on adventures with us," said Annabel as soon as Erta and Marta had gone.

"Don't be ridiculous," hissed Hafwen, but she had lowered her voice so Aunty could not hear.

"We will find the Morever Wand and then go back up to London, and we will find you a star."

Hafwen stared down at the dirty palms of her fat, hairy hands. Her little dark beard twitched on her chin. Annabel watched her. It seemed impossible that in that creature crouched there, smelling of rotten onion, with lank, greasy hair, there was something small and shining inside. But Annabel could sense it. Hafwen's wonderment.

"Sometimes," Hafwen whispered, "when I am up upon the earth, the grasses sing. The trees—they sing, too, and their breath is all filled up with green. The night is very clean. Why is the night like that, so singing and clean that it puts a spell on you?"

"I don't know," whispered Annabel. "But that night is your destiny, Hafwen. Come with us."

But Hafwen did not answer. She only stared at her dirty troll hands, thinking, until Erta and Marta came back. When they did return, they had everything that was required. Aunty shouted orders from her nest. The fire was lit in the corner, and the room filled up with smoke. Annabel and Kitty began to cough, but the trolls didn't seem to notice at all. The pot was put on the fire and filled with the river stones.

"You must put the magic skinny in first!" shouted Aunty. "She will flavor the water."

"You won't be putting me in a pot," cried Kitty.

Erta had the Ondona and she was pointing it at Kitty, pretending to do magic. "It doesn't work," she said.

"Give it to Marta!" bellowed Marta, and she grabbed the wand and pointed it at Kitty, and when it did nothing, she laughed and threw it onto the fire.

"No!" cried Annabel as the wand disappeared in the flame. Her great-aunts' wand! The ancient Ondona. She bent over double with the shock of it. Oh, Miss Henrietta would be very cross indeed.

But what did it matter? They were done for. There was no point. It was the end, she thought, when Hafwen leaned a little toward her and whispered, "Tell me?"

There was the clanging and clamor of pots in the room and a blast of heat as the flame grew.

"Tell you what, Hafwen?" whispered Annabel.

"Would I keep my star in a box?"

"Yes," whispered Annabel.

Then Erta and Marta were upon them, shoving them this way and that. Annabel saw Kitty being dragged toward the pot, terror on her little pale face. She saw Hafwen, too, with her arm upon Kitty, pulling her and prodding her, and she was certain that the troll had only been tricking her, that she'd never meant to help them, when she heard the hiss of water on flame and made out Hafwen's shape beside the pot, before steam engulfed the room.

"Hafwen?" cried Marta, and there was a terrible screech and then the thud of Marta hitting the ground.

"Hafwen?" cried Erta, and a similar thud followed.

Annabel felt hands upon her then, rough hands, untying her rope. She felt for Kitty and found her and never was so relieved to hold such a wild person's hand.

"Now, humanling children from London Above," came Hafwen's voice, very close to her ear. "We must not tarry. We must run."

Annabel grabbed her broomstick from beside the door, and it pulsed in her hand as they bumped and knocked and tripped their way out of the troll hole. The cave shook and dirt rained as Aunty heaved herself up out of her nest to chase them.

Mr. Angel stood on the doorstep of a Bloomsbury mansion and listened to the movements inside. The faded witches, in their ancient, tattered dresses, called to each other softly from room to room. They whispered to each other in the great dusty house, the furniture covered over, their broomsticks in wardrobes, their days of great and wonderful magic quite behind them. The shadowlings pressed their dark faces to each and every window.

"He has arrived, Matilda."

"He is at the door, Esmeralda."

"He waits, Lady Pansofia."

"We will do as the wizards say. Our only hope is the most magical girl."

Lady Pansofia took the Delilah and opened the door. Mr. Angel bowed most courteously. He pointed the Black Wand at them and smiled.

Not long after, the Kentish Town Wizards, stooped and bent, once filled with wild magic, gave him the Kyle. Mr. Angel took it and nodded to them politely, then let his shadowlings sniff at them so that they knew great fear.

Mr. Huxley in Hampstead, with gorse prickles still matted in his fur and his paws still wet with dew, growled and snarled but dropped his wand. Mr. Angel picked up the Little Bear and laughed at its lightness and all the sunny afternoons that would be no more.

His last visit was to Mr. Hamble in Stepney. Mr. Hamble lifted the Old Silver from his mantelpiece and laid it down before the younger wizard. Mr. Angel sighed.

He had been very patient.

Everyone had done his bidding.

He had tolerated their terrified faces, their little tremors of hope that the girl would save them, which they tried so hard to hide.

He had tolerated them all, but now he could not resist it, he simply could not. He raised his Black Wand and turned Mr. Hamble to dust.

14

"A young lady should always, where possible, secure the use of a first-class cabin when traveling overnight on a steam boat."

—*Miss Finch's Little Blue Book (1855)*

Hafwen was fast despite her size. She shouted back over her shoulder: "Follow me." "Down here." "Up here." "Turn here." "Through here." She ran through a wide tunnel, her torchlight racing on the walls before them. Annabel was surprised at the joy in her troll friend's voice. Hafwen was enjoying herself.

Aunty thundered behind them. She filled the tunnel. "Hafwen, stop!" she cried. "Hafwen no farther goes."

Her footsteps rattled the earth beneath their feet.

"Aunty will tell the king!" shouted Aunty.

Aunty was also fast despite her size. As she built up speed, her size added to her momentum. She was a huge wrecking ball hurtling after them through the tunnel. They could smell her behind them, all rotten vegetables and bad breath.

They reached a place where the tunnel narrowed, and they threw themselves onto their hands and knees to crawl.

"Hafwen, run no more," Aunty screeched, plunging after them. She crawled wildly, with her tongue out and her eyes open wide. She crawled so fast that by the time they were in a place where they could stand again she was almost upon them. She reached out one great hairy hand and grabbed Kitty by the ankle and yanked her backward through the air.

"Let me go!" Kitty shouted. "You greasy oaf!"

Kitty looked like a matchstick in Aunty's grip.

"Let her go!" cried Annabel. She would have rushed toward Aunty and been caught herself had Hafwen not held her back.

"Let Aunty have the skinny," said Hafwen. "We keep running."

"No!" shouted Annabel. "She's my friend."

Kitty looked at Annabel. She tried to speak, but she was being squeezed too hard.

"Aunty will snap her in half!" screeched Aunty.

"Kitty, can you throw one of your lights?" shouted Annabel. She had an idea. Her broomstick trembled in her hand, as though it understood.

Kitty was turning purple, her eyes bulging, but Annabel heard her begin to hum.

"Aunty, she's too skinny," said Annabel to distract the great troll. "You take me instead."

"Better a skinny humanling than no humanling," said Aunty, but her grip lessened as she pondered the swap.

A strangled hum was enough. Kitty coughed out a misshapen heart light, weakly gleaming, as Aunty's grip tightened again. The little light orb flew through the air between them, and Annabel ran toward it, her broomstick raised like a bat. Aunty screeched and squeezed Kitty so hard that she turned from purple to blue.

Annabel had played shuttlecock with Isabelle Rutherford at her family's country house in Shropshire. Surely, hitting a light orb was no different. She ran one, two, three steps forward and lifted the twig end of her broomstick. She whacked the heart light as hard as she could, aiming for Aunty's face. She aimed and whacked and the thing traveled at an alarming speed toward Kitty's captor. It slammed into the huge troll's surprised face. It exploded in a shower of light.

Kitty was released as Aunty hollered and held her hands up to her eyes.

"Aunty can't see!" she cried.

Annabel rushed forward and dragged the slumped Kitty away from her reach.

"Aunty be blinded!" yelled Aunty as Kitty began to cough.

The little shards of light sped back into Kitty's mouth.

"Can you run?" asked Annabel, helping her friend to her feet.

"I think so," said Kitty.

"Hurry," said Hafwen. "Bring your friend the skinny after all."

◆ ◆ ◆

They raced through several tunnels until the sound of Aunty's shouting faded. Finally they came to an empty spacious cavern where the walls dripped. Hafwen held her torch high.

"Here is one way up," she said, panting heavily but most pleased with herself. She bared her grayish teeth in a great troll smile and pointed at the rocky cavern ceiling.

"She's mad," whispered Kitty.

"Above be a big house with bells," said Hafwen. "First you must go through the rooms filled with the dead humanlings, stacked up one on top of the other, and from them we take our wedding dresses."

It does seem true that trolls are always getting married, thought Annabel. The thought of them stealing dresses from the catacombs gave her a fresh wave of shivers.

"But there be other places," said Hafwen. "I can take you to the grass."

She was facing them now, her big dirty face smiling and expectant.

"But we don't need to go up," said Annabel very gently.

"But . . . stars . . . be up," said Hafwen.

"Yes, but first we must follow the map and find the Morever Wand," said Annabel.

"But . . . up be stars," said Hafwen, incredulous.

"We aren't going up!" shouted Kitty sternly. "We are going to find the Morever Wand."

Her voice echoed up and down the dripping walls of the cavern.

Hafwen closed her eyes. She drew a breath and held it. By the light of her torch she grew a violent stormy color.

"Hafwen want star!" she screeched, blasting them with her breath and ruffling their hair.

"Hush, hush, hush," said Annabel. "I have promised you a star and you shall have it, but we cannot go up until we have found the wand. You must help us on our way."

"Leave her," said Kitty. "She's served her purpose."

"Stop it, Kitty!" cried Annabel. "We would be in a pot if it weren't for her."

Hafwen's eyes darted between them. She held her breath again.

"Breathe, Hafwen," said Annabel. "Soon you will have your star. I promise you."

Hafwen deflated. "So . . . I must take you where your map does say?"

"Yes," said Annabel. "Lead us through Trollingdom like the brave little troll you are."

She held out her arm and they gathered around her to find which path they would follow next. Hafwen gave Kitty the torch and peered at Annabel's arm. She placed a big hairy finger in the center of a circular cavern.

"Here where we be," she said. Her hulking shape cast a shadow.

"Get out of the light, you filthy oaf," said Kitty.

"You would have been better in a pot," said Hafwen.

"Both of you, stop!" cried Annabel.

Hafwen did not like Kitty. Kitty did not like Hafwen. They

were actually quite similar, Annabel decided. Kitty coughed and glared at Hafwen. Hafwen narrowed her twinkling eyes.

"This be the up cavern I know," said Hafwen. "But to go farther . . ."

She twisted Annabel's arm roughly because trolls do nothing gently. She twisted it so she could see the fleshy part above the elbow. A maze of tunnels led to the vast open space that took up most of the inside of Annabel's upper arm. The rough oblong shape was filled with waves that Annabel had seen but refused to touch. Just looking at the place made her feel dizzy. It was deep. It was fathomless, that place.

She looked at the upside-down words. *The Lake of Tears.*

"No trolls pass here," said Hafwen, pointing to those words. "Only dead trolls on their funeral boats, fed to . . ."

She stopped.

"Only dead trolls on their funeral boats," repeated Kitty, "fed to . . . ?"

Kitty passed the flame back to Hafwen. She traced her finger across the Lake of Tears. There was a shore, and beyond it a single path that snaked its way up onto Annabel's shoulder. Annabel couldn't see where it led after that. The others followed the single path with their eyes. She saw them gaze at her chin, her cheek, her forehead. Their eyes settled back on her cheekbone. They looked away.

"There be a terrible thing," said Hafwen, "after the Lake of Tears."

"And is this the terrible thing?" said Kitty, pointing to Annabel's cheek.

"Things what trolls don't mention," said Hafwen, and she refused to look where Kitty pointed.

"All will be well, Hafwen," said Annabel gently. She was quite good at calming down cranky trolls, she had discovered. A talent that Miss Finch at her Academy for Young Ladies could never have imagined. "We are only trying to understand what is ahead of us. What things?"

Kitty looked back at Annabel's cheek again.

"Can someone please tell me what is on my cheek?" asked Annabel, quite politely, she thought, under the circumstances.

"It is the West-Born Wyrm," said Hafwen.

"The West-Born Wyrm?" repeated Kitty.

"Yes, the West-Born Wyrm," whispered Hafwen. "It eats up everything. Dead trolls best. We feed it our dead 'uns to keep it away. Sometimes it goes up and eats some humanlings."

"A worm?" said Annabel. "It must be a very big one to eat people."

Kitty looked at Annabel as though she were the stupidest person she'd ever met. "A mad troll and pretty girl with not much brains," she said. "We'll never get out of here. A wyrm, Annabel Grey, is a dragon."

She continued the path with her finger, from Annabel's cheek into the center of her forehead.

"And it appears that the only way to the Morever Wand is through the dragon's lair," she said.

◆ ◆ ◆

Annabel didn't like to think of dragons. She tried not to as they trudged up and down troll passageways. She thought instead of her mother, who had been magical but never showed it, when all the time she could have been teaching Annabel. That made her think of why. And how. And what terrible thing could have happened in Mr. Angel's house that her mother had turned her back on magic for good. That in turn made her think of her father, the Great Geraldo Grey, which made her feel the breathless, falling type of sadness, which was almost as bad, she decided, as thinking of dragons that breathed fire and were monstrously big.

Sometimes they heard troll voices in the distance and Hafwen led them quickly in another direction. Annabel hoped she was leading them in the right direction. She hoped there was a way out of the maze of tunnels. She thought of what she had seen in the water of the stream. She knew they had to move quickly.

Be brave. Be good.

"I'm hungry," said Kitty.

Hafwen stopped and pulled a worm from the earth wall and held it out to her.

"Leave off, you dirty lump," said Kitty.

"What was that light that came out your wormhole and blinded Aunty?" asked Hafwen.

"It's Kitty's heart light," said Annabel.

"I don't like it," said Hafwen. "It unnatural."

She put the worm in her own mouth and sucked loudly.

She led them up and down tunnels, in and out of caverns. Sometimes she stopped and scratched her troll head and started again.

"Do you even know where we are going?" asked Kitty.

"I take you to the Lake of Tears," said the troll.

"You are very kind, Hafwen," said Annabel.

Kitty sighed.

"I want my star," said the troll.

"You'll get your star, dear Hafwen," said Annabel.

Annabel had felt the expanse of the Lake of Tears on her arm, but nothing could prepare her for the sight of it.

They stumbled, very suddenly, out of a passage and onto its shore. Hafwen held her flame up, and they saw the dark stretch of water. They could not see its edges. It felt endless to Annabel.

"So, how do you get across the Lake of Tears?" Kitty asked.

"No one crosses the Lake of Tears, skinny," said Hafwen.

"But you said the dead 'uns are sent across the Lake."

"They are dead 'uns in funeral boats," said Hafwen.

"And where would we find a funeral boat?" asked Kitty.

"You would find a boat where the funeral boats are built," said Hafwen.

"And I am sure you don't know where that is," said Kitty.

"Of course I do," said Hafwen, and she puffed out her little troll chest. "I will show you."

She led them along the shore, and the dark water sucked and slapped against the rocks. It was a lonely sound. A hungry sound. An unsettled sound.

"I don't like this place," said Annabel.

"Hush," said Hafwen. "All you humanlings do is talk. We must be quiet or the boat builders will hear us."

There was no sign of boat builders. There were only rocks by the light of Hafwen's little flame. Large rocks, small rocks, slimy rocks. The three of them slipped, clambered, climbed. Sometimes the dark water rushed through spaces and touched their toes. They walked and walked until their legs ached.

"She's tricking us," said Kitty.

But then Hafwen took her flame and extinguished it in the water, and they were in darkness.

"We are close now," she said, and they heard suddenly the sound of hammering from a long way off and the faint murmuring of voices.

They climbed in the blackness then, tripped and tumbled, and Kitty swore so loudly once that Annabel was sure they would be heard, but the hammering only paused and then continued.

It grew louder, the voices clearer.

"You must build it well, and well it must be built," said one voice. "Pay attention, young Calder."

There was a flurry of banging and sawing.

"Has the wyrm ever come our way?" asked a younger voice.

"Why, yes," said the older. "It has come across this lake and in through Trollingdom, eating trolls, sucking them up, here and there—even the then king in all his dandies, straight into its mouth, *crunch*, *crunch*—until there were none left but a few young 'uns huddled somewhere secret. That is why we must build the boats and send him the fresh dead 'uns, the noblest act of any troll, and then he will not come a-hunting us. Put a nail here. Here be a good humanling nail. See how it is made. They are better made than any other. Humanlings be good for naught but making nails."

There was a sharp bang.

"Well done, young Calder. Calder shall be a boat builder yet."

Hafwen stopped still and looked back at Annabel and Kitty. She placed a hairy finger to her hairy lip. She pointed to the water before them, and Annabel saw there were many small boats, some Hafwen-sized, some Aunty-sized. They bumped against each other quietly in the water. They were tethered to the rocky shore by ropes.

Hafwen knelt down and unfastened one of the ropes and motioned for them to get inside. Kitty, with hands on hips, refused.

"It's too small," she hissed.

"Get in," said Annabel.

Annabel clambered into the stern.

215

"Kitty—quickly," she said.

Kitty refused.

"We could have chosen a bigger one," Kitty said.

"Get in," said Hafwen, and she pushed Kitty in as best she could. The boat rocked. Kitty cursed. The hammering on the shore stopped. There was the sound of startled voices. The light of torches flared over the rocks, and several trolls appeared, rushing toward the shore.

Hafwen waded beside the boat, pushing them as fast as she could.

"Humanlings!" the crowd cried.

"Traitor troll!" they shouted.

"Jump in, Hafwen!" said Annabel. Hafwen was up to her round troll waist in water.

"No troll crosses the Lake of Tears alive," said Hafwen, but she looked back at the trolls on the shore. More had arrived. Their angry voices boomed from the rocks.

"Take her to the king!" they shouted.

"He'll chop her up!" they shouted.

"Hafwen—please come!" cried Annabel. "You must."

"No troll crosses the Lake of Tears," said Hafwen, but her voice was not so sure.

"She'll sink the stinking boat," said Kitty. "Leave her."

But it was the wild girl's hands that reached out for the troll's all the same.

Hafwen had one short hairy leg in the boat, and Annabel and Kitty dragged her in by an arm each. The boat rocked under the weight of her. She squeezed between Kitty and Annabel, looked at them apologetically, and smiled.

Annabel smiled in return. She had her broomstick ready. She dipped it in the water and began to paddle. They moved farther from the shore and from the crowd of angry trolls, who called but did not follow. They were too frightened of what lay beyond the Lake of Tears.

"Everything will be fine," said Annabel.

Kitty scowled at her, half squeezed out of the boat by Hafwen. "Yes, a fine night to visit a wyrm," she said at last, and began to laugh.

◆ ◆ ◆

They hadn't gone far before there was a reshuffling in the boat. Kitty complained bitterly until Hafwen stood to let her move to the bow. The boat tilted heavily to starboard when Hafwen sat down again. Annabel was very glad to have Hafwen beside her, her shoulder pressed against Annabel's own. Hafwen smelled of the earth and unwashed clothes and deep, dark places, and for reasons Annabel did not understand, this was comforting. She could never explain such a thing to Isabelle Rutherford.

Hafwen rowed with the wooden torch, and Annabel used the broomstick. They moved the little boat out onto the black water. The troll crowd, which had grown large and loud with boos and hisses, grew smaller and smaller until it was just a glowing line and was then swallowed up by the darkness altogether.

"Can you make a light, Kitty?" asked Annabel.

Kitty hummed for a while and produced a small pale green orb.

"Keep it away from me!" shouted Hafwen, flailing and flapping so that the boat swayed wildly.

"Hush, Hafwen," said Annabel. "It will not harm you."

Kitty blew her heart light close to Annabel's arm. Hafwen leaned as far away as she could. There was the lake drawn upon her upper arm, filled with dark waves. The very same lake that rocked them now to drowsiness. Beyond the lake there were more caverns, one after another, that grew smaller and tighter, winding onto her throat, where she lost sight of them.

Her companions looked at her skin in silence, and then Kitty swallowed her heart light.

"I need to rest." Kitty coughed. "My chest hurts."

Annabel thought and thought and thought in the darkness. She wondered what a real dragon looked like. She wondered if it was always bad or perhaps had a good side, too, the way Hafwen had seemed very bad but had turned out rather charming in the end. Hafwen, who had given up everything. She was a very brave troll. Annabel supposed there had never been a braver one.

Then she thought of London Above going about its business. All the streets and hospitals and churches and houses and inns and taverns and Parliament, with all the lords in

218

their silks, and all the ladies in the parks taking a turn, and none of them, not any of them, aware of what went on down below. That there was a wall made from faery bone and there was the maze of Trollingdom, and that deep below their feet slept a dragon.

Annabel stopped rowing. It seemed the boat was moving itself now, riding the small waves, up and down, lulling them. Hafwen had begun to snore quietly in a rumbly troll way, and Kitty's head was lolling in the darkness. Curled at the end of the boat, she looked peaceful and sweet. Annabel felt the seeing glass pressed against her chest.

She had asked it to show her Hafwen; now perhaps it could tell her how to approach a dragon. She took it from her dress and placed it on her palm. It was blank, of course. Empty. She sighed at her stupidity. She needed light to see inside the glass. Yet as she was about to put the glass away, she noticed a tiny glimmer within. A flicker. She looked up toward the cavern ceiling, which she had thought would be lost in darkness, but she saw that it was studded with pinpricks of light. They were like tiny stars, and she wondered if they were fireflies or some kind of precious stones.

There—the little glass flashed again. She held the ruby-red seeing glass higher, toward the ceiling. If she could align the glass with one of those specks of light, it might illuminate the piece. But it was difficult. The lights high above on the cavern ceiling seemed to be moving, because the boat was moving. The ruby-red glass would flash, and then the boat would glide on, the speck left behind.

She experimented for some time. She tried to match the glass with a speck in the far distance, the farthest she could see, and finally she captured one. The ruby-red glass flashed crimson, and she saw inside it.

She saw nothing useful.

She saw ruby-red glass suddenly glow.

It was a start.

She felt Hafwen breathe beside her and heard Kitty murmuring in her dreams. She looked deeper into the ruby-red glass. There were shadows now. The shadows were moving, and one of them was tall and one short, and that made her breath quicken. Her head said, *Look away*, the way it always had, from puddles and shiny silver spoons and lacquered jewelry boxes, but into the glass she looked.

The shadows moved toward her, and through the glass they grew giant. Now the cavern ceiling was aglow in ruby-red light. The shadows loomed huge across it: a tall woman and a short woman. And though she could not see their faces, she knew they were her great-aunts, and it filled her with joy.

"Miss Henrietta," she started to cry, but her great-aunt's shadow on the red cavern ceiling held a shadow hand up to her shadow face and hushed her.

"You have come a long way, Annabel Grey," the small shadow said. Or the waves said, the stones said, the cavern ceiling said.

"But I don't know where we will go next, or how we

will . . . ," started Annabel. "You see, there's a dragon. You didn't tell me about the dragon!"

The taller shadow flickered darkly against the stones but did not speak.

The two shadows swam murkily on the ceiling, became nothing, and then formed bodies once again.

"You must not fear the dragon," said the short shadow, who Annabel knew must be Miss Estella. "You have the broomstick."

"Oh," said Annabel.

That seemed easier said than done. She wondered if Miss Estella or Miss Henrietta had ever been anywhere dangerous or met a dragon. How could she defeat a dragon with a broomstick?

"Time moves quickly," said the shadow Miss Estella. "The darkness is gathering."

"We're trying awfully hard," whispered Annabel.

She thought of the Ondona thrown on the fire, and her heart beat faster.

"Never mind that," said the little shadow.

The shadows unshaped themselves again and reshaped, and a shadow tree appeared, its shadow limbs stretched across the ceiling vault before dissolving.

"All of good magic depends upon you," said shadow Miss Estella when she reappeared.

The taller shadow stepped forward. She moved closer and closer, the way a mother leans down over a child in bed to place a kiss upon its head. Annabel thought perhaps that was what the shadow Miss Henrietta was about to do, and if the real Miss Henrietta had done that in the magic shop, she would have been horrified, but here on the Lake of Tears she was quite looking forward to it.

The shadow giant Miss Henrietta came closer until Annabel's face was covered in the velvety Miss Henrietta shadow, but she did not feel a kiss. She felt nothing, and then the shadows were gone. Annabel's glass moved out of alignment with the tiny speck of light, and the ruby-red glow of the cavern vanished. There was only darkness and the three of them drifting across the lake.

She remembered what the wizards had told her about visions that spoke. *If someone speaks to you directly from a vision, then that person is dead or very close to death, hovering between the two worlds.* Annabel had not wanted to remember those words. She put her face in her hands and began to cry.

Mr. Angel carried the good wands to the machine room. He ran his hands over them, and the shadowlings leapt and danced upon the walls. There were five hundred now, more. He had raised them from the bottom of wells and behind paintings. From tea chests and unopened trunks. From unused ballrooms and forgotten stairwells. From quiet vestries.

Now they watched him.

When he leaned forward to examine the dark-magic gauge, they copied him. They grew themselves tall and thin and leaned forward with shadowy monocles pressed to their empty eyes. The needle had moved past two-thirds full. Mr. Angel snapped the wands, one by one, like twigs. He fed them to the machine, which groaned. The gauge needle trembled and climbed.

He destroyed the good wands that had raised fires in hearths and made dead trees blossom. That had coaxed babies from dying mothers and ignited love in unexpected places. The good wands that had helped ruined cakes rise and summoned good rains and bought sudden afternoons of much-needed sunshine. The wands that had given good dreams and seeded good friendships and soothed grieving mothers and healed injured limbs and fixed broken wings.

It was the end of good magic, the end of the Great & Benevolent Magical Society. And the machine, sensing this ending, sang up in ecstasy.

15

*"A young lady always ascertains she has her hand luggage
before disembarking. There is nothing more vexing than
to find oneself in the rain without an umbrella."*

—Miss Finch's Little Blue Book (1855)

Annabel stopped crying almost as soon as she'd started.
Where would crying get her? She simply would not believe that her great-aunts were gone. She couldn't be separated from her mother and find out her father was not a dead
sea captain and then lose her brand-new great-aunts as well.
It was impossible.

There was a job to be done, and she would do it. She was
the most magical girl, and there were prophecies about her,
and . . . She stopped because that seemed more impossible
than anything. But she pulled her cloak close to herself and
straightened her shoulders and took a very deep breath.

Emerald-green ice skates, she thought. The emerald-green
ice skates she'd had her heart set upon before her whole

world turned wrong. The green ice skates her mother had promised her for her birthday.

"Why, it must be my birthday," she said to herself very quietly, and Hafwen snored beside her in a comforting, grumbly way. "Many happy returns, Annabel Grey."

Just saying that made her smile because she was not at all who she thought she would be when she turned thirteen. She was someone completely new, and she liked the new her. She was brave and good, and she had magic inside her.

Her smile vanished when she saw a light in the distance and realized it must be the far shore of the Lake of Tears. The fires were pretty from a distance but horrible up close. The rocky shore was littered with centuries' worth of funeral boats, pile upon pile of sticks and wood and spot fires smoldering. The place smelled terrible, acrid with smoke, pungent with death. She woke Kitty and Hafwen, speaking softly so they were not startled.

The hull of their boat scraped against rock, and Hafwen, her little gray troll face all creased and confused, looked happy at first, until she realized where they were.

Kitty rubbed her eyes. "I'm starving," she said, and Annabel could tell she was pretending to be unafraid.

"I'm sure the West-Born Wyrm is, too," said Annabel.

They laughed nervously, except for Hafwen, who had begun to tremble.

It was very, very quiet.

"We need a plan," said Annabel, lowering her voice. It was

the type of place that made you want to whisper. "A perfectly proper plan for how we can either defeat or avoid this wyrm creature."

Miss Finch always said a young lady should make a list of her day's chores. Rise and dress, recite her French conjugations, answer letters, and do something delightful like sketch in the park. Annabel decided that finding the Morever Wand should be no different. They would consult the map. They would find their way to the dragon's lair. They would ask it very politely to allow them to pass.

She shook her head. Even she knew that was an impossible plan.

They stepped as quietly as they could into the shallow dark water. Annabel took Hafwen's rough hand, and Hafwen held tight. By the light of a smoldering boat, Hafwen and Kitty looked at the map on Annabel's shoulder. Kitty traced a line from there up to a spot on Annabel's cheekbone.

"A hole here. Then cavern after cavern, leading to its lair, and beyond it lies the Morever Wand," she said. "No other way."

They looked at the small rocky shore and its awful rubble. There in the cavern wall was one entrance, narrow and dark. Hafwen whimpered.

"Well, if there is no other way, there is no other way," said Annabel. She closed her eyes. She was meant to know what to do. What had Miss Estella told her? The answers were in her head and in her heart. *You must not fear the dragon. You have the broomstick.*

She looked at the broomstick. Well, that didn't make an ounce of sense.

Hafwen and Kitty watched her. It made her feel uncomfortable.

You must not fear the dragon. You have the broomstick.

She knew many things. She knew how to wear her hair, how to walk gracefully, how to play the pianoforte. She knew which mountains were bigger, the Vogelsbergs or the Carpathians. She knew how to nod agreeably, even when things were not agreeable. How to read French, which she was not so good at, and Latin, which she was very bad at. But she didn't know how the broomstick could help.

She felt Hafwen clutch at her hand.

"What is it, Hafwen?" she asked.

"Listen," said Hafwen.

Annabel could hear nothing.

You must not fear the dragon. You have the broomstick.

Hafwen clutched at her elbow. She dug her fingers into Annabel's skin.

"What is it now, Hafwen?"

Hafwen's eyes were wide. She looked at the ground, and Annabel followed her gaze. The pieces of wood they stood on were shaking. There was a tremor beneath their feet.

"It's coming," said Hafwen, and Annabel didn't think she'd ever seen anyone, troll or human, more terrified.

"We must hide," said Annabel, and she made for the boat they had arrived in.

"Not that one," said Kitty. "It will look at that one first."

227

They picked their way quickly through the remnants of boats along the shore until they found one that was no longer smoldering. It was well shielded by the wreckage of several other boats, a jumble of wood and smoke. The ground was shuddering now. Hafwen's face crumpled, and she began to cry.

"Don't fear, Hafwen," said Annabel. "All will be well."

She was surprised at how calm she sounded.

"Quickly," she said, unfastening her cloak. She hurried Hafwen into the bottom of the small boat and lay down beside her. The broomstick shivered in her hand.

You must not fear the dragon. You have the broomstick.

She tried to think it in the shadow Miss Estella's voice, but it still didn't make any sense.

"Hurry, Kitty—lie down."

Kitty moved sullenly beside Hafwen, and Annabel tossed her cloak over them. There was pushing and shoving beneath, and Hafwen cried out. Annabel patted her gently on what she thought might be her hand but was actually her nose.

"Stay very still now. Put your hands around my waist."

She felt Kitty's and Hafwen's arms around her and more fighting.

"It's no good—she's too fat," said Kitty.

"We should have left your good friend the skinny behind," said Hafwen.

The ground rumbled beneath them; the boat trembled. Hafwen held Annabel tighter.

A deep, low growl came from within the tunnel, a growl that shook their very insides, a growl that rattled their teeth. They held each other as a hot wind rushed out of the opening, followed by the dragon.

The rumbling grew greater, and Annabel peeked from beneath the cloak. The West-Born Wyrm was coming from its lair. It was unraveling itself, twisting and turning and writhing. Oh, the smell of it! It slid out of the tunnel, shedding filthy scales. Oh, the size and darkness of it! It was as long as a train at Paddington Station and darker, far darker than the darkness itself. It had terrible black eyes.

Annabel felt Hafwen's quivering, Kitty's heartbeat, the broomstick's shivering. She hoped the cloak covered them. The dragon oozed itself out of the tunnel. Its black wings unfolded slowly, almost mechanically, sounding brittle, like a thousand umbrellas being opened in unison. They opened and closed twice, three times, sending huge downdrafts of wind to press against the cloak. The wings fluttered then, frantically fast, until their sound filled the cavern.

The West-Born Wyrm was graceful. It hovered just above the rocks, coiling the great length of its body, its tiny legs tucked up against its monstrous belly. It moved toward the funeral boat that had carried Annabel, Kitty, and Hafwen across the Lake of Tears. It expected its dead-troll offering. It nudged the boat with its wet snout. It sniffed and buried its nose inside the thing, and when it realized there was no troll inside, it coiled its body whip-quick and, with its great black tail, smashed the boat to splinters.

You must not fear the dragon. You have the broomstick.

Hafwen broke wind. Kitty cursed her.

The dragon sniffed the air deeply, and the cloak rustled. It slipped its body over the rocks toward them. Annabel was aware of the smell of Hafwen beneath the cloak. Oniony, smoky, earthy Hafwen. The dragon was looking for the troll that belonged in the funeral boat, and it slid toward them, all black and oily. The broomstick shook violently beside her.

You must not fear the dragon. You have the broomstick.

The dragon came toward them, closer and closer. Its hot breath ruffled the cloak. It was almost upon them.

"Fiddlesticks!" cried Annabel.

◆ ◆ ◆

Annabel leapt up from the bottom of the boat. She knew what had to be done. The broomstick shot forward in her hand, and she threw herself on it, and off they soared, straight past the dragon that snapped its terrible mouth, straight past its black eye, murderously gleaming.

The dragon recoiled. It opened its great dark mouth and hissed.

Inside its mouth there were teeth. Row after row of teeth strung with rotting flesh.

"Annabel!" cried Kitty.

"Stay down!" shouted Annabel.

She did not tell the broomstick to fly faster with words.

She screamed it with her body, with every part of her being, with her toes and her fingers, with her set mouth, with the very tips of her hair. She leaned forward and shot up past the dragon into the air.

The dragon thrashed its body. It whipped its great tail so fast that it hurtled toward Hafwen and Kitty in the boat, and they threw themselves beneath the cloak again. Its black eyes were fixed on Annabel on her broomstick. It snapped open its wings and with one dreadful shriek launched itself into the air.

Annabel looked behind her and saw it coming. Its great mouth opened, and it let out a blast of orange fire. *Down!* her body told the broomstick, and she plummeted straight toward the dark water, the dragon on her heels. She skimmed along the surface, then exploded upward again just as the dragon let out another shriek and spewed fire at her.

Annabel rose and fell; she swerved and skidded. She could not tell in the darkness where the cavern ceiling was, yet she trusted the broomstick. *Faster!* she thought, and her hair blew out behind her, and she rose and fell like a stone being skipped across a pond. She flew far away from the shore where Kitty and Hafwen huddled. She flew far out over the deep, dark lake.

The dragon was fast. It surged forward, it gushed fire, it roared.

Annabel willed the broomstick on. *Faster!* she told it with her heart. *Faster! We must throw this dragon into a wall.* She curved and turned, and the thing followed and she did not think she could outwit it, so graceful was its flight. She felt the burn of its flames against her boots. She saw the hem of her dress begin to smoke. The West-Born Wyrm was nearly upon her.

Faster! thought Annabel. She urged her broomstick on. *Her* broomstick. *Faster. Faster. Faster.* She flew so fast that she could barely open her eyes against the roar of the wind. *Faster. Faster.* She let out a scream. One long, high-pitched scream, and the broomstick jolted forward in a great surge of speed, and the dragon, thinking it would lose her, surged after her, toward the cavern wall.

Annabel Grey flew toward the cavern wall without slowing. Annabel Grey, who had never once done a dangerous thing, not once, until she met this broomstick. She flew without slowing.

She shrieked another wild, unladylike shriek that would have made Miss Finch turn gray in an instant.

She was oblivious to the rocky shore. She did not notice the wreckage of boats or the spot fires burning. She did not see Kitty and Hafwen standing to watch her, their mouths open. She hurtled toward the wall without slowing, until it grew so huge, so close, that there was nothing but the great rocky face and she would slam into it within seconds. And then she flipped the broomstick upside down and turned with such swiftness that she felt she had left her stomach behind. She turned out over the lake, which was so wide and open in comparison that she smiled and remembered to breathe.

She heard the dragon hit the wall. She flinched at the

sound of it. It hit the wall with such a crash that the whole cavern shook. The jumble of funeral boats collapsed, clattering and banging, and the water rose up in a huge wave and thumped itself against the shore.

Annabel swept her broomstick around.

"You really are very good, dear thing," she said, and it skittered and swerved so playfully that it almost threw her from its back.

The West-Born Wyrm lay upon the rock before the entrance to its lair. It huge black body was not completely still. It twitched and lifted its giant head, shaking it slowly, eyes closed. It groaned and slumped again.

"We must hurry," said Annabel, landing before Kitty and Hafwen. "Perhaps it will not sleep for long."

Hafwen still had her mouth open. Kitty shook her head, and a brief smile of admiration passed across her face before she hid it away just as quickly.

They had to climb over the dragon's tail to enter the tunnel. It was scaly and slimy and covered in pointed barbs. Annabel held the torch, which they lit from a smoldering funeral boat. Her broomstick was tucked back inside her sash on her back. She held out her hand to Hafwen, and Hafwen held out her hand to Kitty, who refused, of course. Sometimes the dragon convulsed suddenly and they clung to the spikes on its tail. It was treacherous business. They scrambled over the side of the dragon into the dark entrance, where Annabel held her flame high. Hafwen smiled her huge gray-toothed smile.

"Dragon slayer," she said.

"Oh, not really," said Annabel, but her cheeks flushed.

"She wouldn't have needed to if you hadn't been so stinky," said Kitty, but Hafwen smiled as though it were a compliment.

The tunnel was a black hole. The worst hole. It was sticky and slimy and coated with scales. It filled Annabel with dread, but she also knew it was the only way to find the wand. If they found the wand, she could go home, and home was what she wanted. Yet it wasn't the house of her Mayfair mother she thought of, but the little magic shop in Spitalfields and her two great-aunts and everything they might teach her.

The full moon rose slowly through the fog. Its first beams hit the great brass moon funnel, and the Dark-Magic Extracting Machine sang up one gear. The shadowlings slid themselves across the ceiling backward, away from it.

Their number had grown. All through the house they clung to the ceilings and to the staircase balustrades. They swayed and shivered against the walls. They filled up the darkened sitting rooms, whispering black thoughts into each other's ears. They touched their faces to the windows and looked out upon the city with their empty eyes.

The moonlight hit the moon funnel, and the machine fed.

Its cogs and wheels turned. The light filtered down through its brass tubules. The moonlight combined in glass reservoirs with the dissolved remnants of sorrowful things. The black hats and mourning rings, the unfinished letters and the dead baby's booties. It mixed with the pieces of stopped clocks and the poor girl's boots and the strap used to whip poorhouse orphans. It filtered and combined. It breathed and sighed. Moonlight and air. Fabric and paper fragments. Onyx slivers and black glass glitters. The strange substance dripped into the spinning black heart, which turned faster and faster until it made dark magic.

The machine shuddered and bulged with the weight of it.

The needle in the dark-magic gauge inched closer to full.

"The swiftest and strongest," said Mr. Angel to the shadowlings. He took Mr. Keating's handkerchief from his pocket and held it high. "There are two girls, and if they succeed, they will come up again aboveground. It is the Grey girl I need. Seek her out. Bring her to me, unharmed, and I will feed her to the machine. . . . Behold, the moon rises."

16

"On arrival at her destination, a young lady should sit quietly and wait for her friend or host in a position that is readily visible. She should not explore the station, nor visit the refreshment rooms alone."

—Miss Finch's Little Blue Book (1855)

The passage was narrow, and they had to squeeze themselves through it. Annabel supposed it was the worst place she had ever been, but still she led the way. Her broomstick shivered on her back, and she touched it tenderly.

"Nearly, dear thing," she whispered. "Soon you shall have sky."

Annabel wished there were a more scenic way to the chamber of the Morever Wand—which was drawn very neatly upon her forehead, according to her two companions. They had peered at her forehead in a way she did not like. By the flame she had looked at her arm where the map had disappeared. The ladder to the secret river . . . the Singing

Gate . . . the maze of Trollingdom—now all gone. The deep waters of the Lake of Tears had almost completely vanished, too, but she could still feel that place inside her. She could still feel all those places. She wondered if they would stay inside her forever.

The map written on her skin had changed her. She knew it.

"We have come such a way," she said, trying hard to sound cheerful. She felt very tired but also quite brave.

Behind her she could hear Hafwen muttering to herself about a star. She was very fond of the troll and glad she hadn't been eaten by the dragon. She turned to check on her friend and saw that Kitty had fallen behind. The wild girl was shivering, and her cheeks burned red.

"Dear Kitty, put my cloak on," she said. "Are you taken ill?"

"There's nothing wrong with me," said Kitty. She refused the cloak.

"Well, we'll be home in no time," Annabel said as sunnily as she could.

It made her think of homes again. Hafwen's home, which she had left behind and to which there was no returning, and Kitty's home, which was nowhere at all. Her own home and, of course, her mother. It made her shake her head, but she kept walking. The passage stank. Something horrible stuck to her ruined boots with each step.

They squeezed themselves, slid themselves, lowered themselves onto hands and knees. The passage opened into small circular caverns littered with strange objects. There were bones and brooches and tattered banners. Troll clothes and pretty ladies' shoes. Great tufts of hair in piles. They picked their way through the terrible clutter.

Annabel encouraged Hafwen, who grumbled behind her. She looked back at Kitty, who moved slower and slower. Kitty's coughing echoed about them. The passage became more and more muddled with dragon treasure. Chairs and bassinets (oh, that made Annabel shiver), shields and horses' saddles. Piles of bones and shredded clothes. They stepped over such things and Annabel recited to herself, very quietly, *Be brave, be brave, be brave.*

At last they entered a much larger cavern, filled with even more treasure. The place stank of the dragon, and everything was coated with its oil and scales. They slipped on the floor and held on to each other for balance. Annabel raised the torch, and they saw small mountains of coins and embroidered pillows, shields and swords, and the entire skeleton of a horse. They saw armor, ladies' parasols, empty birdcages, clocks, and mirrors. A man's coat, spectacles still neatly in one pocket.

Piles of clothes.

Piles of hair.

Piles of bones.

Kitty fell quite suddenly, her eyes closed.

"Kitty!" cried Annabel. "You *are* taken ill!"

"There's nothing wrong with me," Kitty said, but she moaned and struggled to sit up.

Annabel touched her friend's burning skin. "Stay still,"

she said. "Is this the last cavern before the chamber of the wand, Hafwen?"

Hafwen looked at the map on Annabel's face. Her eyes followed the line of passageways and stopped. She counted on her fat, hairy fingers and puffed out her troll chest in her dirty yellow dress.

"This is the last cavern before the wand," she said very solemnly.

Annabel looked about. There seemed no opening any-where.

"Can you see the opening on the map?" she asked Hafwen.

Hafwen's chest grew even bigger with the responsibility. She peered up at Annabel's face with her sparkly troll eyes. She planted her finger squarely on Annabel's forehead.

"It be right at the back, opposite the place we came in," she said.

"Oh," said Kitty, closing her eyes again. It was a terrible "Oh." She looked tiny and fragile, the light quite gone out of her.

"Stay still, Kitty. Rest a little," said Annabel, taking her hand.

Kitty coughed. Perhaps Aunty had broken something in her. Perhaps it was the wound from the bone wall.

Hafwen began to remove the clutter from the place where the opening should be. She was strong and fast. She did not complain. There was a chair and more shields, two wom-en's hats, tall and conical, quite ruined. There was a car-riage wheel.

"I want to see the sky," whispered Kitty.

"And you will see it," said Annabel. "We're nearly home. We'll see the Miss Vines. They'll be very pleased with us."

Kitty smiled weakly.

"You could stay with us," Annabel said. "Oh, I'm sure they'd let you. They'd teach us magic, and then one day my mother would come home."

Kitty shook her head and sat up further. "Do you never stop talking?" she said, and coughed again, wincing as she held her chest.

Hafwen removed bones. Troll bones. Troll pots. Troll pans. She removed a troll washing line, still pegged with troll underwear. She found the hole. It was a small hole. She looked inside.

"I see it!" she cried.

"Good girl, Hafwen. Now you must help me lift Kitty," said Annabel.

"Leave off," said Kitty, standing up and swaying, refusing their help.

They heard a noise. A terrible noise. It was a roar loud enough to rattle the armor on the floor. The coins slid from their piles.

"Quickly—to the hole!" cried Annabel, and together they helped Kitty to the place.

The opening was at waist height, and Annabel and Hafwen lifted Kitty and squeezed her through the hole. They heard her slide, then tumble through into the adjacent chamber.

"Ouch!" she said as she hit the stone floor.

Annabel looked at Hafwen. She looked at Hafwen's stout legs and Hafwen's round belly. She looked at the small hole. Hafwen looked at Annabel and raised one hairy troll brow.

Hafwen stood on Annabel's bent knee, and once the troll had her head and shoulders through, Annabel began to push. She pushed and prodded and shoved. She smoothed down rolls of troll belly so that they would pass through the opening, and she leaned with all her might against Hafwen's bottom until, with a sudden plop, the troll was through. Annabel quickly passed her the torch.

The lair of the West-Born Wyrm was filling with sound.

A violent hissing and a wild churning. The walls rattled, the shields and swords fell over, the armor clattered to the ground. The dragon was returning.

The shadowlings flew. They screeched and skittered. They moved in a seething, shadowy cloud against the rising moon. Londoners already afraid of the black night shuddered at the sound. Mothers checked on their babies once, then again. Slumbering old men in nightcaps opened their eyes at the sound.

They breathed, those shadowlings. They breathed the breath of dark stairwells and damp cellars and old chests long forgotten. They breathed the breath of empty, closed spaces where they had slept for centuries. And they searched.

They searched for Annabel.

They opened their blank mouths above the sewer grates. They threaded their long shadowy arms down drainpipes. They whispered her name up and down streets and lanes. They rushed across railway yards. In one church door and out another. They looked for cracks, for fissures, for holes. They looked for where she might come up. Until, finally, they tasted her.

In his dark mansion Mr. Angel pressed his monocle to his eye and saw that the dark-magic gauge was almost full. A matter of hours and the Grey girl would remedy that. When the shadowlings brought her to him, he would tell her the story of her mother and then feed her to the machine.

He climbed the staircase, up past the moon funnel that chanted a sad, lonely song, out onto the platform that looked over London. He breathed in the dark miasma, wept at the great wretched fog. He looked over all that would be his.

17

"No matter the heat, a young lady shall not remove her gloves in the ballroom."

—Miss Finch's Little Blue Book (1855)

Annabel clambered through the hole. First one leg, then the other. It was most unladylike. She twisted onto her belly and slid herself through, and as she did, she saw the dragon coming. She saw its black snout and its black eyes. She saw its huge enraged shape sliding into its lair, filling the space. She ducked down and crouched with the others, low to the ground.

A blast of hot wind shot through the hole, followed by a huge flame. It was a golden dragon flame, and it licked up the wall above them as they huddled on the ground. By the light of the flame, Annabel saw that the circular wall of the chamber rose as far as the eye could see. They were at the bottom of a very deep well.

And there, in the center of the chamber, on a small raised dais, was the wand.

The Morever Wand.

"The White Wand," said Annabel and Kitty in unison.

They were quiet for several seconds, and in the quiet they could hear the dragon breathing. It nudged its snout against the hole, sniffing them out. There was nothing for it. Annabel was up. She ran as quickly as she could to the middle of the chamber and clutched the thing in her hand.

It was a stick with a jagged bend at one end and thousands of tiny words and symbols written all over it. It was light. So light that it felt like air. She scuttled back and threw herself flat as another blast of heat came through the hole, followed by a golden flame. She smelled singed hair.

"Now for the way home," she said.

The dragon was angry. Very angry. It threw itself at the wall at the sound of their voices; it slammed its nose against the hole. Hafwen grabbed Annabel's hand and uttered several troll prayers.

"But how?" asked Kitty.

Another flame burned through the hole, this time aimed low, and they rolled to one side, farther from the opening. They looked up again and, by the flame's light, saw the brickwork stretched above them until it disappeared into the darkness above.

Annabel touched the map on her forehead with her hand, but she knew that even as she did, it was vanishing beneath her fingertips.

Another blast of golden flame erupted through the hole.

It was hot, so hot in that place. The dragon thrashed and thumped against the wall, and bricks rained down. A fireball shot up into the darkness. How would they get out? There must be something that Annabel was meant to do. She was the most magical girl.

She was the Valiant Defender of Good Magic.

Miss Estella had touched her head and her heart.

All Annabel's answers were there.

She was not alone. She knew it then. She was most definitely not alone.

"We must go up," Annabel said purposefully, her shoulders back, her chin held high, exactly the way she had been taught at Miss Finch's Academy for Young Ladies.

Up.

More bricks fell beside them, and the dragon's snout appeared. They screamed.

"But how?" said Hafwen and Kitty together, looking upward at the seemingly endless tunnel.

"I know exactly how," said Annabel.

◆ ◆ ◆

The broomstick thrummed in Annabel's hands. *Her* broomstick! The broomstick she'd chosen herself from the pile in the magical storeroom. The broomstick that had saved them over the streets of London Above. The broomstick that had saved Kitty from Aunty.

It bucked in Annabel's hands. It wanted up the moment she thought it, and she had to keep it from flying off without her.

"Everyone climb on!" shouted Annabel as another great dragon fireball exploded into the chamber and burned a trail upward. The dragon's snout was in the room now, its hot breath upon them.

"All of us?" shouted Kitty.

More bricks rained from the opening, which was growing bigger by the minute.

"We have to try," said Annabel. Another flare erupted and licked across the floor and up the wall beside them. They skittered quickly to one side. By the light of a new flame that rushed just above their heads, Annabel saw Hafwen's wide eyes and knew what she was thinking.

"Never," said Annabel. "You know I wouldn't, Hafwen. You know it."

She held out her hand to the troll, who jumped on the broomstick behind Annabel.

Kitty scrambled on at the rear. "You'll kill us all!" she shouted.

Annabel ignored her. She waited for the dragon's fire. It burst through the hole and the huge flame ball rose up the chamber.

Up, commanded Annabel, and the broomstick flew up.

It leapt high and fast into the air.

It stopped and hovered. It strained under the weight of the three girls and began to fall.

Up! cried Annabel again.

But the thing began to plummet backward.

There was no time to think. No time to yell. She thought of the Miss Vines, of the Finsbury Wizards, of her mother. A new fireball exploded from the hole in the wall. The dragon's head was through.

Up, she commanded her broomstick. She meant it with every cell in her body. She meant it with her heart. She had never sounded surer. A great jolt of power coursed through her hands and into the broomstick. It stopped sliding backward. It bucked and surged forward, and with flames licking their toes, they shot upward toward the world.

III

DARK-MAGIC GAUGE FULL

18

"Upon arrival at her destination, a young lady says farewell to any acquaintances she has made. She does so warmly but without undue extravagance or familiarity. Addresses should not be exchanged unless mutually agreeable."

—*Miss Finch's Little Blue Book (1855)*

They lay where they had landed, breathing hard. It was very dark—not the darkness of Under London's caverns and troll holes but an airier, more open blackness. Annabel took a deep breath of London Above and smiled. As her eyes adjusted, she saw there was an expanse of marble floor and great stone steps and, above them, a magnificent ceiling. She thought it was perhaps a castle, but then, after she had stared a while longer, she realized it was really only the great hall at Euston Station. She'd been there once before with her mother to catch a train to Birmingham. There was a glimmer of light from a high window, and when she looked, she saw the brownish blurred face of the moon appearing.

"Look—the moon is quite high," she said, and sat up quickly.

She looked down at her torn cloak and mud-coated dress. Her hair was filled with straw and dragon scales. In one hand was her broomstick; in the other, the Morever Wand. The map was gone from her arm and her face, but she still felt the weight of it inside her. Its fullness. All of Under London was inside her, and she would never get it out again.

"Now, my star," said Hafwen, sitting up just as quickly, for she had remembered.

"Yes, dear Hafwen," said Annabel. "Your star. But first we must take the wand to the Miss Vines."

First they must stop Mr. Angel. First they must save all of London. Somehow.

Annabel wondered at the Morever Wand's magic. She looked at the strange words written all over it. How did it work?

They sat at the edge of the hole they had flown from, which was already disappearing. The marble floor was growing over it, shimmering in the muddy moonlight.

"We could have come straight here and flown down and got the stupid thing without all the trouble," Kitty said.

"I don't think magic works like that," said Annabel.

Kitty smiled, but it was a weak smile, and she coughed again as she sat. Her cheeks were very red. She closed her eyes, and half her dirty little face shone in the moonlight.

Hafwen smiled her large gray-toothed smile.

"Did you enjoy that adventure, Haffie?" asked Annabel. She had decided that was what she would call her troll friend.

"No," replied Hafwen, putting away the smile, although little bits of it still twitched at the edges of her mouth.

Soon there was nothing to show for the hole to Under London, just a patch of marble floor a little glossier with rusty moonlight than the rest. Annabel tested it with her toe. Yes, solid marble.

"We must take the wand to the Miss Vines. They will know what to do," said Annabel. She didn't want to think of her vision on the Lake of Tears. It wasn't good to think of that at all.

She stood and swayed with hunger and tiredness. She had the Morever Wand in her hand, and she had returned to London Above. It should feel like an ending, yet, standing there in the great hall of Euston Station, she felt tired and very brave but as though her journey had not finished. It was an unsettling feeling, like being asked by Mr. Ladgrove to recite a Latin passage and not having a clue what it meant.

Kitty coughed and nodded as though she understood. She refused the hand that Annabel offered her, scowled, and stood.

Hafwen held out her hand to be assisted, and Annabel, laughing, helped her up.

Yes, they were the best friends she had ever had. Isabelle Rutherford seemed like a paper doll in comparison. Here were her true friends. Her heart soared in such a way that she had to put her hand over her chest to hold it in.

"To the magic shop," said Annabel.

"To the magic shop," repeated Hafwen. "To find my star."

◆ ◆ ◆

They went out into London Above. Out past the darkened ticket windows and the refreshment rooms. Out past the ladies' cloak rooms and gentlemen's cloak rooms, out through the great arch into the night. Annabel never knew it could feel so good to take deep breaths of foggy London night air. But she also felt frightened. The fog was thick and the gaslights shone weakly, with pale halos. There were strange sounds: the slow heartbeat of faraway horses' hooves, a lone bell, muffled, as though it were deep underwater.

How much time until the moon reached its full height? It was already high in the sky, a pale smudge behind the fog.

Annabel held Hafwen's hand. London was full of many unusual things, but stout, hairy Hafwen would probably still stand out. She took her little troll friend and hid her behind her skirts. There was another sound, a whispery sound, and a faint breeze made the fog swirl around them.

"It is Euston Station," said Annabel nervously. "But I'm quite sure I don't know the way from here."

She imagined the magic shop and the Miss Vines waiting for her. She longed to see Miss Henrietta's face when she showed her the wand.

"It's that way," said Kitty, leading them out to the road. "You and Hafwen will fly."

The breeze grew stronger, a sudden wind now, blowing against their skirts and lifting the red cloak.

Hafwen didn't like it. "What is that talking air?" she asked.

Annabel tried to smile at the little troll's expression. "But why do you say only Hafwen and I?" she asked Kitty.

"Because I have done what I told the Miss Vines I would do, and more."

"But, Kitty . . . ," whispered Annabel.

Kitty wanted sky. She wanted to walk all the way to Highgate and curl herself beneath a tree and wake with sunlight on her face. She wanted no more journey. No more trolls. No more wands. She didn't want to look at the disappointed face of the Grey girl, who all her life had gotten exactly what she wanted.

"But, Kitty, you can't mean that," said Annabel. "After everything we've done."

"Traitor," said Hafwen.

"Shut your gob," said Kitty.

"The Miss Vines would have you. They would—I know they would," said Annabel. "Please say you will."

Kitty was her friend. She'd never had a friend like Kitty. It seemed all wrong. How could she be the Valiant Defender of Good Magic without Kitty?

Kitty shook her head. In all her life she had never met a girl like Annabel Grey. She was bright as a star and good and brave.

"It is not my place," Kitty said, but the wind grew louder still, and it whipped up her words and blew them away.

It came in a sudden rushing gust, blew up from the

pavement, and sent rubbish flying. It worried their skirts and grabbed the wand from Annabel's hand, and the broomstick too, and threw them out onto the road.

"Whatever is . . . ," Annabel began but did not finish.

The fog was quite blown apart before them, and out of it flew a terrible shape.

A monstrous shape.

Out of the fog a huge dark carriage drawn by six shadowy horses came. It made a sound like a thousand angry hornets. It flew straight toward them, so that there was not a moment to think. It rushed toward them, so that Annabel knew it would crush them, smash them, end them.

But it passed through her. The horses passed right through her, and as they did, she felt a great tugging sensation and she was lifted clean off her feet. She felt Hafwen's hand slip from her own. She was yanked violently upward and into the thing and onto a hard seat, and then the carriage was lifting, soaring away from the ground.

"Kitty!" Annabel screamed as she went up. "Hafwen!"

"Annabel!" she heard Kitty shout before the most magical girl was taken by the shadowlings and carried away into the sky.

Mr. Angel stood on his rooftop platform and raised his Black Wand. He lifted the fog. He lifted it from tenements and tiny lanes.

He lifted it from the grand mansion streets. He lifted it from the closes and circuses and cathedrals. He lifted it from churches and charnel houses and factories. Like a blanket he lifted it up from the marshes, from the shining still river, from the great parks. He tossed it up into the sky like a blanket, and it drifted away.

The full moon gazed down, new and clean. It shone into the moon funnel, and the machine below fed. It was full of dark magic and ready for him. The house bulged with shadowlings. They swarmed in rooms and on the staircases. They filled the ballroom. They tapped their claws at the windows. They mimicked the sound of the machine, its great whirring and sighing and whining, as it waited for its last meal.

19

"When out walking, a young lady does not stop or turn to stare at those she passes. She keeps her gaze steady and pays little attention to that which does not concern her."
—*Miss Finch's Little Blue Book* (1855)

Annabel flew through the air in the claw chair, the shadow carriage around her, rustling and hushing and saying her name. Up and down the thing went, riding the wind, until she felt dizzy and sick. She gripped the seat, and just touching it terrified her, but there was nothing else she could do. Her bottom lifted off the seat with each undulation, only to slam down hard again.

"Oh," she cried. "Please stop."

But it wouldn't. They wouldn't. She could see their open empty mouths, and all about her they breathed. Through the little spaces between them she caught glimpses of moon-washed parks and churches and road after endless road. The shadowling carriage flew her over London. It swept her over rooftops; it rushed her through the night air.

When it did come down, finally, it was into a street of well-to-do houses with well-to-do gardens. Without warning the shadowlings unlaced their claws and dropped her onto the grass before one such house.

"Ouch," she said, and stared at the tall, dark building.

She shivered, for she knew it at once.

The curtains were drawn, and the black windows stared back at her. It was the house from her visions. The shadowling carriage dissolved and vanished in a plume. The shadowlings twisted and turned like a murmuration of starlings, up to the rooftop and inside.

Annabel stood.

She felt instinctively for her broomstick and the Morever Wand.

She was empty-handed.

The front door opened slowly, and Mr. Angel appeared. He bowed deeply.

"Annabel Grey," he said. "At last. We have been waiting for you."

His black hair fell over his shoulders, and his cheeks were filled with darkness. He was horribly crooked and more wickedly gleeful than ever. Behind him in the house she heard a noise now. It was a droning and thrumming. She realized that the pavement shook beneath her and the roof groaned and the walls creaked as though they might explode.

"The moon is high, Annabel," said Mr. Angel. "The time is nearly come."

He bowed again and motioned for her to enter.

Annabel looked at the house and remembered her vision: the black wave washing out from this place, ready to smash everything in its path. Here she was, the most magical girl, standing empty-handed at her destination. She had failed. She had failed her great-aunts. She had failed the wizards. She had failed all of the Great & Benevolent Magical Society. She put her hand to her heart and took a deep breath.

She would not cry.

"Come inside," Mr. Angel said quietly in his lonely voice. The loneliest voice Annabel had ever heard.

Annabel raised her chin. She straightened her spine. She smiled just the way she had been taught at Miss Finch's Academy for Young Ladies, for when things were terrible or even just a little bit bad.

"Thank you, Mr. Angel," she said, as though he had asked her in for tea, and she followed him inside.

◆ ◆ ◆

The trouble with Annabel Grey, thought Kitty as she picked up the broomstick and the wand from the ground, was that she talked too much. She was like a clanging bell, and she liked everyone she met and wanted to know their story and how she might help them—even trolls—and it was exactly that sort of thing that had gotten her swept up by a shadowling carriage and into the sky.

Kitty had crouched. She had heard the thing coming and had crouched. She knew such things. She looked at the

Morever Wand and felt its weightlessnes but knew it to be magical. She turned it over in her hand. It had faery magic written all over it.

Hafwen lay on the ground, facedown, crying.

"Get up, you big baby," said Kitty.

Hafwen lifted her tearstained troll face. "I want Annabel back," she said. "Why did the wind take her?"

Kitty sighed and took Hafwen's hand and helped her to her feet. She wished the carriage had taken the troll as well.

The wind had lifted up the fog in the street, and the moon now shone down on them. It turned the writing on the stick silvery. All the fear had gone out of the place with the departure of the flying shadowling carriage, but it was now somewhere else in the city. Kitty had to go where that fear went. She knew it. The way was there in her worn little boots. She needed no map drawn upon her skin. The whole of London was inside her head, all its leaning lanes and ragged roads, all its grand squares, all its locked gardens and last meadows.

"Hush," she said quite gently to the troll now. "I must listen for the way."

The trouble with Annabel Grey, she thought, was that she made you love her however hard you tried not to and she was always needing to be saved.

20

"A young lady's most enviable talent is her artful conversation."

—*Miss Finch's Little Blue Book (1855)*

Inside was very dark, and it took Annabel's eyes time to adjust after the bright moonlight. She and Mr. Angel were in a black parlor, and everywhere, she heard the rustling of shadowlings. They hung upside down from the ceiling and whispered against the walls. They brushed her skin as she passed. They hissed her name quietly and rattled their claws.

The house rumbled around her. It shuddered and shook.

"What is that noise?" she whispered. There was a grinding sound coming from above. A rhythmical thumping and rasping.

"It is the Dark-Magic Extracting Machine," said Mr. Angel.

He led Annabel down a murky corridor and into the dining hall, where a table was set with two places. When they entered, the shadowlings erupted from the walls. They swarmed until Mr. Angel raised his wand and commanded them to be quiet. They disappeared into the ceiling and the folds of the curtains again.

"Be seated," Mr. Angel said. He took his place at the end of the table. Annabel peered at him through the dimness.

"We will eat before the ending," he said, and his voice was so soft that she could hardly hear him. "A last supper, shall we say."

She saw him smile his lopsided, half-melancholy smile.

"You are as fair as your mother is dark," he said. "But also so like her."

Annabel thought it was very familiar of him to talk of such things. She did not reply but instead pretended to be interested in her napkin, which she placed upon her knee.

He laughed a small, papery, whispery laugh. "We shall eat, and then I will tell you the story of your mother," he said.

"Mr. Angel, please pardon, but I don't believe there is anything you can tell me of my own mother," said Annabel, and she was surprised at the strength in her voice.

She felt angry. She did not like him. She did not want his version at all.

"Oh, but there is, child," said Mr. Angel, and he began to laugh again, louder this time.

He took his Black Wand and waved it at the table, and food appeared on Annabel's plate. It was a roast, and the smell of it brought water to Annabel's mouth—she could not help it.

"Eat, and I will tell you," he said. "And then it will be time to feed you to the machine."

◆ ◆ ◆

Kitty stood before Euston Station. She coughed, and her chest hurt. She would curl into a ball and sleep if she could. She knew places nearby, the colonnade platform or the rail yards farther north, but now was no time for sleep. She shivered in the new wind but was glad for it. On the new wind she could find her bearings. Her way to Mr. Angel's dark mansion.

"Be quick," said Hafwen, who didn't like the wind. She was used to close tunnels and damp, dark places. The wind had taken her humanling friend.

"Be quiet," said Kitty.

The fog was gone, and the moonlight had woken London. Kitty listened to its scratchings and passages. Mail carriages previously waylaid were moving again, and out on the river was the sound of whistles and horns. Cattle were being herded at Smithfield, and all through Covent Garden wagons were rumbling. Above it all she heard the sudden clear voice of the quarter bells at the Clock Tower.

She listened. She wanted the wind to tell her something. *Hurry*, she said to it silently, but she knew that would do no good. She had to be patient. She heard the young voices of ash trees in Regent's Park, rustling and anxious; the bean trees in the Inner Temple rattling their pods; and then, far away, so very distant, the ancient green voice of the Totter-idge yew. She closed her eyes.

Come this way, the old yew tree said, very calm on the wind's worrying. *Come now.*

She had never understood its voice before, but tonight it was very clear to her.

She turned in her worn little boots, with her eyes still closed, listening for the way to go. She listened for the yew's voice in amongst all the others: the carriage wheels and coachmen's horns, bells and barking dogs, an organ-grinder who saw fit to celebrate the lifting of the fog with a tune. She turned and listened. She had Annabel's broomstick and the Morever Wand in her hands, and she knew London would not let her down.

Come, said the Totteridge yew, and Kitty stopped and opened her eyes.

"This way," she said to Hafwen, and began to walk.

21

"A young lady only ever takes small portions of food upon her fork."

—*Miss Finch's Little Blue Book (1855)*

Feed her to the machine? Annabel listened to it up above. It whined and whirred and made the ceiling tremble. How could she be fed to a machine? She took a very small bite of bread, and Mr. Angel watched her from the far end of the table.

"Please accept my thanks for the meal, Mr. Angel," she said. "But I'm afraid my appetite seems to have disappeared."

She knew it was impolite to refuse food and that Miss Finch would frown upon such a thing, but she felt very unwell. She worried for Kitty and Hafwen. She worried for her broomstick and the wand. All that time crawling through dirty tunnels only to have it snatched out of her hand by the wind. All of good magic had depended on her and now she had gone and ruined everything.

She thought of Miss Henrietta and Miss Estella. She thought of her mother. She thought of the Great & Benevolent Magical Society. What would become of them? Of London. Moonlit London. A thousand chimneys, with family after family slumbering, old ladies in nightcaps, and maids in attic bedrooms and babies in bassinets. Kittens in baskets and poor girls in dormitories and weary newspapermen in candlelit offices telling the story of the end of the fog for the morning paper. Ladies sleeping on goose-down pillows and waifs sleeping rough with leaves in their boots. All of London unknowing.

What did she have?

What could she do?

What had Miss Estella said? All the answers were inside her. In her head and in her heart. She touched her forehead there at the table, and then her heart. She placed her hand over her dirty, ragged dress and felt her seeing glass. Her breath caught.

She smiled at Mr. Angel. Her politest smile. "The story of my mother, if you please, Mr. Angel," she said.

◆ ◆ ◆

Kitty and Hafwen went through the park, past the noisy barracks and the zoological gardens. Hafwen stopped still when she heard the elephants stamping their feet and trumpeting at the moon, and Kitty had to coax her forward.

"Hafwen, you'll have your star," she said, trying placation first. "Annabel wouldn't lie about such a thing."

The troll trembled and shook her head.

"It will be the brightest star that you could ever imagine."

The troll refused.

"Hurry, you big oaf, or it'll be too late. Annabel is in peril."

They tried the broomstick. Kitty straddled it and commanded it up, but it wouldn't move. Hafwen shoved her angrily out of the way and tried it herself, but it refused to take off. Kitty sighed and thought she should've known as much; it would not fly because it was completely attached to the girl that everyone loved, wizards and trolls alike. And there in the moonlit park she did not feel angry but only smiled and coughed.

The giraffes lifted their slender necks to watch them go.

They ran through Primrose Hill Park and, far ahead, the oldest willow and the oldest ash called Kitty's name. *This way*, they said. *This way.*

Sometimes Kitty stopped. Breathing was hard, and her chest ached. She stopped and she listened. She knew this way. She knew the railway line and its tussock grasses. She knew the heath in the distance and was glad for it. All the milkwort and the bedstraw she brought the Miss Vines, the hawthorn and red clover for the Kentish Town Wizards, the secret places the faeries lived—oh, she could almost smell them tonight. On the heath the new air would be thick with the honey scent of them. The wind rushed through her, and sedge grass far ahead whispered, whispered, whispered, *Hurry, Kitty.*

The old oaks and the greater mother oak called.

And far beyond came the steady, quiet voice of the great Totteridge yew again—*Onward, Kitty*—and she navigated the streets toward it, like a sailor following a pole star.

22

"Yes, Annabel," said Mr. Angel. "It is a story that will make you cry, dear child. A great tragedy. And when I have told it, you will be quite ruined. And ruination is what the machine desires. Desolation, sorrow—pure and simple."

As if it could hear his words, the machine took a great breath above them, and the house shook to its very foundations. It whirred and grumbled and the dark paintings rattled on the walls and the dark chandeliers shivered.

"It was your mother's sorrowful tears upon a handkerchief that first gave me the idea for the Dark-Magic Extracting Machine. That handkerchief was the first object placed into its heart. I have built around her tears for thirteen years. Thirteen years of full moons. And now, tonight, you will complete the circle."

Annabel clasped her hands together in her lap to stop them from shaking. She lifted her chin.

Mr. Angel watched her carefully. "Your mother was a most magical young woman," he said, and he stood.

He walked, all crooked at the top, back and forth behind his chair.

"It was said she once flew on her broomstick all the way to Elgin and back in one night for a potion. She saved a child almost sure to die. She was good, your mother, very good."

Annabel didn't like the way Mr. Angel used the word *was*. As though her mother wasn't coming back. As though she wasn't good anymore. It made her heart hurt. The floor rattled beneath her feet. The shadowlings whispered against each other's cheeks.

Mr. Angel smiled. "She was a healer, and she had the sight, and she was wild and young and full of promise. She was even given her own wand, not normal for one so young. The magical world spoke of her—oh, how they spoke of her, Annabel. There had not been such a witch for some generations. But then she fell in love."

Mr. Angel stood motionless for some time, thinking. The shadowlings crept from their hiding places and grew their necks long toward his thoughts.

"In my humble opinion," he said at last, "love ruins most things."

He waved his wand, and the shadowlings descended, and in seconds the food and tableware were gone.

Annabel imagined her mother wild and passionate rather

than graceful and poised. She imagined her riding a broomstick all the way to Elgin, which she knew from geography was a very long way indeed. She needed to take a deep breath, for the image did not shock her so much as make her feel suddenly happy. Happy despite everything. Happy despite sitting before Mr. Angel, who was about to destroy London. Of *course* her mother should ride a broomstick, her black hair unwound. She should scream out at the wind and the clouds and in the mornings, when she returned, smell like the rain and the sky.

Mr. Angel banged the wand down on the table. "Vivienne Vine fell in love with a man by the name of the Great Geraldo Grey. That was his stage name. An apprentice to the Great Horaldo. They were magicians only. Card sleight–performing tricksters. No more than that. But how she loved him."

The Great Geraldo Grey, thought Annabel, and she bit her bottom lip. Her hands went up to her face, trembled. She tried very hard not to be sad. *The Great Geraldo Grey*.

"The Miss Vines forbade the liaison. The Finsbury Wizards refused his request for marriage. But Vivienne and Gerald married in secret anyway, and soon after, your mother was heavy with you."

Annabel had many questions. Mr. Angel was going too fast. One minute her mother was flying to Elgin for a potion and the next she was getting married. Who was Gerald Grey? What was he like? Where did they meet? Did he have fair hair or black hair? She needed to ask her mother these things, and now she would never have the chance. The machine up above let out a long, thin wail, and the walls of the house shivered. Mr. Angel's eyes widened with pleasure.

"Now, one evening not long before you were born, the Great Geraldo Grey had a terrible accident. He said goodbye to Vivienne and set off for the theater, and perhaps he was not watching where he was going or perhaps he was thinking of your imminent birth. We shall never know. But he stepped in front of a coach on the Euston Road and it was the end of him."

Annabel's mouth was open. Her heart quite stopped.

But it *couldn't* be the end of him. She'd only just met him in the story.

Mr. Angel laughed his soft, papery laugh at her distress, and the shadowlings mimicked him.

"Vivienne heard the commotion. All the traffic was stopped on the Euston Road. Dear Annabel, how she wept over his body, lying there in the dirt and manure. But in her wild grief she remembered something. She remembered the story of me, Mr. Angel, banished by the Finsbury Wizards for my resurrection machine. Do you know what that is, Annabel?"

Annabel shook her head.

"A machine that can bring those who are departed back to life. I had tried it several times on rabbits, several more on cats, but never on a human soul. Shall I explain its workings?"

"No, thank you," said Annabel.

"It was a simple matter of dark magic, necromancy, and steam," he said, ignoring her. "The soul can be called back— but getting it to stay in the body is another matter. With the resurrection machine, I was trying to fix that."

Annabel wanted to know how her father spoke. How he walked. How he laughed. However hard she tried to stop them, two tears slid down her pale cheeks.

Up above, the machine bellows sighed.

"There was a knock at my door, Annabel, and there stood Vivienne Grey with her newly departed husband, the Great Geraldo Grey. The perfect human subject for my machine. Up the stairs he was carried by two footmen, and into the machine. Shall I tell you what it looked like?"

"No, thank you," whispered Annabel again.

"It was a little like a coffin and a little like a bed, with the subject attached to various tubules by way of needles. The tubules were attached to various receiving bells, and it was all completely powered by steam."

Annabel wished she couldn't hear. She wanted to know how her father danced, how he listened, what special tricks he could do. If he was a good man. And now she would never know.

"Your father was attached. The engine ignited. The pistons fired. His soul was called back, and thus my first human subject's resurrection was a success. The Great Geraldo opened his eyes, Annabel Grey."

◆ ◆ ◆

Hafwen gazed up at the stars as she and Kitty walked on the heath. She gazed up so much that she frequently bumped into Kitty, who cursed her in a new way each time. She called Hafwen a grubby worm-eater, a fat piece of dragon cake, and an onion head. Hafwen listened, and each new name made her gray-toothed grin grow. Kitty could not help but laugh.

"But how would Annabel Grey have such a star?" Hafwen asked.

"How would I know?" said Kitty. The laughing had made her cough.

"Where did she pluck it from? Which part of the sky?"

"I don't know, you big greasy buffoon," said Kitty, and she bent down and coughed until she could spit into the grass. By the moonlight the spittle was dark.

She closed her eyes, and her heartbeat was very loud in her ears.

On the heath there was a grass that shone a certain way beneath the moon, lit up all silver along its edge. Since she was small, she had called it the moon grass. She had seen one hundred full moons or more, she thought, though she couldn't say for sure, not knowing her age or her beginnings.

She didn't have a mother the way Annabel Grey did. She did not have great-aunts or a long-dead father. She had London Town. The lap of the heath where she had often slept, the cluttered-up streets, the wild dark tenement heart. Yes, the city was her mother, a confounding, beautiful mother, with her lonely churches and warm stables and flowing park skirts.

Kitty touched the moon grass, and she coughed and coughed until her body felt quite hollow with coughing. From up high she looked back upon the city beneath the moon and was glad for its mothering.

Annabel Grey, she said to herself.

But the Totteridge yew called *her* name, and she wondered at that. The yew's voice was much clearer now. *Onward, Kitty, onward.* She hummed up her heart light, half to frighten Hafwen, and when it came, it was the deepest green. She marveled at how easy it had come, as though the cage she kept it in, her body, had grown more fragile. It slipped out of her simply.

Hafwen peered at the light from the corner of her eye and looked worried. "Is it far, skinny?" she asked.

"No," said Kitty. "Not far now, Hafwen."

23

━━━◆◆◆◆◆━━━

"If a young lady does not wish to join in parlor games,
then she must occupy herself with a quiet pastime, such as
needlework or reading."

—*Miss Finch's Little Blue Book (1855)*

Annabel didn't want to hear any more. She tried to think of the emerald-green ice skates, but her mind was used to that trick. It would not conjure them up. It said, *Here is the story of your father's last moments. Pay attention, Annabel Grey.*

Mr. Angel pointed the wand at the long table and blasted it with purple light so that it disappeared into a pile of dust. The shadowlings writhed with amusement. All that was left was Annabel and her chair.

Mr. Angel walked slowly toward her.

"The Great Geraldo Grey opened his eyes, Annabel," he said. "And he looked at your mother. He had been gone, Annabel, and now he had been returned. He looked at the tubules and the pistons and the way he was pinned to the apparatus. He looked at the great receiving bells that sat above him and had called his spirit back. Can you picture it?"

"Yes," whispered Annabel.

"The horror of it?" asked Mr. Angel.

"Yes," whispered Annabel.

"He was quite gone from this world and now returned. 'Gerald,' said your mother. 'Gerald.' And how she clutched at him. 'Vivienne' was his reply. 'What have you done?'

"His only words, Annabel. 'Vivienne, what have you done?' The machine was new, Annabel, never tested on a human. He seemed filled suddenly with confusion and rage. He tried to sit, and the needles were ripped from his skin. 'Vivienne,' he said, reaching for her blindly, and she tried to calm him, Annabel. 'Vivienne!' he cried, for he could no longer see her. She held him by the hands. 'Vivienne,' he said, and then he fell backward and was gone."

Mr. Angel watched Annabel. He watched the tears that slid down her cheeks. He watched the way she trembled. There were volumes of tears in the child. Tears of abandonment. Tears of confusion. Tears of loss. Tears of sadness. She tried to contain the ocean of tears, and it made her all the more pitiful.

"You tricked her," she whispered. "You tricked my mother with your terrible machine. You made her think he would be back the way he was. She never would have done such a thing otherwise."

"I gave her no such assurances," said Mr. Angel. He gazed upon Annabel sadly. "I offered her my services; I told her there were no guarantees it would work. How she wept over him, Annabel. The Great Geraldo Grey—not so great after all. I gave her my handkerchief, of course, and when she left, when she ran from that room, she left it lying on the floor. It gave me an idea. That handkerchief and the glass tubules, the receiving bells. A new and more wonderful machine."

Annabel did not want her father, whom she did not know, to have died not once but twice. She wanted him to be at home, at that very moment reading a newspaper or practicing magic tricks with cards. The tears would not stop. They slipped down her cheeks and dripped onto her hands in her lap.

"The machine, dear Annabel. Now is the time," said Mr. Angel, and then to the shadowlings: "Guard her. I will prepare the machine for its last meal."

◆ ◆ ◆

As soon as he was gone from the room, the shadowlings drew closer. They slipped from the walls to stand about her in a circle.

"I'm not afraid of you," she said to them as they moved around her, their shapes blending and changing. They made themselves into copies of Mr. Angel peering down at her. "I am not afraid of you, do you hear?"

But she was. They breathed against her skin, and she flinched. They watched her every move.

She took the ruby-red seeing glass from her bodice and placed it on her palm. There was barely any light in the

279

room, but she hoped there was enough. *Please*, she said to herself. *Please. Please, someone tell me what to do.* She looked into the glass and saw nothing but dimness.

Her mind raced. She needed the Miss Vines to appear, or the Finsbury Wizards. Oh, it would be good to hear kindly advice from them. She peered into the dark glass, but nothing came.

She remembered the cup of her mind. She examined her thoughts, and there were many. She was running out of time. Hafwen would be frightened. Kitty was unwell. Her father had died twice, and it just wasn't fair. Her mother should have told her the truth. She should feel angry, but all she felt was longing. All of London was in danger. She was the Valiant Defender of Good Magic, even though she didn't want to be. There, she'd said it. And now she'd let everyone down.

She peered into her ruby-red seeing glass and waited. The shadowlings crowded around her. She saw darkness, she saw dimness, she saw the sudden silvery moonlight on long grass.

Hafwen and Kitty trudged through a heathland. Kitty held the wand and the broomstick. Hafwen gazed in awe at the stars.

Annabel didn't think she had ever been happier to see someone. "Hafwen!" she shouted. "Kitty!"

But they faded just as quickly as they'd appeared. Now there was nothing but the opaqueness of the glass, and when she looked up, Mr. Angel was waiting at the door to take her upstairs.

◆ ◆ ◆

Kitty heard the shout. It wasn't so much a word as a sudden change in the landscape. The wind blew out one hard breath, and the trees shook their leaves, and the grasses banged down their tips once to the earth. Hafwen stopped in her troll tracks.

"Did you hear it, too?" asked Kitty.

Hafwen nodded.

"We are close," said Kitty.

She held her aching chest and coughed another violent cough. When she spat, there was more dark blood on the ground.

"We must not tarry, skinny," said Hafwen. "You can keep going?"

"Yes, Hafwen," replied Kitty. "But I must listen."

She closed her eyes. Her ribs ached, and every breath caught and snagged inside her as though she contained a thorn. She listened. She listened to the night. Annabel's shout was gone, but it had left behind a faint echo, the way a bell leaves a sound where it has broken the air on a clear, still day. She heard a new sound. A dark sound. A grinding, turning, rattling sound. A noise that did not belong there. It pulsated in the night air. She felt it in her body and knew it to be wrong.

"Yes," she said, but that one word made her cough, and her knees crumpled beneath her, and she fell to the ground.

24

"Before climbing stairs, a young lady arranges her skirts in such a way as to make the task possible, but so gracefully that none would notice she had done so."

—*Miss Finch's Little Blue Book (1855)*

r. Angel led the way. The passageways creaked and groaned beneath their feet. Up above them the machine clanked and sighed. Mr. Angel climbed the stairs before her, and the shadowlings came after her. Hundreds of them, clouding the air, whispering in her ears. They said her name and her mother's name, and they hissed the words *the Great Geraldo* and giggled. Every part of the story that Mr. Angel had told, they repeated.

Annabel felt the machine. It rattled the banister. It shuddered the floorboards. She wished for Kitty and Haffie. She did not want to be here alone.

Nothing could have prepared her for the sight of the Dark-Magic Extracting Machine. Even the darkness of Under London was nothing compared with the darkness of the machine. In the gloom it vibrated and twitched, and its giant bellows, as if sensing her, snapped open and then huffed shut. The room was cold, so cold.

"It knows you are here," said Mr. Angel quietly. "See how it senses you. It is alive with terrible magic."

Annabel stood in the doorway, and her skirts lifted toward it; she felt the pull of it on her skin. What was she meant to do against such a thing? As the most magical girl, she must be meant to do *something*. She looked at the huge funnel that stretched up toward the ceiling with its great and jagged hole. Pure bright moonlight hit the brass funnel.

"Come and look upon the city," said Mr. Angel. "I will show you all that will be mine."

She didn't want to go near the machine. The closer she got, the greater the pull. He guided her around the perimeter of the room, and the machine sang a strange song of grindings and moanings. He led her up the small staircase that wound its way around the moon funnel. Her legs trembled as she looked down into the machine, at all its gleaming moving parts. The shadowlings breathed softly behind her.

On the rooftop they were above London. They looked over streets and parkland and toward the city. The moon washed everything silver, and Annabel didn't think she'd ever seen London look so beautiful. It shone on Mr. Angel's face and made him look even lonelier. She thought it must be a terrible thing to be so bad.

"All the parks and palaces. All the people," Mr. Angel said. He pointed out over the rooftops. "All mine."

"But pardon me, Mr. Angel, why must it all be yours?"

He sounded like a spoiled boy. She wanted to say so, but he raised up the Black Wand and sang out loud, "Umbra, antumbra," and from everywhere, from rooftops and the church spires, shadowlings appeared.

"Because, Annabel Grey, darkness *should* reign, and darkness *will* reign," he said. "And I will be the king of all darkness."

◆ ◆ ◆

She wished that her mother could have seen her in Under London, with the Ondona raised at the bone wall. It was a simple wish. That her mother see what she had become. Now the time she said good-bye to her mother before their house had turned into the last time, and Annabel didn't think she'd ever felt sadder. Her heart ached beneath her breastbone, and it wasn't even the crying type of sadness but a more desolate thing. The machine down below sensed it. So did Mr. Angel, and he took her back down the stairs into the room.

The new shadowlings he had raised from the rooftops and belfries flew down the stairs behind them.

"Up," he said, and they flew to the perimeter of the room, where they opened and shut their wings and buzzed like angry bees.

From beside a chair Mr. Angel took a small pair of shoes.

"Behold the machine, Annabel," he said, and he stepped carefully into the center of the room and held them up. "They are the shoes of a pauper I found frozen in a lane behind Hackney Station last winter. It has a fondness for such sorrowful things, the shoes of departed children being among its favorites."

He leaned his crooked body into a space that seemed no different from any other space, yet his cloak lifted upward toward the machine. He released the pitiful shoes, and they were taken quite suddenly by a great sucking wind, pulled with great speed into a slit at the machine's side.

It was alive, that machine. Annabel knew it then.

"So, here you are, Annabel Grey, after your journey into Under London to find the Morever Wand. Here you are, with nothing to show for your trouble," he said.

Annabel let out a little sob.

"Raised in a house filled with such secrets," he said. "By a mother who did nothing but lie."

He smiled at her in the darkness, and his white teeth glinted.

She let out another sob, but this time she felt angry.

"Annabel Grey, the most sorrowful creature of all," he said, and he took several steps toward her. The machine wailed in anticipation.

The shadowlings droned.

He was going to grab her.

She did not want to be grabbed.

She did not want to be told she was sorrowful.

"I am brave," she whispered.

She was. She had entered Under London and returned.

"I am good," she said.

She was. She knew she was.

Mr. Angel strode toward her, his awful smile stretching across his face.

"I am brave! I am good!" she shouted now. She had no other weapon.

He was beginning to laugh. The shadowlings laughed with him.

Then he had her by the arm, and he was dragging her toward the center of the room, before the Dark-Magic Extracting Machine.

◆ ◆ ◆

Mr. Angel was strong. She pulled against him. She tried to unclasp his gloved hand. She kicked at him with her boots and twisted her body to get away from him. For one instant she was free and sprinting, but he grabbed her skirts and pulled her backward, held her hard about the waist, and dragged her, feet lifted from the ground, to the machine.

"The tears of the mother came first!" he shouted above the shrieking of the machine and the laughter of the shadowlings. "And now the small, sad daughter!"

And as he said it, the moonlight hit the moon funnel squarely and the machine made such a noise that his words were drowned out. A light filled the room. His cloak blew upward with the pull of the machine. He was turning her toward the place where he would let her go. Time slowed.

She listened to her own ragged breaths. Her heart beat in her ears.

Then another noise.

A slam. A bang.

Mr. Angel turned his head toward the noise, bringing her with him.

In the doorway to the ballroom stood Hafwen.

Stout, hairy Hafwen, holding the broomstick like a walking crook. The only troll in Trollingdom with a twinkle in her eye.

And on Hafwen's back was Kitty, with the Morever Wand in her hand.

"Let her go!" shouted Hafwen. Her voice was almost lost in the noise of that room. "Let Annabel Grey go."

"Take them!" cried Mr. Angel, removing one hand from Annabel to wave at the shadowlings.

The dark creatures leapt down from the walls toward the pair, but Kitty opened her mouth and released a heart light. It was small and pale green. She grew it so that it was as large as them, and they were surrounded by its light. She slipped from Hafwen's back and stood supported by the troll, with the wand in her hand.

The shadowlings skittered backward from the light, and Mr. Angel was distracted by their reluctance to follow his command. His grip lessened long enough for Annabel to break free. She pulled herself away from him just as Kitty crumpled to her knees, throwing the wand so that it raced across the ballroom floor.

Annabel rolled and crawled until she felt the wand in her hand. The lightness of it. The airiness of it. The goodness of it. But the machine, the great inward-drawn breath of the machine, seized her foot and began to drag her along the floor toward its blackness, the slits opening and shutting fast with a noise like a tent buffeted by wind.

"Help!" she screamed, and Hafwen rushed toward her. She wrenched Annabel by the hand out of the space.

Mr. Angel was coming toward them.

"Stand back!" Annabel shouted as she clambered to her feet, pushing Hafwen behind her. "Stay back."

She raised the Morever Wand at Mr. Angel, and he raised his Black Wand in return.

"I cannot be defeated!" he shouted, and out of the Black Wand's tip came a blast of mauve light.

◆ ◆ ◆

Afterward, she could not say if it was her word alone that saved them. The mauve light came toward her, and she shouted the word *Benignus* at the same time. She shouted the word so loudly that it seemed to break the air, as though it were a force itself. It was louder than the terrible machine, mincing and grinding its sorrows; it was louder than the shadowlings, shrieking on the ceilings and on the walls. It was louder than the city, oblivious to all that was happening in the dark mansion.

Annabel Grey shouted the word *Benignus.* The wizards' word. The witches' word. The Great & Benevolent Magical Society's word. She shouted it and knew in that instant that it meant "by good, kind magic," "by the magic of gentle ancient wizards and gentle, kind witches," "by the magic of the old trees and heaths and meadows," "by the magic of girls like Kitty, heart-light singers," "by the magic of the small folk sleeping in cemeteries," "by the magic of old places, secret rivers, and sacred wells and springs."

"Benignus!" she shouted, and a great golden light came from the end of the wand and met the mauve force that rushed toward her.

Kitty threw her heart light at the very same moment. She threw it from the far end of the room with the last of her strength, and all three forces collided. There was a great explosion of light, so bright that the shadowlings stood stark against the walls. They'd no sooner opened their dark mouths and claws in fright than they dissolved. They were illuminated and ended in seconds.

And in the brightness there came a thundering roar and a great galumphing of feet. Annabel saw the shape of Hafwen hurtling toward Mr. Angel. The little troll dived across the space, pushing him to the floor and into the place before the machine.

The machine caught him.

It held his ankles with its inward breath.

He looked at Annabel. He scrabbled at the floor, his

fingers frantically looking for purchase. She went toward him, but Hafwen held her back. It sucked him slowly at first. It dragged him backward toward its terrible mouth. It took a great breath then and sucked him up fast and gobbled him quickly through its leather slit. The sound of his cry was brief.

The machine cried one long note.

There was a great blast and more white light, a giant expanding ring of white light that blew out the bellows and spewed glass and petals and paupers' shoes. A ring of white light that exploded outward with paper and mourning pins and blackwork samplers. It hit the walls. It blew out the windows. Rubble rained down around them.

Then the machine's screaming faltered. It dropped several octaves. The gears and cogs, protesting, ground to a halt. There was a dull thud. The machine was quiet.

Annabel lay on the ground breathing hard, the Morever Wand in her hand. A single white handkerchief fluttered down from the ceiling, shining in the moonlight. It landed upon her heart.

She took it and held it to her face and began to cry.

25

"A young witch will rise well before dawn. She will make yellow tea and look at the weather and feel how it impresses itself upon her spirit. If it is fine, she should stay indoors. But if there is wind and rain, she will take her broomstick and ride with delight for just a little while."

—Miss Henrietta's notes, kept for Annabel Grey

I t is exactly the kind of day she sees things. The rain comes in squalls, and the sky is wild with rushing clouds. She rises at dawn and dresses quickly. She is good at her buttons now. She ties her apron strings. She wraps her long fair hair into a bun. In the silence of the house her footsteps echo. She tiptoes in and out of the rooms in the half-light. Sweeps the cinders, starts the fire in the small kitchen, brings water to boil.

She lets the porridge cool so Hafwen can sleep later, trolls being grumpy if they are woken too soon. To rouse her, she must go through the shop and the magical storeroom. She likes to stop still in that place, just for a moment, to hear it murmuring to itself, the broomsticks rustling and the seeing glass chiming and the peat mud bubbling in jars.

She goes down the dark staircase and through the old parlor and into the riverbed chamber. She hears the secret river and thinks of all the places she has visited deep down below. They still sting on her skin, those places, even though the map has vanished.

When her great-aunt Estella spoke to her on the Lake of Tears, she had indeed been hovering close to death. The wounds from Mr. Angel's Black Wand and the shadowlings were too much for her old body to bear. She is gone from the bedchamber now.

That is a new pain for Annabel, one of many, and she busies herself to seek solace from it.

There is Hafwen to care for, sitting up and waiting in her small bed filled with clean straw. Everywhere in the cluttered room are the things she collects: shiny teaspoons and scraps of paper on which she is learning to draw, old dresses, ribbons, green grass pulled from the earth, ladybugs in glass jars.

Hafwen is holding her prized possession, her glittering star.

"Look how it sparkles this morning," says Annabel.

Hafwen smiles and shuts the lid on the star brooch. She holds it to her heart.

"But is it a real star?" Hafwen asks with the box still held close to her chest as they climb the stairs.

"No, it is not a real star," says Annabel. "But you know I have said I am sorry."

Hafwen opens the box again in the kitchen and gazes upon her jewel. "Yes, but I love it all the same," she says.

She is full of questions in the morning, this troll: Why do you think the world has oceans? Why do humanlings like bells? Where do birds learn their songs? Why is there a queen in London Above, but not a king? And could Hafwen fit another star inside her box?

Annabel makes tea, listens, half listens, drifts. Three heaped teaspoons and the pot turned widdershins and left to brew. She pats her broomstick, which is leaning near the back door, and she feels its delight at her touch. It wants up and flying and the sky.

"Soon, dear broomstick," she says.

She throws slops out into the laneway for the birds and looks upon the puddles. She walks between them slowly until one speaks to her heart and she kneels. She wishes for a vision of Kitty, just one vision, but this morning the chosen puddle shows her something unexpected.

Her mother.

Her mother is wearing a blue dress and standing in a boat. She is holding a wand. She looks very grave. Her black hair is unbound, and she raises her hand slowly, and Annabel knows immediately that she is coming home.

She is sending word, just as she promised.

Annabel stays kneeling on the ground, smiling, long after

the vision has vanished. So long that Hafwen comes out and very grumpily asks for more porridge.

"I saw my mother," Annabel says in the kitchen. She can barely breathe. "She's coming back."

Hafwen looks at her suspiciously. "Will you still love me?" she asks.

"Of course I will, Haffie," says Annabel.

And it makes her think of Kitty again and how much she misses her. The betwixter girl disappeared from the ballroom, and only Hafwen saw her go. Annabel has asked her to tell the story again and again, and each time Hafwen tells it just so: "She stood up. She looked about. She smiled. And then away that skinny went, out through the door."

"But did she leave no message for me?" Annabel asks again in the kitchen this morning. "Did she say nothing?"

"The skinny left no message," says Hafwen.

The Finsbury Wizards have not heard from her. Kitty has not brought them their brownie tea. "The wizards tell me I should not stop hoping," says Annabel.

They search for Kitty—they search for her daily—and when she is found, Annabel will be the first to know. They have sent out their pigeons to all those remaining in the Great & Benevolent Magical Society. *Search all the pockets of woods and the shady groves, search all the cemeteries and hedgerows. Send word to the faeries that she is missing and deeply missed.*

Yet Annabel remembers her vision in the lacquered jewelry box all those years ago. The little coffin carried by the very old men.

She takes a deep breath, stands up. She'll be late. It's time to tend to Miss Henrietta's wounds.

Miss Henrietta is awake, sitting propped up, pale. Her black hair flows over her shoulders. She smiles today, a small smile, when Annabel enters.

"Tea and medicines, Miss Henrietta," says Annabel.

Annabel still does not know how her great-aunt survived Mr. Angel and his shadowlings. She grows agitated with any questioning. Her physical wounds are just as deep. Ugly wounds upon her legs and arms and several jagged gashes upon her cheeks. But they are healing. Each day they improve. Annabel uses the medicines and potions that the Finsbury Wizards and the Bloomsbury Witches send her. There is a yellow ointment that smells like the sea and a purple balm that stains her fingers.

Miss Henrietta complains now during the dressing of her wounds, so Annabel thinks she might be mending.

"You hurt me," she moans, and Annabel soothes her and gives her tea.

She is often confused.

She has asked after the girl they sent down into Under London; after her sister, Estella; and after Vivienne, who turned her back on magic.

But today she says, "Annabel?"

"Yes, Miss Henrietta."

"You are a good girl. You are very brave," and then she sleeps again.

It's Annabel's turn to smile. She goes about tidying the room and opens the curtains to the day. There is light at last, streaming through the window. She likes to think of Kitty lying somewhere, in such a patch of sunshine, held in the crook of a tree, listening to the strange language of the leaves. *There are not many girls like Kitty anymore.*

She touches the Morever Wand where it leans against Miss Henrietta's bed. She looks at her own hand. There is so much magic inside her, she knows, but she does not understand it yet. Should she tell Miss Henrietta of her vision in the puddle today? That her mother is returning?

No. There are floors to be swept and the shop to be opened. *Tomorrow*, she thinks, *tomorrow is time enough for such things.*

ACKNOWLEDGMENTS

There is much thanks in my heart for my beautiful mother, who has gone away now. She was always my good friend. She was a great listener and unflinchingly believed in all my harebrained ideas. She was a storyteller, too. She told the story of us, our family, so that we knew it like the verses of the Bible. She was the teacher of patience and persistence, kindness and forgiveness. She taught love. I could never have written a word without her lessons.

Many thanks to Catherine Drayton, again, for her invaluable insight into messy first drafts and for always knowing exactly what to say. Erin Clarke for always knowing just how to make a story work.

Finally, special thanks to my good friends and family. Jane-Anne Boyd for cheering me on. Rachel Paterson and Linda Porter for their kindness. Sonia Blake and Ruth Foxlee for always listening. And Alice, of course, for making life beautiful.

Thank you for choosing a Piccadilly Press book.

If you would like to know more about our authors, our books or if you'd just like to know what we're up to, you can find us online.

www.piccadillypress.co.uk

You can also find us on:

We hope to see you soon!